Outbound Train
A Novel

by

RENEA WINCHESTER

FIREFLY
SOUTHERN FICTION
LIGHTHOUSE PUBLISHING OF THE CAROLINAS

OUTBOUND TRAIN BY RENEA WINCHESTER
Firefly Southern Fiction is an imprint of LPCBooks
a division of Iron Stream Media
100 Missionary Ridge, Birmingham, AL 35242

ISBN: 978-1-64526-241-1
Copyright © 2020 by Renea Winchester
Cover design by Elaina Lee
Interior Design by Karthick Srinivasan
Author photograph by Quintin Ellison

Available in print from your local bookstore, online, or from the publisher at:
ShopLPC.com

For more information on this book and the author visit:
ReneaWinchesterAuthor (Instagram); Renea Winchester, Author (Facebook),
goodreads.com/author/show/4452520.Renea_Winchester (Goodreads).

This is a work of fiction. Names, characters, and incidents are all products of the
author's imagination or are used for fictional purposes. Any mentioned brand
names, places, and trademarks remain the property of their respective owners,
bear no association with the author or the publisher, and are used for fictional
purposes only.

Scriptures are taken from the *Holy Bible*, King James Version.

Brought to you by the creative team at LPCBooks:
Eva Marie Everson, Lucie Winborne, and Evelyn Miracle

Library of Congress Cataloging-in-Publication Data
Winchester, Renea.
Outbound Train / Renea Winchester 1st ed.

Library of Congress Control Number: 2020904014

Printed in the United States of America

PRAISE FOR *OUTBOUND TRAIN*

Renea Winchester's storytelling is as real and authentically Southern as the clear water music of an Appalachian creek and the song of Cicadas on a front porch summer evening.

Lisa Wingate,
#1 New York Times Bestselling author of
Before We Were Yours and *Before and After*

Renea Winchester has gifted us with an engaging, starkly realistic story set in the shanty side of Bryson City, North Carolina. In turns, Barbara Parker, a young mother reeling from her own personal history, and her sixteen-year-old daughter, Carole Anne, narrate the variables that comprise their Appalachian lives. They live humbly in a trailer park with Barbara's mother, Pearlene–a character so fully drawn as to add delightful, regional attitude to this slice of life story. It is a unique story of women strong enough to reach for more yet savvy enough to "make do" as they wield deep secrets and hidden agendas. As products of the hard-scrabble environment to which they were born, each character lures the reader with a plausible motive as they work toward bettering their circumstances. This finely woven story has much to recommend from its inciting opening scene to its satisfying ending.

Claire Fullerton
Multiple award-winning author of
Mourning Dove, Little Tea, Dancing to an Irish Reel, and
A Portal in Time

This is the story of my people--those who came up hard, survived in the margins, and persevered. Winchester does us proud in this delightful, well-told tale. You will enjoy this read!

Lauretta Hannon
The Cracker Queen

Renea Winchester writes with all of her heart and soul and we are the luckier for it. She had me rooting from the start for the three generations of fierce and admirable "make-do girls" from the Parker family; her rich storytelling keeps the pages turning in this tale of determination and steadfast love.

Lynn Cullen
Bestselling author of *Mrs. Poe* and *The Sisters of Summit Avenue*

Outbound Train traces the hardscrabble lives of three generations of Parker women with heart, wisdom and hope. Winchester sharply characterizes the residents of Bryson City, North Carolina who swill RC colas, toil in the mills, and listen to the whistle of the train, dreaming of an escape from their bleak existences. "Southern fiction at its very finest."

Karin Gillespie
Author of the *Bottom Dollar* series

Renea Winchester writes about the people of the hardscrabble south with compassion and conviction. Her debut novel, *Outbound Train*, is an inspiring story of three generations of women who not only seek to survive a life of poverty in Appalachia but also dare to dream. With pitch-perfect dialogue and believable characters, Winchester has crafted a story that will make readers stand up and cheer.

Michael Morris
Bestselling author of
Man in the Blue Moon and *A Place Called Wiregrass*

A powerful tale of heartache and healing delivered with the skills of a true southern storyteller.

Julie Cantrell
New York Times and USA TODAY bestselling author of *Perennials*

Outbound Train is the moving and uplifting portrait of three generations of working-class women and their struggle to survive the brutality of poverty, hopelessness, and oppression. Bryson City, North Carolina in the mid-1970s is a small mountain town governed by railroads, mills, and football. I fell in love with the smart, strong, funny characters in this community of make-do women, and I predict you will, too.

Pamela Duncan
Plant Life

Unflinchingly honest and heartfelt, *Outbound Train* by Renea Winchester explores the relationships between mothers and daughters, the lengths we go to pursue our dreams, and the lengths we go to abandon those dreams when our past won't let us get away. Barbara and Carole Anne are a mother/daughter duo that won't be soon forgotten.

Jolina Petersheim
Bestselling author of *How the Light Gets In*

Outbound Train is a journey you won't want to miss. It is a thrilling and heartfelt journey into the collective soul of the Parker women from the mountains of North Carolina, who will teach you the meaning of courage, strength and, most important, love. Outbound journey is a novel you will not put down or ever forget.

Peter Golden
Nothing Is Forgotten

Renea Winchester's *Outbound Train* is a story about survival, hope, and reclamation. It is the multi-generational story of the women of the Parker family as they each confront the boundaries of their small-town world, dealing with the "is" while hoping for the "might be." Winchester's skill with the written word captures the angst of life in the rural South and will make readers believe they are right there with the Parker family. This bold debut novel tells a timeless story with a deft and nuanced touch, and long after its conclusion, readers will hold Barbara Parker and her family in their hearts and wish them well.

Raymond L, Atkins
Set List, Sweetwater Blues

"If gumption was all I needed to succeed, well, I had plenty of that," says teenager Carole Anne Parker, and Renea Winchester's *Outbound Train* gives us an accounting of that gumption she shares with her mother Barbara and grandmother Pearlene, a family of working-class women making do and getting by. The girl is obsessed with escaping the trailer park and dreary factory in the small mountain town of Bryson City, North Carolina, her mother obsessed with the dark secret of a long-hidden crime. Every day seems to bring a new struggle, a new obstacle to them all, but stubbornness and a fierce love for one another drive them all toward a new day where life might be a little easier, full of new possibilities.

Rita Sims Quillen
WAYLAND

Renea Winchester is a natural-born storyteller. She has crafted a debut novel with a strong sense of place and a colorful cast of characters nursing old wounds and fighting for better lives in a small North Carolina town. *Outbound Train's* small mill-town setting is reminiscent of *An Officer and a Gentleman*. While revealing the heroic battles of the human spirit—especially those of Barbara Parker and her daughter Carole Anne—she maintains their dignity. She deftly captures the voices of the people in Bryson City in the 1960s and '70s.

Susan Cushman
Friends of the Library and *Cherry Bomb*

Outbound Train is a novel of struggle and survival. Set among the backdrop of the Great Smoky Mountains, the focus is less on the beauty of nature and tourism than the traps we find ourselves in and dreams of escape. Realistic and alive, you will find yourselves rooting for Barbara, her mother, and her daughter. *Outbound Train* is a must read and joins the ranks of the best Southern novels.

Niles Reddick
Drifting too far from the Shore and *Lead Me Home*

Like all great writers, Renea Winchester writes best about what she knows. And not many folks know the people, places and culture of the Great Smoky Mountain region more intimately than Renea. Known previously for her superb non-fiction literary work, Renea's stellar debut novel takes her writing to a whole new level. *Outbound Train* is a rollicking coming of age story that bonds the past, present and future of three generations of remarkable mountain women, and their love-hate relationship with their equally remarkable community of Bryson City, N.C. Sometimes heart breaking, other times hilarious, *Outbound Train* is the book that Winchester was born to write. And the first of many more great novels to come.

Bob Plott
NC historian and author of *Plott Hound*

The year is 1976, and 16-year-old Carole Anne can't wait to leave the relentless poverty of Bryson City, N.C. Her mother, Barbara, once had the same dream only to see it thwarted by a horrific event. Grandma Pearlene, meanwhile, is funny, wily and determined. Filled with unusual insight and authentic detail, this beautifully written story examines the resilience, quirks, secrets, daily hardships, and deep personal courage of three Appalachian women. It is their kinship that saves them. *Outbound Train* is a book I will remember for a long, long time.

Amy Hill Hearth
New York Times bestselling author of
Streetcar to Justice, Miss Dreamsville

ACKNOWLEDGMENTS

On July 4, 2010, while sitting beneath a shade tree with my family, I heard the unmistakable sound of horse hooves pounding pavement.

"Wagon's coming," Dad announced. "Passes by every day heading to town to pick up tourists."

After quickly loading my daughter and nephew, my brother and I settled into the back of the wagon. Traveling at this slow pace, I saw a different side of Bryson City, one hidden from tourists. At the edge of town, eight trailers were parked end-to-end with only a sliver of dirt between them. Children played outside. Dogs lived under the trailers, protecting their owner's meager possessions. Broken-down cars in various stages of repair, rested on blocks, their open hoods waiting. A wrestling ring, like the ones on WWF, butted against the outside door of one of the trailers.

And then I saw a freckled face girl with her nose pressed against the window glass. At that moment she was my Carole Anne, fiercely determined to leave the trailer park by any means necessary.

"There's your book," my brother said while pointing to the trailer park. "You need to write about this Bryson City, about the town we grew up in, not the tourist trap it is today."

Looking into the eyes of this young girl, I promised myself I would tell her story. I would tell people that she mattered.

Today, I am grateful for the readers I've met along the way with my books about farmer Billy Albertson. His story provided fodder for my career. God planted this seed and readers sustain me. My success, always, depends on readers.

To my Atlanta Writers Club critique group who believed in this story enough to break out the red pen. Early readers Laurie Paisley and Angie Kinsey proved their love for the written word and offered priceless feedback during the life of this novel. Ladies, I am forever grateful. George Brossi, whom I admire and consider the expert on

Appalachian history and literature, moved me to tears when he said, "gracefully navigated and artfully done."

Writers: Bren McClain, girl I flat out love you. What more can I say? Claire Fullerton whose generous heart reached from the California Coast into the hills of North Carolina and invested in me, a stranger. You are phenomenal. Eva Marie Everson, the best friend a writer could ever have who literally hung the moon. God sure did bless me when He connected us. To every author who gifted me their time to write a blurb, I am in your debt. Thank you.

To Carol Crawford who coordinates the Blue Ridge Conference and Terry Kay who became my mentor years ago at the conference after announcing, "Renea, you're a writer!" with such intensity I actually believed him. You sir, are my treasure.

Booksellers and literacy advocates: Cat Blanco. Gina, we did it! Bookmiser owners Annelle and Jim Gerson; Book Exchange, Jennifer Gillman; The Foxes at FoxTale Book Shoppe; Chris Wilcox at City Lights and to every brick-and-mortar bookseller, thank you. The SIBA powerhouse, Wanda Jewel and Nicki Leone, you are loved beyond measure. Julie Cantrell and Kathy Murphy whose encouragement carried me through the valley. Elizabeth H. Potts, a champion for libraries, thank you for believing that books still matter.

To Mom, I hope I made you proud. Saving the best for last, for my beloved husband, who believes in me still, and my brother. All my love, always.

As the trailer park faded from view I saw in Carole Anne's eyes a dare. Tell my story, tell it and make people see me not for what I am now, but for who I can become.

DEDICATION

To Den

Bryson City, North Carolina

1976

The people of Bryson City didn't need an alarm clock to signal the start of another day; Norfolk Southern Railroad provided one each morning. Three engines passed through town: the midnight, three-thirty, and five-thirty rails. In the darkness the trains sounded alike. A rhythmic clack of steel against steel, the roar increasing as each engine pushed through the darkness. Followed by the sound of a whistle piercing the night, blowing two short toots then one longer howl, warning anyone who might be out after dark–and there weren't many–to clear the tracks.

Beneath a blanket of darkness, Bryson City seemed peaceful. Some Mill Town occupants slumbered in houses they rented but would never own outright. Others slept in trailers set up on blocks with wheels removed and sold for extra money. Hardworking people slept soundly until the first train clacked into town. Then they stirred, but not to the point of fully waking. They continued this half-sleep while the second train sounded its horn until finally their train–the five-thirty–sounded.

The five-thirty, whose engineer kindly held the chain longer than the two previous men, converted the warning whistle into a town-wide wake up call. One long, wake-the-dead scream for those who were so dog-tired they could barely face the morning. It was then that the good people of Bryson City arose and blindly measured three scoops of JFG coffee for their machines. Some lit a cigarette and sat hypnotized as pitch-black coffee sprang to life in the percolator bulb. They removed bits of tobacco from the tips of their tongues while the aroma of liquid sunshine escaped through cracks in the walls. A new day dawned, and

1

some folk, but not many, dreamed of a life beyond the one-stop-sign town.

Chapter One

Barbara Parker
1960

On the night of the championship game, three chartered buses headed downstate: one for the team, another for cheerleaders and band members, a third for fans willing to pay $38 for a round-trip ticket to Raleigh. Those too poor to afford tickets, or too afraid of big-city traffic, crowded around their radio and listened as WBHN-AM broadcast the game live. It was those fans who later flooded the streets chanting, "Maroon Machine, Maroon Machine!"

I'd heard this battle cry and the cheers all season. The voices tumbled down the valley and mingled with the clang of cowbells and ecstatic roars each time the Maroon Devils scored another touchdown. Exuberant roars rushed down the railroad tracks into my open bedroom window, reminding me of my place within the social standing. Mama never let me go to the games. She believed when crowds gathered, they generated nothing but trouble. She didn't care that I wanted to join the cheerleading squad. She just refused by saying, "No daughter of mine is going to strut around half naked."

Mama was strict like that. She was afraid I'd get married or let the first boy who came along get me pregnant. Later, I wondered if her fear conjured the evil that found me on the night the Maroon Devils won the championship game, or had it simply been my fate.

I didn't listen to the radio or cheer for the team while the football team played downstate. Instead, I took the keys to the Oldsmobile and drove to meet my friend Victoria.

I didn't need a radio to know when the Maroon Devils won the title by beating the dickens out of those city boys. In the wee hours of morning, a white bus with maroon lettering pulled into town with all the windows down despite the cold. Cheerleaders broke the "players- only" rule and packed the team bus. They waved pom-poms as players leaned from open windows and slapped the side of the bus. Fans whistled and clanged cowbells. Following behind, Bryson City's ambulance, fire truck, and a sheriff's cruiser formed an impromptu parade, their emergency lights flashing. After arriving on Main Street, the chartered buses let everyone off and residents rushed to greet their champions.

And while they celebrated, I looked forward to graduation and the rest of my life. My plan: to leave Bryson City—a town so small it suffocated me—and never return.

The crowd was larger than I expected and I couldn't find Victoria where we agreed to meet. She'd whispered excitedly about Marlboros, moonshine, and *maybe* doobies if Zeke didn't pass out while listening to the game. I wasn't interested in going, but Victoria insisted she didn't want to go alone. I didn't see any of my classmates in town, which was no surprise. Not finding Victoria wasn't that big of a shock; I felt sure Victoria and Zeke were celebrating in Mr. Cutshaw's barn.

Avoiding the crowd, I parked the Oldsmobile behind the Piggly Wiggly, cut behind the pawn shop, and walked the tracks leading out of town, planning with every step just how I'd leave after graduation. Planning and plotting and dreaming ... until he slipped up behind me, cat-like, and wrapped thick fingers around my long hair. He gave a firm tug, snapping my head back.

Clouds that seemed far away a moment ago rolled in and veiled the moon's face. My tennis shoes kicked up gravel as I fought to free myself. "Let me go!" I sounded weak, like a small child being bullied on the playground, something I was all too familiar with.

My weakness gave him strength. His arm clamped tight around my waist. "Lookie what we got here, boys." A voice, thick tongued and dangerous, sounded against my ear. Rough fingers traveled across my body to remove the keys from my back pocket, then tossed them. I heard the catch of them in someone's hand. Someone behind me.

"Where's your car? Care if we take it for a spin?"

"Let's take *her* for a spin first," the voice spoke at my ear. I bucked at the implication and tried to run, but his arm held firm and pulled me closer toward him. Close enough for me to feel his hardness.

His strength made me realize I was no match for him. Fear punched hard in my gut as I heard more voices. A knife clicked open. A zipper lowered.

"Boy, put that knife away," my captor said. "And zip your pants before you cut off that little worm."

A shudder ran through me when I recognized the voice—Ted Camden, captain of the football team. He sensed my recognition, too, because the moment my body tensed, he whispered, "That's right, little monkey, I gotcha now."

That name. They'd called me "Monkey" just hours before when Connor Brown snatched me up like a football and carried me through the elementary school playground to the metal monkey bars installed specifically for football players. Connor had lifted me high in the air where he dared me to hang on or fall while the players circled and waited for me to do just that.

"Stand watch, boys," Ted now barked.

I tried to free myself but there was no use. Ted eased down the embankment dragging my kicking body as easily as he would carry his girlfriend Rebecca's purse until he had me where he wanted me. His weight pinned me down. Thin blue-jean fabric ripped. Tears streamed from my eyes and traveled down the sides of my face, pooling in my ears. "No," I said, knowing my words were useless.

"Just relax," Ted said, leaning down to graze my lips with his.

I caught his lower lip between my teeth and bit down hard, the sweet metal of blood lying thick on my taste buds.

"You little—" he said with a quick backhand across my cheek.

Ted leveled his weight on my body and leaned in close. I squeezed my eyes shut and turned my face away. His tongue found my ear. I winced. There was no shutting off his voice—hot and mean. "Open your eyes," he commanded.

I squeezed them tighter, thankful for the darkness.

His hands came around my neck, gentle at first then slowly building pressure. "Look at me or I swear I'll snap your stupid head off."

I ignored him, not caring anymore. Part of me had died already.

His sour breath moistened my face. He took my ear in his teeth and bit down while his hands squeezed tighter.

I opened my eyes with a gasp, looked past his face, and caught a brief glimpse of the moon hanging in the heavens, watching as helpless as I had become.

"Thata girl," he purred. "That's a smart little monkey."

Ted lifted my shirt. Ripped my bra free. Bit my skin. My blood for his.

"Why?" I asked. One word, weak and useless.

Laughing blue eyes broke through the night. "Because tonight I own this town."

His hands returned to my neck, his mouth to my ear. "Now I'm going to do something all the girls like."

But that wasn't true. Instead, Ted Camden ripped my innocence to shreds and wounded my soul. Tears pooled into my ears, broke free, and slid down the back of my neck wetting my hair. My protests didn't matter. My screams meant nothing. *I* meant nothing. Gravel cut at the backs of my legs. I prayed for time to speed up. Prayed for him to release his vileness in me because, I knew once he was done, I could get away.

"You like that?" he asked.

When I didn't answer his hands found my throat again. His fingers pressed hard. "You like that ..." His words were not a question.

"Yeah," I lied.

"Good, 'cause we're just getting started."

I tried once more to scream, but the sound would not come. Ted's thumbs pressed against my throat and locked my voice within. I struggled to breathe, my eyes focused on the moon, peering through the parting clouds. I told myself to keep my eyes on the moon and it will soon be over. *Eyes on the moon.*

The others were watching. I heard them cheering, beer cans crushing. Ted's face hovered over mine. His fingers pressed tighter and tighter until eventually I had no more breath. Finally, finally … his darkness swallowed up the light from the moon until everything turned black.

***

When it was over, the moon stared down sorrowful and helpless. Crumpled cans and broken bottles settled around me. Around here people tossed unwanted items from open car windows without a second thought, forgotten items that tumbled down embankments into ditches where kudzu covered them in the summer until they eventually rusted or rotted. I winced as I sat up, then I scoured the embankment for my clothes.

Crab-crawling up the graveled bank, I eventually found my pants and pulled them on, aware more now that my skin was sticky with a dark layer of ugliness.

The most absurd thought skipped in then: How could I go back to school and act like nothing had happened? How could I walk the halls and pretend nothing was wrong?

I couldn't. I wouldn't.

I wanted to die.

In the distance the three-thirty train called out an answer.

The train. That's how I'd do it. I'd lie down in the middle of the tracks and wait for the engine to end my misery. Gravel shifted and I stumbled, then used my hands to pull myself up little by little. Locating my ripped shirt, I pulled it over my head and waited for my shaking hands to settle. Eventually, I crawled to the siderails. There, where the light from town illuminated steel, I waited.

The tracks began to vibrate. The engineer sounded the first warning. I knew I should leave. Spying the shoe that came off when Ted snatched me, I hobbled over, bent to retrieve it, and slipped my right foot into the canvas.

Just lie here. Lie still on the tracks. Eyes on the moon.

But I couldn't face the moon; his face was too sorrow-filled. Instead,

I turned my head toward the light.

Yes. That's it. Just be still and let the train do what it does best.

For a moment I wondered if the train would cut my body in half, separating the parts of me like Ted had. Would the train ease my suffering, or would I spend eternity bruised and damaged?

Don't move, Barbara. Just be still. Wait for the train and it will all be over.

The whistle sounded a third time.

Oh, God ... I was tired. So tired. I held my breath, closed my eyes, and readied myself for the end.

Chapter Two

Carole Anne Parker
1976

I had just asked Mama what the letters on the side of the JFG coffee can meant. She looked questioningly at the bright blue can then glanced outside our plastic-covered kitchen window and said, "Just frickin' great!" At the time, I wasn't sure if she was talking about the JFG coffee, or the fact that I had missed the school bus. Missing the bus was a terrible offense and meant asking Doretta's mama for a ride. Playing hooky was never an option. Walking to school wasn't either, because even though I'm sixteen, Barbara Parker has a non-negotiable rule: *no daughter of mine is walking to school. Not when my taxes pay someone to drive a big ole yellow school bus straight to the door.*

Mama's afraid someone will kidnap me like those poor kids in Chowchilla, California. I've tried to explain that California is on the opposite side of the country from Bryson City and that those kids were kidnapped while *riding* a school bus. "Doesn't that make the bus more dangerous?" I asked.

But she won't listen. "Someone could grab you and take you anywhere in the world. Then what would you do?"

I'd sing hallelujah that's what I'd do.

I haven't told her that when I can't sleep, I *dream* of being taken, because if anyone ever kidnapped me there'd be no way in the world my family could come up with enough ransom money to bring me home. Then I'd be free of this town, free to see something other than the fake wood-paneled walls of a 10 x 60 tin-can trailer.

Mama wrestled her arms into her coat. "Call Doretta. See if her mama can come get you on her way to work. And whatever you do,

9

don't wake Pearlene." After a final slurp of coffee, Mama headed out the door.

Granny Pearlene lives with me and Mama. People around here say Pearlene Parker is crazier than a bedbug … and they might be right. I think the last sickly spell affected her mind more than we thought. Lately it seemed like I was always tiptoeing around one of them, unless I'm playing nursemaid to Granny Pearlene or waitress to Mama when she comes home too tired to do anything other than soak her aching body in the bath.

That's when Mama reminds me, "If we're gonna make it we've all gotta pull our weight."

Most days I feel like I pull more than my fair share.

Instead of calling Doretta like I was told, I rang Connor Brown who lives a few trailers up the road. He passes our trailer every day. He's told me it's no trouble to pick me up, says the school is on his way. Connor works at Keith's Garage and can repair anything broken, even mornings that start off wrong. Just last week he unclogged the toilet. In a way it was embarrassing, but Connor fixed it speedy-quick and left before Mama got home from work. Last month, I called him in a panic when I came home from school and Granny Pearlene was missing. He drove me around till we found her looking in the window of Rite-Way Pawn. When I nudged her arm and told her it was time to go, she answered, "Five more minutes and my stories will be over."

Connor and I didn't bother telling Granny Pearlene she was watching her own reflection. We just waited until she was ready to go. Connor and I decided to keep that little adventure to ourselves. Mama doesn't need to know everything, and she certainly doesn't need to know about my plans to play Cupid.

If you believe the talk, Connor's personal life has hit a rough spot. Of course, around here no one's personal life is private. According to the ladies at the beauty shop, Connor is "soon-to-be divorced and back on the market." These same busybodies report with excitement that Connor's wife "left him in the middle of the night with a stack of unpaid bills and a pile of dirty laundry." Gossipy women say that living in a trailer park wasn't what his hifalutin wife had in mind when she said, "I do."

Some believe Connor and his wife will reunite. I don't. He's sweet on Mama. I can hear it in his voice, the way he asks about her when he drives me to school. The way he comes speedy- quick, even if I need only a little bit of help, like this morning.

I held the screen door wide enough to ease through, stopping at the section where rusted metal hinges announce my escape. I had greased the hinges with lard so many times it attracted blowflies, but no amount of grease would quiet the whine. I glanced toward Granny Pearlene's bedroom, hoping the light wouldn't turn on when the door creaked open. With her room still dark, I bolted from the trailer. Swinging a thermos full of coffee, I hurried to the end of the driveway. Mama didn't know I'd made a full pot this morning and that I already had the thermos ready for Connor before I missed the bus. These days, she's too tired to notice much of anything, especially about me.

Connor took the thermos in one hand and then offered the other so I could pull myself into the cab. "Rough morning?" he asked as the truck bounced across the tracks.

I wiggled my feet between piles of tools on the floorboard and said, "Aren't they all?"

Connor laughed and passed me the thermos. This was our dance; a banter to pass the time. He drove. I poured coffee. We chatted about nothing important.

No, this wasn't the first time he'd taken me to school. Mama would pitch a fit if she knew how many times he'd driven me. Or that some mornings, like today, I miss the bus on purpose.

Mama doesn't need to know everything.

Steam escaped and fogged up the window when I popped off the plastic cup and poured. Nodding a thank you, Connor held the cup in the air and asked, "Sip?"

When I shook my head he said, "Sure you don't want to give it a try?"

He did this often, tempted me with coffee. I love the smell but cringe at the thought of having the same bitter breath as Granny Pearlene.

"No, thank you. I don't drink the hard stuff, especially not this early in the morning."

Connor laughed. "You're a smart girl. No hard stuff for you." He pointed his chin toward the gearshift and pressed the thermos cup to his lips. I placed my hand on the knob and slid the truck into third gear.

Connor believed all women should know how to drive a stick, so while he worked the clutch, I changed the gears.

I wouldn't object one bit if Connor moved in with us. Our trailer doesn't have one inch of space to spare but maybe, if he did, I could bunk with Granny Pearlene or sleep on the couch. I'm tired of not having a man around and especially tired of wondering about my daddy. I had already taken a hard look at Connor and determined we looked *nothing* alike. I figured if Mama wouldn't tell me about my real daddy, I'd pick out my own. I picked Connor.

Like most trucks in Bryson City, Connor's vehicle doubled as a mobile storage unit, so the smell of coffee blended with tool grease and dried sweat. We were separated by the stick shift, a dented red toolbox, and his aluminum lunch box that banged together each time the truck hit a pothole. Loose tools jostled around my ankles and rattled beneath the seat.

After draining the cup, Connor passed it back and declined a refill. Using his shirtsleeve, he wiped the windshield until a peephole appeared in the fogged-up glass.

"I'll probably be over this weekend. Want to talk to your granny about the car."

I could never figure out why Mama walked to work when we have a perfectly good car parked under a tarp out back of our rented lot. Granny Pearlene claims ownership of the Oldsmobile. Mama argues she bought it free and clear and that being a co-*signer* doesn't make you a co-*owner*. When they start arguing I hide in my room.

"You do know that car is really Mama's ... right?"

Connor shrugged. "So, I'll ask her."

"Won't do any good. Mama says it's hers to do with as she pleases."

"Then why isn't she driving it?"

I had wondered that myself. Sure, the tires are flat, but those could be fixed. I didn't tell Connor about the number of arguments Mama and Granny Pearlene had over the stupid car. Connor didn't need to know about the times Granny Pearlene reminded Mama how much trouble the car had gotten her into, or that Mama had said, "I don't need no car to remind me of my mistakes when you do a great job reminding me every single day."

"Don't know why you want the car," I mumbled. "Probably won't even crank."

Connor reached over and patted my knee. "I'm not worried about that. I can fix anything, remember?"

Afraid that Connor might catch Granny Pearlene or Mama in a selling mood, I said, "I think they are saving the car for me."

Connor smiled. "Well now, if that's the case you're going to need to know how a car works, how to change the oil, fix a flat, check the radiator, change the battery. I know just the person to teach you."

Excited, I leaned over and asked, "Who?"

"Why me, of course."

We were almost at school and I frowned. I wished I could ride with Connor forever, wished he would drive right past my school, wished he would run the stop sign at the edge of town, point the truck west and never look back.

"I don't think they'll ever sell the Oldsmobile," I said. "But if you think you can help me fix it up then stop by this afternoon and talk to Mama."

The truck came to a stop behind a line of parked school buses. Connor reached across me to open the door. The aroma of coffee lingered on his skin as he pulled the handle. "I might just do that. Have a good day at school."

I grunted and slid off the seat.

"And Carole Anne, tell your mama I said hello."

I smiled and shut the door. Connor had his work cut out for him. Maybe he could fix the Oldsmobile *and* Mama at the same time.

Bus Number 28 had already unloaded. Doretta stood among the seniors taking one last drag from their cigarettes before first bell. She greeted me with a chewing gum bubble that filled the air with an undeniable watermelon fragrance. She deflated the bubble with her tongue and sucked it back into her mouth then walked toward me and said, "I can't believe you missed the bus. Today, of all days."

Doretta believed that Principal Walker and our English teacher, Miss Love, were having an affair. She suspected that before the morning announcements and pledge of allegiance, they scheduled a phony staff meeting with the sole purpose of enjoying a little uninterrupted hanky-panky. Doretta had noticed that each Tuesday Miss Love wore high heels and a tighter-than-usual short skirt. While I argued that a wardrobe change isn't hard evidence of hanky-panky, Doretta–who had read every Nancy Drew book ever written–described more clues.

"Every Tuesday she's late to her first-period class. Once, her lipstick was smeared."

"So," I had countered. "Smeared lipstick isn't a big deal."

Doretta always gave her reasons with five fingers stretched out, palm open. Then she curled the fingers inward toward her palm, starting with her thumb; a puzzling way of providing what she called "indisputable proof."

"First, she dresses differently on Tuesday." She blew a bubble with each clue as she popped the gum for emphasis. "Second," she curled the pointer finger this time, "Miss Love either soaks in Calgon or bathes in perfume every single Tuesday." When I rolled my eyes Doretta added, "Carole Anne, that is a legitimate clue. She's obviously trying to mask their love juices."

"Oh, gross, Doretta. That's nasty."

"I'm serious. Some mornings we can't catch our breath. We have to crack the windows. On Tuesday she wears her hair piled on top of her head. Plastered stiff with at least one full can of hairspray."

"So. What does that prove? Maybe she goes to the beauty parlor

Monday night."

"It proves she don't want to mess up her hair. Then there's that one time when she turned to write on the blackboard and her pantyhose were tucked in all crazy, poking out of her waistband."

"C'mon now, Doretta. She could have just been in the bathroom and hurried to class."

Doretta wasn't convinced. "Nope. Not possible. That leaves the biggest clue." She blew a bubble and quickly popped it. "Every single Tuesday Principal Walker takes a shower in the boys' locker room."

Now I was interested. "No way!" I said, leaning in closer. "Who says?"

"I say. I've seen him."

My math book slid from my grasp, falling open with a thud. "What do you mean, you've seen him?"

"Look. I notice things and I'm telling you right now they're doing the dirty deed. Some things are undeniable, indisputable facts. This is one of them. There's no logical reason why Principal Walker should use the school's shower."

Doretta punched my shoulder. "I know what's going on. They're doing it in the shower. That's why she wears her hair twisted up, so it won't get wet."

"That's just nasty." I wanted to tell Doretta I thought her idea was crazy talk, but Doretta had a way of making crazy talk sound sane.

"I'm telling you, Carol Anne, every Tuesday it rains cats and dogs. Tuesday the weather forecast calls for rain, frog-strangling after-sex showers the likes this town has never seen before."

Doretta had established a weather-related code so we could speak openly about her suspicions without others knowing. Any conversation that referenced the weather was secret-talk for Miss Love and Principal Walker's affair. Talk of frost or snow meant Miss Love had been rejected and was in a horrible mood. She gave pop tests and extra homework on those frigid days. Thunder and lightning meant it was Miss Love's time of the month. Rain implied hanky-panky. Talk of rain also meant Doretta would have an easy first-period English class, certainly no pop tests. Meanwhile, I'd sit on the front row of Mr. Womick's class and try to understand algebra.

I bent over to pick up the math book. Doretta followed and acted like she was tying her shoelaces. "You tell a soul and I swear I'll hang you from the flagpole by your underwear." She grabbed my wrist, pulled hard, and said, "C'mon, we've gotta move if we're going to catch them in the act." Then she raised her voice, looked to the sky, and said, "Look at those clouds. It's about to come a downpour."

Her words were so convincing that the smokers lowered their cigarettes and lifted their eyes toward the heavens. With a giggle she pulled me toward the three-story brick building.

Doretta leaned against the wall. "Now when I give the signal, make a run for the bushes. We'll see everything from there."

It didn't matter that students were everywhere, there's no stopping Doretta on a mission. Worried, I looked up. The second floor housed the administrative offices. We'd be caught for sure if anyone happened to look out the window.

Before I could ask, "What's the signal?" Doretta grabbed my hand and dragged me behind her. Limbs tugged at my pants. Pine needles tickled my ankles. As we crouched behind the bushes, I felt like an idiot.

"He has to pass by here," Doretta whispered. "When he does, take a good look at his hair."

Gazing upon Principal Walker was easy. Most of the female population took notice every time he walked down the hall. He was the complete opposite of former Principal Hargrove, who was short, bald, and—Doretta insisted—the twin brother of the cartoon character Mr. Magoo. Principal Walker made an impression starting with his first day in Bryson City. The school board hired him all the way from Charlotte. A move that set most folk against him from the start, what with all the godless heathen activity common in big cities. That first morning, his platform shoes made a distinct *thunk-thunk* as he heel-toed down the halls and introduced himself to each class. Principal Hargrove moved stealth-like, silently lurking around corners listening, observing, and

using any type of information he acquired to keep upperclassmen in line.

Newly hired Principal Walker wore a pale-blue polyester suit, no tie, and a partially buttoned checked shirt that afforded a generous view of his thick curly chest hair. A gold necklace adorned his neck and glistened when he walked. Some days he wore two necklaces. The Foster boys called him "queer" but all the girls knew they were just jealous because no one had ever given the Foster boys the time of day. Principle Walker, with his sexy looks and ultra-cool attitude, became a heartthrob from day one. He insisted students call him "Stu," which was short for Stuart.

Female students—myself included—adored Stu. I fell in love with my high school principal the first day. Standing in front of the bathroom mirror, I practiced saying his name in the sexiest voice possible. I hoped he stayed in Bryson City forever. Or at least until I got out of town.

Male students hoped his tenure was short.

On the second day of Stu's tenure, virtually every female in school, faculty included, arrived wearing makeup. We fidgeted with uncooperative hair when his footsteps grew louder. Then inhaled a big gulp of air and sat tall, stomach tucked, shoulders back, breasts held high. He looked around the room, nodded a good morning, then closed the door as the girls deflated, slumping over their desks with their hearts pressed against the flat wooden surface.

No man in Bryson City would have been caught dead wearing any type of jewelry other than a thin wedding band. Before Principal Walker moved to Bryson City, women bought their husbands flannel shirts and wool socks for Christmas. After his arrival, women all over town searched for gold chains with which to adorn their beloveds. The department store couldn't keep pale-blue polyester fabric in stock.

"If he's been in the shower, and I know he has, you'll see what I'm talking about. His hair will be slicked back," Doretta explained.

"It's always like that," I answered hoping she didn't recognize the dreaminess in my voice.

"I know that," she snapped. "But there's a curl in the back, near his collar." Doretta pointed at her own ear. "After it rains, he's in a hurry to get back to the office in time to make the morning announcements. You think Miss Love scratches his back with those claws she calls fingernails?"

"Gee, thanks for the visual," I said with a shudder. "Now I need to Clorox my eyeballs."

Dragging me deeper into the bushes Doretta hissed, "Hush. Here he comes." She then fished a wrapper from her pocket and placed the chewing gum inside. I guess she didn't trust herself not to pop the gum. "Ah-ha," she whispered. "I knew it. See that duck curl?"

From my hiding place I couldn't see a durned thing. Doretta pulled my head toward her, then moved it with her hands. "Behind his left ear. See?"

My heart beat fast. Principal Walker wore a dark-red suit with white stitching around the collar and pockets. A paisley shirt with blue designs lay flat against the polyester fabric. He took the steps two at a time, stretching the fabric tight.

Miss Love was a lucky woman.

"Did you see it? Did you see the curl?" Doretta asked. "I bet you believe me now. I'm telling ya they're doing the dirty deed. It's raining all the dang time."

I didn't have the nerve to tell Doretta my eyes hadn't traveled any higher than Principal Walker's back pockets. Before I could answer first bell sounded. Grabbing my books and lunch box I said, "Gotta run. Can't be late for algebra or Mr. Womick will give me a zero."

Doretta popped a new piece of gum in her mouth. "Honey, I can take my own sweet time. Miss Love will be in a *fan*-tastic mood." She blew a large bubble then filled it with smaller ones. After several pops of gum, Doretta skipped across the pavement with her arms open wide singing, "It's raining, it's pouring …"

Chapter Three

Barbara Parker
1976

I woke fighting for air. It took a moment to realize the train had not killed me, that it wasn't 1960, that Ted wasn't choking me. Only the demons played tricks with my mind.

They also only came at night, hovering above the bed like dark clouds pregnant with rain. They hid in the brown spots of the ceiling, up where the rain leaks through, and found pleasure dropping into my subconscious. Where they scampered around until I woke. Devouring my energy, the demons knew that with very little prompting I will replay the past and spend hours blaming myself for what happened sixteen years ago. They whisper, "*Yes, it was your fault.*"

They have whispered it so much, I now believe them.

I'm an expert at wasting time wondering what I could have done different that night.

"Go away," I whispered through gritted teeth. "Leave me alone."

I repositioned my pillow and took a deep breath, then another, willing myself to let go of the past until a sound startled me and I bolted upright like a jack-in-the-box. I listened and cocked my head, my breath caught. There it was again, a pitter of toenails ... a rat gnawing through the wall, pulling away what little insulation remained.

That's the thing about demons, they know what winds me up. They send the rats, and the nightmares. Demons and rats make perfect bedfellows.

Fully awake, my mind whirled. I thought about the night Carole Anne was conceived and how hearts were easily broken. I thought about what I wanted from life when I was my daughter's age. I despised myself for giving up on my dreams and settling for this discontented life in Bryson City. I should have taken the Oldsmobile and left, but Mama had raised me to stay, to dig in and stare down trouble.

It would be nice if I could talk to Mama about my feelings, but Pearlene Parker isn't known for her nurturing ways. She believes in lowering her chin, plowing through challenges and never looking back. Not me. I kept one eye on the past, because looking at my future makes me want to tie myself to the train tracks—this time with different results.

Even to this day, I remember the moment clearly, down to the millisecond when harsh blue eyes stared into mine, when I squeezed my eyes tight and turned my face away.

On a better note, the demons have taught me a thing or two about lies and their usefulness. A well-placed lie serves a purpose and omissions of truth weave strong webs. And so, I continue the lie of omission and will continue to do so until the day I die. Carole Anne doesn't need to know the truth about the night she was conceived. No one does.

Carole Anne. God must have made a mistake when he saw fit to give her to me. Back then, as my bruises faded, a restless spirit settled in my soul. I began to worry. Fret. Pray. Oh, how I prayed. Prayed that my period would come. Prayed to forget every moment of that night. Prayed for the chance to rewind my life. But I soon learned that some prayers weren't meant to be answered. One missed period and then another. Mornings where I rushed to the bathroom hoping not to wake Mama.

But Pearlene already knew. The demons tattled. Ever since I was little, I'd been told that secrets carry on the wind. Late one night the rotten-tongued demons whispered my secret into Mama's ear. Even when I tried to hide the pregnancy, she knew. Mama always had a way of knowing things.

When I refused to name Carole Anne's father, it created a rift that no amount of praying on Mama's part, or hoping on mine, could change. Mama took me straight to the Wednesday night prayer meeting at First

Baptist, just like Zeke's mama had after she realized a "bag of grass" isn't the same thing as the cuttings raked from her yard.

Zeke had an assigned seat in front of me in English. Most days the seat sat empty while Zeke skipped class, so I wasn't surprised in the least when he got caught. I'm sure the deacons lectured him, repeating what we'd been taught in Sunday school—*be sure your sins will find you out.* Once Zeke confessed his sins privately to the deacons, he got off with an apology along with a promise to weed-whack the lawns of every church deacon for the summer. But things are different for girls. A boy can sell weed to half the town and can even get a girl pregnant without much fuss, but girls get a bad name. Around here, football players are untouchable, incapable of wrongdoing, while most people believed textile girls like me were trash. Especially pregnant, unmarried, textile girls. And now, years later, here I am, living with Pearlene and Carole Anne in a trailer on the poor side of the tracks. Not a darn thing's changed.

I think Pearlene took me to Wednesday night prayer hoping the ladies would surround me with love and cover me with prayer. She had noticed a difference in me, a troubled quietness she couldn't help. The church ladies might have offered comfort if it weren't for the deacons who called a "business meeting" to discuss my pregnancy. Afterward, they announced that if I wanted to remain a member in good standing, I must confess my sins before the congregation.

Pearlene's look was first of hurt, then quickly changed to anger. "Who died and made y'all judge?" she demanded.

Not wanting any more trouble, I quickly said, "I'll do it."

Pearlene tucked her purse beneath her arm then grabbed my hand. "No ma'am you most certainly will not. Your sins are between you and God, not you, God, and them." She pushed me toward the door and said, "None of y'all are spotless. Not a single one." Pointing, she spoke with a short-clipped tone. "Not you. Or you." Raising her chin a notch, she added, "And especially not you, Mr. Chairman of the Deacons!" She had pulled me toward her and said, "My Barbara's not perfect, but neither are you. None of us are. I'm pretty sure the Bible says, 'let ye who are without sin cast the first stone.'"

And with that, we left without a single stone tossed.

***

I looked at the clock. Five twenty.

I needed a moment of peace, just one, before walking out the front door and into the repetitive task of sewing. The warped linoleum floor of this trailer let in the cold and made me irritable and fussy, much like Carole Anne had been as an infant. I curled my feet under me, closed my eyes, and listened to the coffee pot.

After bringing Carole Anne home from the hospital, I determined it best to keep her bottle beneath my pillow. I reasoned the bedroom was too cold to sour the milk and body heat worked just as fast as the decrepit stove. Waking when she stirred, my hand searched for the bottle. I soon mastered the art of nighttime feedings—removing the nipple cover and finding Carole Anne's mouth with remarkable accuracy, not once needing to turn on the light.

Those times were gone now. Carole Anne had grown into a teenager and I could feel deep in the marrow of my bones that the demons have grown tired of playing with me and had set their sights on my daughter.

I poured coffee and wrapped both hands around the cup. Homes with wheels weren't meant for teenage mothers who have no idea what they're doing. I don't pray much anymore, but when I do I pray God prevents Carole Anne from repeating my mistakes and supernaturally transports her from this hovel of poverty into a better life.

I stopped praying for myself a long time ago.

I left the kitchen and walked to the bathroom. During the night ice had formed a layer inside the windows. It was almost time to buy heating oil. The price always shoots up after the first killing frost. No matter how hard I tried, I couldn't drive out the cold, or darkness. Wind filled the room with frigid puffs of air. I had already taped bedsheets to the ceiling and walls, cursing the cascading folds that barely blocked Mother Nature's cold breath.

Mine wasn't the only trailer with sheet-covered windows. By

November, everyone in the trailer park had cloudy plastic or bedsheets taped to their walls. Not that it mattered; no matter what you hung cold air always found a way inside.

I was awake now, fully awake and afraid to blink. If I closed my eyes even for a minute, I could feel prickly whiskers scraping my pale skin. Tan muscular arms holding me down, sweat mixing with my blood.

Outside, train tracks vibrated. Familiar sounds shook my core as the rhythmic pulse of pistons plucked at memories, pounding harder and harder. Tears stung my eyes. Peering out the window, I saw a tiny speck of light growing larger as the train approached. Its scream was a warning. While most people in Bryson City took the signal as a reminder to clear the tracks before it was too late, for me the piercing noise beckoned: *Come. Lie down on the tracks and end your pain.*

I reached for a pack of Marlboros. Shoving my fingers inside the crinkling package, I fished out the last one and threw the empty wrapping in the trash.

Two days till payday and I'm out of smokes.

The match ignited and spat fire. I held the flame to the tip and inhaled. Watching the red glow of the cigarette blend with the train's increasingly bright light, I took a hard drag and held my breath. Smoke burned my lungs and filled the room.

Coffee dregs danced in the bottom of the cup as the train roared past. Glancing at the mirror, I realized how old I looked. Faded youth, worried lines with a trace of despair dotting my cheeks.

I took another drag. The mirror danced on the wall and threatened to leap to the floor. Hypnotized by the piercing light, I longed for the hope-filled days. Light had a way of piercing the darkness, stripping away youthful dreams and replacing them with the cold, blinding truth. I leaned forward, crushed the cigarette into the coffee cup, and stared out the window. The engineer held the chain, filling the morning with one final teeth-shaking howl of the whistle. As the train passed, light illuminated my face. I pressed my hand to my forehead and squeezed my eyes shut.

"Go away," I said to the images boring into my brain. "Why won't you just go away?"

Freight cars rumbled past. The trailer rocked and despite the darkness behind my eyelids memories of that night remained. I heard Carole Anne's bedroom door close. Awake and restless, just like her mother. Sometimes I wondered if she instinctively knew what had happened that night.

Wetting a cloth, I washed my face and remembered a night many years ago when the train had been so close my hair smelled of creosol. On that night I had welcomed the train and its force, its power to destroy anything that dare approach the tracks. On that night, bruised and bleeding, I waited on the tracks, desperate to end the pain.

But, then ...

Chapter Four

Carole Anne

Thanks to Doretta's comments, I couldn't get images of Principal Walker and Miss Love doing the horizontal hokey pokey out of my mind. Doretta was prone to exaggeration, and as she constantly reminded me, I am naïve, but the proof was there all curled up behind Principal Walker's ear.

I shuddered. *Gross.*

The afternoon bus ride was always short. Trailer park kids were the last picked up in the morning and the first dropped off after school. It's like the driver wanted trailer trash kids riding for the shortest possible time. As the bus came to a stop, a thunder of tennis shoes approached, vibrating the floorboard. Brad blew past me in a flash, followed by the Foster boys—Mark and Luke, biblical in name only. Doretta and I usually roll our eyes when they gallop off the bus, but she was staying after school for cheerleading practice, and what she called a "little bit of detective work."

"I'm going to see if it rains after school, too," Doretta had whispered during our lunch break. "I'll call you tonight."

"Be careful," I warned. "If you get caught, there'll be trouble."

Doretta didn't really care about trouble. Sometimes I think she welcomed it. She possesses a cat-like curiosity; it is one of her best qualities. Like me, Doretta is an only child. I used to think she became my friend out of boredom. But, as our friendship grew, I realized our little trailer was a place where popping gum isn't frowned upon and watching soap operas doesn't come with judgment that damns your soul to hell. At my house, she's free to paint her nails any color she wants. Even the color she calls "whore red," even though the label reads

Candy Apple. She wears the shade all day while we talk about our future husbands and children, reluctantly changing the color back to "virgin pearl" when it's time to go home.

I said good-bye to the driver and winced as gravel pressed into my thin-soled shoes. I live in the second trailer on the left, wedged between Willa Rae Jameson and Trummie Woodard who has tried for years to woo Mama into selling Tupperware.

Our dog, Smokey, emerged from beneath our trailer with a tail-thumping welcome. When I released him from the chain, he took off like a flash, like he was eager to escape, like he was abandoning me and leaving Bryson City never to return. As he reached the mailbox, he circled fast, kicked up gravel, and ran back to me. Bending, I offered him the crust from my peanut butter sandwich. "Hey, boy. Miss me?" I asked.

Smokey wolfed down the crust and didn't offer a hint about Granny Pearlene's mental status today. I never knew what to expect when I got home from school. Sometimes she acted fine, but on confused days she called me by Mama's name. I'd be doing homework at the kitchen table and she'd say something odd like, "Barbara, remember that time you fell on the school playground and almost knocked out your front teeth?"

I never wasted time correcting her. Today, as I placed my hand on the doorknob, I hoped she recognized me. Entering the trailer, the smell of ammonia almost knocked me down. Our black-and-white television sat on the kitchen counter blaring *One Life to Live*. Granny Pearlene sat in a chair with a towel pressed tight against her forehead while her best friend Claudette stood behind her shaking a clear plastic bottle of perming solution.

"Tip your head forward," Claudette commanded while she drenched the rollers with milky liquid. The bottle belched and air refilled the almost empty container. "Pearlene, I don't know why in the world you won't let Barbara give you a perm. Lord knows she's better than me."

"Humph. You're just as good," Granny Pearlene said, her words muffled beneath folds of terry cloth fabric. Yellow rollers formed a track across her head. She never used red rollers. Said they made her hair too kinky.

Claudette didn't look up from her work. "Carole Anne, did you know that girls used to beg your Mama to fix their hair?"

I looked at Granny who didn't dare move lest a drop of curling solution trickle into her eyes.

"Sure did," Claudette continued. "Girls used to line up at the crack of dawn on the morning of the prom. Your Mama created the most elaborate updos."

"Humph," Granny Pearlene grumbled from beneath the towel. "She'd make a sight more money doing hair than sewing pants. I tell you that much for true. I still don't like the way she rolls my hair ... too kinky."

Perm solution dripped from Granny Pearlene's ear. Once the bottle was empty, Claudette dabbed away excess liquid with a cloth and fitted a shower cap around Granny Pearlene's head. She cranked an egg timer and said, "While your hair processes take a look at what I brought."

Dumping the contents from a paper bag onto the kitchen table, Claudette said, "C'mon Carole Anne, you can help."

Colorful sheets of paper slid across the table. Claudette placed her hands on the pages and touched them like a gypsy reading a crystal ball. "These come in the Sunday paper every week. They're coupons printed by companies who want us to buy their products."

She produced three pairs of scissors from her purse. "Let's start clipping."

"Where did you get so many newspapers?" I asked.

"Oh, it was easy," she said with a smile. "Sheldon got them for me. He asked the ladies along his trash route to stack their papers on top of their cans."

Granny Pearlene pushed the shower cap away from her eyes with the palm of her hand revealing gray and thinning eyebrows that had disappeared when the cap slid down her forehead. With her soap operas ended, she turned off the television. "Some people think poor folk are lazy and ignorant. I'm here to testify we are some of the smartest people I know." She reached out and pulled a stack of coupons toward her. "You know what they say … one man's trash is my treasure."

Claudette pulled out a chair and patted the seat. "So after we get all these coupons clipped, we use them at the grocery store and buy whatever we have a coupon for. Sheldon got a big load of papers and we can really stock up." Sliding some pages toward Granny Pearlene, Claudette said, "The Piggly Wiggly subtracts whatever this says." Her fingers tapped the picture on the paper. "This one is for fifty cents off a four-roll pack of Charmin toilet paper."

Granny Pearlene flicked her wrist and the coupon twirled toward Claudette. "Good land of the livin,' woman. I can't afford no fancy Charmin, even with one of these here cue-pins. It's all I can do to buy the True Value brand rolls when they go on sale."

Rolling her eyes, Claudette sighed and said, "I know that Pearlene, but I have it on good authority that this Wednesday Trent Smithfield is going to double the amount printed on every coupon. In addition to the five percent senior citizens discount, that little scrap of paper you threw at me will be worth one whole dollar."

Granny Pearlene snatched the slip of paper back into her possession. "You mean I could buy me a pack of that fancy Charmin and it would only cost me a dime?"

Claudette nodded. "Now you get the picture. The best part is that the Piggly Wiggly isn't going to advertise the double-coupon special. So, this means Sheldon can get us another load of papers before people find out. You know once word gets out people will be stealing newspapers outta driveways in the dead of night."

Granny Pearlene said, "Carole Anne, put on another pot of coffee. We've got some serious clipping to do."

We removed every coupon, even for items we didn't use. Stacks accumulated beside us. We sorted the piles into categories: baby items, beverages, canned goods, pet food, and paper products. As we sorted the clippings, Granny Pearlene came across something she didn't recognize. "Claudette, what's this?" she asked while holding an odd-looking coupon for examination. "This one don't say how much it's worth."

Claudette adjusted her glasses. "That's a rebate form. Way down at the bottom it says, buy three cans of Alpo dog food and get one dollar back. Just follow the instructions printed on the bottom of the sheet. This one wants you to mail in the labels from three cans of dog food. Some rebates don't need labels, you only need to write the UPC code on the slip of paper and mail it."

"What in the Sam Hill's a UPC code?" Granny Pearlene interrupted.

I said, "UPC codes are those numbers printed on the back of everything we buy. Remember when you thought they were the mark of the beast?"

"Oh yeah. Now I remember … and I still think those numbers are the mark of the beast." Granny Pearlene readjusted the shower cap. "Gov'mint is always watching us too."

Claudette continued, "Anyway, follow the rebate instructions. Send in the label, or the UPC, whatever they ask. A few weeks later the company mails a check just for using their product."

I slapped a dog food coupon on the table. "Here's twenty-five cents off three cans of food for Smokey. That'll be fifty cents when doubled. If we can find these on sale and send in the rebate, we'll earn sixty-three cents for something we use every day."

"Minus the price of stamps and envelopes," Claudette reminded. "When you take advantage of a rebate there are some upfront expenses."

"We'll put the money in our emergency jar," I said.

Lately both Mama and Granny Pearlene preached the importance of having a little stash of "emergency money." I'm still wondering how that's possible considering we never have any extra money to spare much less stash. It is impossible for me to make money. It's not like I can go out and get a real job. My job is looking after Granny Pearlene every single day after school and the pay sucks. That's why I help Hubert at night while Granny Pearlene and Mama are asleep. I've got plans for my money that do not include them.

Granny Pearlene laughed, "So they will pay us forty-five cents instead. We'll still make money and I for one am willing to take every penny someone cares to give me. No more True Value dog food for Smokey." Sorting through the piles she said, "What other rebates we got in here?"

"Looks like a lot of diapers and baby food," I said while placing them in a separate pile. "Mama can take these to the ladies at the plant. Someone always needs diapers."

Granny Pearlene grabbed my hand. "Whoa there. Not so fast. I might be willing to give someone a dollar off their diapers but I'm not so sure I want to add a two-dollar rebate to go with it." Displaying the offers in front of her like a hand of cards Granny Pearlene said, "I think if we play this right, we could make us some real money. We're smart gals. We just need to put our heads together and figure out how to claim all this free cash."

"Kind of impossible since none of us have babies," Claudette said while lifting her empty cup.

I refilled their coffee. The women slurped and pondered.

"I've got it," Claudette said. "Sheldon picks up the trash for the whole town. He can just save the trash from people who've got babies." She looked at us for affirmation.

Granny Pearlene shoved the sinking shower cap out of her eyes. "Claudette, have you lost your ever-lovin' mind? Yore husband can't put poopy diapers in his truck. No. That won't work."

Claudette crossed her arms across her chest and said, "You got a better idea?"

The vinyl seat creaked as Granny Pearlene sat back. "As a matter of fact, I do. Let's make a list of the labels we need to go with these here rebates then we'll just mosey down to the trash dump and find the labels. Carole Anne, fetch me a sheet of paper."

Expecting Claudette to shoot down the idea, I stayed put.

"Sheldon has the key to the gate ... right?" Granny Pearlene asked.

Claudette nodded.

"Then all we need is to drive in there after they lock up, pick through the bags, peel off the labels, and we're done."

"What if we get caught?" Claudette asked.

"Not gonna happen. We'll lock the gate behind us. Carole Anne can stand guard."

"Do what?" I said, shocked that I was included.

Ignoring me, Claudette asked, "What if Sheldon says no?"

Pearlene rolled her eyes. "Persuade him. You know … use your womanly charms on the man."

I blushed and remained quiet. Both women had lost their minds.

Claudette held the coffee cup to her lips, considering Pearlene's suggestion.

"C'mon, Claudette." Granny Pearlene picked up the rebate forms. "Here's a dollar for dog food; two dollars for diapers; another dollar for Kotex. That's a lot of free money."

"Don't forget about the postage," Claudette said.

"Enough with the blasted postage; I don't give a rat's hind-end about postage." Granny Pearlene fished a dollar out of her bra and slammed it on the table. "Here! That'll buy enough stamps to get us started. Ladies, what we have here is an opportunity. We've got a group of people who don't use these cue-pins. Whether they are too proud or too ignorant, I don't care. As long as Sheldon can get his hands on these papers and get us into the county dump, we'd be fools not to take advantage of this chance." She looked from one to the other of us. "C'mon, how about it? Folk like us don't get many breaks. Claudette, you said it yourself, once word gets out people will be stealing papers. They'll be digging in the landfill too. Mark my word."

Picking up a colorful slip of paper, Granny Pearlene looked Claudette straight in the eye and said, "Claudette, you're always complaining that Sheldon controls the checkbook. Now you've got the chance to hoard up some money for yourself. You ain't no fool. You ain't gonna throw good money away. So, whaddaya think?"

Claudette raised her cup like one of those high-browed ladies on television. Then she and Granny Pearlene clinked their cups together, sealing the deal while holding their pinkies high. The timer dinged. Claudette walked over to the kitchen sink and ran the water until it warmed. "I could pretend I was going to church, toss a change of clothes in the trunk."

"Hallelujah sister. Now you're talking," Granny Pearlene said. "Ain't nobody ever gone to hell for missing one Sunday."

"All right, I'll do it. Now come over here and let me rinse your hair. It's time to apply the neutralizer."

Water splashed out of the tiny sink and collected in beads along the counter. Claudette opened the neutralizer bottle and squeezed liquid across the rollers. The women chatted about all the money they'd make and agreed to set out for the trash dump as soon as folk got settled into their pews Sunday morning.

They decided Claudette was in charge of convincing Sheldon to unlock the gate or let her borrow the key. I was responsible for making a list of the items we needed and assembling digger rakes to tear open trash bags without touching them. And Granny Pearlene was in charge of telling us what to do and counting all the money we would earn.

As much as I hated the thought of digging through someone else's trash, the lure of money is a strong incentive. I'm kinda trapped here with Granny Pearlene. But that'll change if Connor gets Mama's Oldsmobile working. That's why I'm giving this rebate gig a go. With the money I've stashed from working with Hubert and my share of the rebate profits, I'll have enough to leave Bryson City and never look back.

Ten minutes later, the timer dinged. Claudette rinsed Granny Pearlene's hair and lathered it twice with Prell shampoo. But the stench of ammonia lingered as did my nervousness about their plans.

Chapter Five

Barbara

It's a long walk from my trailer to the wall-mounted time clock at Cleveland Manufacturing. Opening the door, the morning air chilled my face as I stepped down the cinder block steps and onto the frost-covered graveled driveway. I shivered and wrapped a knitted scarf around my neck then lowered my chin to block the wind. Winter was on the way. I despised winter, a time when the earth seemed naked, lifeless, dead. Glancing toward the Oldsmobile parked behind the trailer, I frowned and curled my bare hands under my arms for warmth.

I should be driving instead of walking.

The Oldsmobile hadn't budged since the night Carole Anne was conceived. The vehicle once served as inspiration, a means of transporting me to beauty school, or perhaps a college where I could earn a four-year business degree. Now every time I look at the car, I remember that night sixteen years ago and realize the futility of dreams. Sometimes it's best to save your energy and just take what life offers.

Tucking my chin further in, I walked faster. Wind cut through my flimsy coat and chapped my lips. Pressing my lips tight, I sealed them closed, protecting them from the wind, while guarding any secrets that might escape. My grandmother had raised me to keep secrets locked up tight, never telling another soul, not even a whisper, because the wind carries our secrets and scatters them like dandelion petals.

"Even the best-kept secrets are eventually revealed," she had warned. "Secrets are collected, plucked from hidey-holes and planted on the tongues of busybodies and troublemakers."

I shuddered. *I hate cold weather.*

My grandmother, God rest her soul, despised winter so much that she believed dying in the winter was God's curse. She used to say, "Why else would God freeze the dirt so hard folk can't dig a proper grave?" She'd tell stories and shiver. I'd dash into the bedroom and return with a patchwork quilt. We'd snuggle under the covers partially for warmth but more for comfort and protection from haints and spirits.

Pearlene would say, "Stop talking about the dead, you'll give Barbara nightmares."

The dead never gave me nightmares … not like the living.

Scurrying past the Baptist Church cemetery where Grandmother was buried, I remembered her words. *Guard your secrets, Barbara. Be sure your sins will find you out.*

I prayed that my secret remained hidden.

Pearlene Parker would never admit it, but she was just like her mother. Mama keeps secrets too. She told me Daddy died in the month of January. Whether that's the truth or not, it doesn't matter. I was still kicking like a mule inside Pearlene's belly and, according to her, having a bad case of the hiccups the day he died. I used to think my daddy was buried somewhere in town. I searched the graveyard, but stopped asking what happened to him, stopped asking Pearlene why we didn't decorate my daddy's grave with paper flowers like other people. Not knowing about my daddy used to bother me, until I became a mother. Now I understand that lies provide a necessary shield of protection. Children don't need to know everything.

The tiny town of Bryson City faded behind me as my feet found US Hwy 19 and the blacktop leading to Cleveland Manufacturing. The road was once dirt, feeding into cow pastures and tobacco rows, which is why the builders selected the property, being the largest plot of land flat and wide enough for tractor trailers to turn around. Locals knew the real reason Cleveland Manufacturing chose this spot was to avoid paying both city and county property taxes.

Wind found its way through my thin coat. Maybe God's curse wasn't dying in the winter but surviving. I switched my handbag to the other shoulder and kept my chin inside my coat. On the right, Mill Town was aglow with workers just rising from their peaceful slumber.

The smell of bacon and eggs triggered a growl from my stomach, and I wondered if Carole Anne ate breakfast this morning.

People called this community Mill Town because the homes were built for millworkers. Here, folk opted to have rent withheld from their paychecks and did everything within their power to keep their homes, because only trailer trash lived on my side of the railroad tracks. Despite the large tenant population, neither the town of Bryson City, nor the state of North Carolina saw a need to widen US 19 ... *or* build pedestrian sidewalks, which is why I pay special attention every morning listening for trucks traveling too fast around the curve.

After saying a quick prayer, I crossed the road with my pocketbook banging against my hip.

Working at the plant is the only possible job when other options like finishing high school and attending college vanish. Single women like me worked extra hard, taking in other work like sewing, washing someone else's laundry, selling homemade cakes. Anything to earn extra money and make life a little easier.

When I was growing up, the extra money did more than keep oil in the furnace of our Mill Town home. Extra income bought an RC Cola at Bennett's Drugstore and provided me with an extended family of brothers and sisters, a community of playmates known throughout Bryson City as the Mill Town Kids. We played outside from the minute we stepped off the school bus until dusky dark. We climbed trees and dared each other to swim in the plant's retention pond. The company dumped used fabric dye in the pond, so no one was brave enough to take that dare. Bored, we kicked cans down the tracks and dreamed of train robbing until Hoke Montgomery told us that the white gold in the boxcars was just plain old ordinary cotton on its way to the lint machine. After that we abandoned our train-robbing plans, scheming instead to hop a railcar, become hoboes, and ride the rail as far as it took us. Except none of us figured out how to hop aboard a 200-ton machine traveling 25 miles per hour.

Trains didn't stop in Bryson City. There was nothing worth stopping for.

Mill Town Kids always traveled as a pack. We placed discarded cigarette butts on our lips and walked around with a thumb latched inside our belt loops like the Marlboro Man. We collected gravel and threw it at the windows where the trailer park trash lived so close to the tracks we wondered if the open glass panes touched the passing railcars. Mill Town Kids enjoyed houses that didn't leak and a community where kids did everything together, parting only to return home for supper when the security lights came on at dusk. Secretly, my friends and I were glad we lived on the other side of the tracks in an area we called "the good side of town." Everyone knew trailer park people were nothing but trash. Surviving on food stamps and cast aside handouts.

Back then, I wasn't rich, or poor, but somewhere in between blissfully living where shag carpeting kept the floors warm at night. On the Mill Town side, we were three generations of Parker women comfortable with our life, until Granny developed a cough she just couldn't shake. We knew Granny had what they called "linters lung" but back then women didn't take off from work, even if they were so sick they could barely make it through the day.

They still don't.

Her cough began with a tickle, like the one you get when a piece of cornbread takes the wrong path down your windpipe; except patting Granny's back didn't make the cough go away. Night was the worst. Granny wheezed. Her lungs rattled and begged for relief that no amount of Vicks VapoRub or Save the Baby medicine delivered.

I was old enough to take care of Granny after school. I kept the house tidy and our clothes clean. Next thing I knew, Pearlene's hours increased and she didn't get home until well past dark, leaving me to nurse Granny. Instead of playing with my friends, I'd slather Vicks VapoRub on her wrinkled chest while coughs wracked her body. Sometimes she managed a weak thank you. When I worried, which was often, Granny opened the Bible and read scripture. "Fear not," she proclaimed with as much gusto as a Baptist preacher. "Everything will be fine."

Everything stopped being fine when Granny died and Pearlene

couldn't make enough money to keep us in the little house on the corner.

There it is, my little yellow house. I miss it so much.

I'm happy someone lives there now; I only wished it were still me.

Each morning as I walked to work, I tried not to think about where I grew up, about fun times with my friends, the little taste of the good life and how short that delicious flavor lasted. I didn't want to think about Carole Ann's life and how it mirrors mine back when I was the same age; how she takes care of her grandmother, when taking care of an old woman is really not her responsibility.

I hurried past the community where I once lived. The smell of coffee tickled my nose and pricked my remembrances.

Maxwell House, Good to the Last Drop. Not JFG bought on sale and brewed so thin you could see through it.

My taste buds salivated with longing as my mind replayed a memory of Pearlene letting me sip from her cup. The flavors of cream and sugar had lingered on my tongue. Coffee from my childhood tasted different … strong and full of hope, made with two heaping scoops instead of the weak liquid I tossed down my throat every morning.

I don't remember much about all the places I've lived. I only remember that after Granny died Pearlene Parker always needed money and I never fell into a deep sleep because I worried she'd wake me in the middle of the night so we could slip off undetected. That's the best time to skip out on the rent, under the cover of darkness when the landlord can't see you cramming everything you own into the car. But there's really no good way to strap a mattress, a bed frame and your television on top of the car, although we did when we first moved, and again the second time. But by age sixteen everything I owned fit into a pillowcase except for a record player housed in a bright orange suitcase-size box—a Christmas present from the year I turned ten. I lugged it from house to house until the electrical cord pulled from the base. I tried holding the wires together with electrical tape, but the adhesive was too weak.

Try as I might for otherwise, remembrances of my past still haunt me. I guess that's what makes me and Pearlene different. She had a way of forgetting things long before the doctor told me about her dementia. Maybe that's why she can't remember much anymore, because she'd spent years trying to forget and eventually got her wish.

Back then, Pearlene liked to call us the "make do" girls. When there wasn't enough food or money we had to "make do." I heard the phrase *we'll just have to make do* so many times I wanted to scream. That's why I worked my butt off to buy the Oldsmobile. At age sixteen, while Mill Town Kids smoked cigarettes and dared each other to jump off the train trestle into the lake, I made money waitressing at Big Joe's Pizza and swore I'd have a better life. But now I want to scream because Pearlene's words sometimes rolled off my tongue before I could stop them. At least I haven't moved Carole Anne from pillar to post.

Maybe I learned to make do by staying put. Even when I wanted to run far away.

A scattering of cars dotted the parking lot as I rounded the corner and opened the side door of the plant. I entered the production floor and shivered. Half of the workers suffer from menopause and never complain about the temperature. I look forward to midday. After the sewing machines start humming the room heats up fast.

I shucked off my coat, hung it on a hook. Looking at the threadbare garment, I understood how Carole Anne felt, how she noticed what other kids wore and longed for something better than what she had. That's one of the reasons I arrive early, I don't want to stand in line with those who have it better than me. Living on the trailer park side of life isn't fun, at any age.

My eyes adjusted to the light as I reached for my timecard housed inside a tall metal rack. After years of punching a clock, my arm knew where to reach; my hand trained to the exact position where the card waited. The machine banged and paper rattled as metal teeth stamped the hour and minute. Seven-twenty: ten minutes early.

Now that I'm an adult I understand how difficult it was for Pearlene to afford our Mill Town house. I remember hearing Pearlene talking with other women about needing extra hours, pleading with supervisors and promising to work twelve, even fourteen hours a day. When her schedule remained the same, she asked if there was an opening in production. Being put on the production line provided an opportunity to earn a good living. The more shirts or jeans you produced, the fatter your paycheck. Doing this type of work meant feeding pieces of fabric into the metal mouth of a ravenous sewing machine. Securing pieces together one cotton fiber at a time, as quickly as possible, while praying your fingers stayed out of harm's way and remained attached to your hands where they belonged.

Sewing machines are hungry beasts.

Janelle appeared at my station before I had the chance to sit. Janelle likes to tell people she "helped build the plant from the ground up." Which is true. She was first hired back when the company had twenty machines and only a handful of orders.

"Slacks today," she said with a nod toward the bin. "No jeans." Inside, a mound of cotton slacks waited for zippers. It took three workers to assemble a pair of slacks, four if you count the pattern cutter. One seamstress sewed the pattern, another the zipper, and a third attached snaps or buttons. Sitting beside me, a pile of pale purple beauties; a new spring line that I couldn't afford.

"How's your back?" I asked knowing that Howard the plant manager frowned upon conversational dallying. We called him The Eagle because he could spy an unproductive employee from the other side of the room and hear gossip above the roar of a hundred sewing machines. When he sensed a lull in productivity, he blew the whistle that dangled from his neck and pointed at the offender. He'd even fired a few on the spot.

"Fine. Better," Janelle said while handing me a spool of thread.

That's another reason I come in early, so we can chat before machines make talking impossible. Janelle's day began at five-thirty when she walked into a room chock-full of bins piled high from the previous day. The unfinished garments needed zippers, buttons, snaps, hemming. Her job is to pair incomplete RUSH orders with the fastest employees. After inventorying the daily workload, she delivers a bin to each sewing station. Sometimes she'd have time to leave thread, buttons, whatever is required to complete the task. If not, a runner we called The Button Boy brought supplies needed to finish the job. The idea was to equip every worker so they need only take a seat and drive the machine from the beginning of the workday until the four twenty-five bell.

Janelle didn't fool me. I could tell by the way she shifted her weight from one foot to the other that her back still hurt. "You know my locker combination. I've got some aspirin in my purse. If you need some, help yourself."

"Thanks," Janelle responded.

She wouldn't take me up on the offer. Janelle is the kind of woman who believed that enduring pain was her lot in life.

The blue-jean plant is the largest employer in Bryson City, sewing for Family Dollar, JCPenney, Sears, and Belk. Only the quick and accurate received production assignments. Women who sat hunched over a piece of equipment with very little opportunity to stretch their legs; a woman who had no choice but to work until her neck hurt, her muscles ached and her eyes strained to focus on a needle begging to taste flesh; women like me, who gritted their teeth and followed in their mama's footsteps.

I tightened the zipper foot on the machine and settled into my station.

"Got a rush order on these," Janelle said with a chuckle.

Around here all orders were rush orders. Desperate women made the best production workers and it was no coincidence that many were single moms. They'd push fabric through the machine until calluses formed on the tips of their fingers. They blew cotton fibers away from the metal foot plate so tiny pieces of lint wouldn't collect and slow down the needle. Eager for their children to have a better life, these mamas set their sights on the future and dreamed of a bigger polyester payday.

That's what workers called Friday, *Polyester Payday.*

During lunch the women huddled together in groups either outside or in the break room. Here they said, "One day I may keel over dead at my station, but I'll be durned if my young'un will end up here. Pushing this fabric through the machines might kill me, but my kid's gonna have a better life."

Some kids do obtain the better life only if they abandon Bryson City, but many dropped out of school and took a seat at a station near Mama.

With a nod toward my pile of work I asked, "How many of these?" Not that the number mattered. You sewed until it was time to go home. Still, I liked to keep a running total of my production in my head. It helped me know my value with the company. A few workers were faster than me, but not many.

"Looks like about twenty-five hundred ordered this week."

Production workers were rarely sick, never late, and didn't argue when the supervisor cheated them out of a piece or two. Those who questioned their paychecks were quickly let go.

Reaching into the bin, I felt my shoulders relax a little. Today's work would be easy, less pressure on my fingers and wrists. Thin fabric slid under the machine's foot and the needle pumped faster, didn't get gonged up like bulky jean fabric. I smiled, on the inside of course. There wasn't much to be happy about when hunched over a sewing machine other than the joy of looking into a bin full of purple cotton slacks that, to me, looked like money.

"JCPenney I think," Janelle said, guessing who had placed the order. "They look too fancy for Family Dollar."

"Hmm. Probably right. I left you a little something in the break room."

A sparkle brightened Janelle's eyes.

"I didn't forget. I slipped it in the fridge ... put a note on it so no one would bother it."

Janelle grinned, not enough to reveal her teeth, but enough to show a little happiness.

"You deserve something delicious on your birthday." I tilted my head to the right. "Best get to moving. Eagle's got you in his sights."

"He always does," Janelle said as she turned to retrieve another bin for the next station. Janelle didn't need to thank me for the birthday cake. She'd parked her gratitude beside me, an easy sew that would generate extra income. Blue jeans are always in demand and some workers can sew them with their eyes closed. Pairing quick-jobs with a fast employee kept The Eagle off Janelle's back, and a bit more money in my pocket. Janelle hadn't worked in the plant for twenty-five years without understanding a thing or two about running a business.

I shuddered. Twenty-five years punching a clock. Lord help. Could be worse; I could be standing in the unemployment line. I snapped a bobbin in place then threaded the machine just like the women in this town had for years. Toby stopped at my left elbow. "Good morning, Barbara," he said while parking an empty bin to my right. The lever squeaked as he pressed the brake so the cart wouldn't roll forward when I slid the finished slacks from one side of the machine to the other.

Toby was a man of few words and very little time. As a runner, his job was just that, scurrying around, driving bins between machines and making sure each seamstress had a place to deposit her finished work. He knew exactly where to park bins so the seamstress could slide their work with minimal effort. Heaven forbid a single item fall to the dingy concrete floor. The walkie-talkie attached to his belt banged against my machine. When you needed extra zippers, buttons, or ran low on thread, you raised your hand. One finger meant buttons; two, zippers; three signaled you were almost ready for a new bin. Upon seeing the signal, Toby or Janelle dispatched a Button Boy to replenish your stock. Make no mistake, Toby might be helping The Button Boy right now, but I knew he was a mini-Eagle, a fledgling in training, tasked with conveying information to the all-seeing boss man.

"Looks like Janelle gave you the new spring line," Toby said.

A rookie employee would see Toby's comment as an opening, a way to get on his good side. They would attempt to befriend the man who reports to The Eagle. I knew better. Toby had no good side. He was baiting me, creating an opportunity for chitchat. I'd seen this trick before. With a click, I lowered the metal foot and held the cloth in place. Excess fabric collected in my lap.

"Yup." The engine purred as I drove the machine hard like a getaway vehicle. I released the foot and used the needle to hold the zipper in place while I turned the slacks. Needles were either a powerful tool, or a dangerous weapon.

With the garment repositioned, I pressed down hard on the foot pedal and powered through the other side.

Finished. That's one down, and a binful to go.

I liked to compare how many garments I completed before lunch with my productivity after. I find that the closer it gets to quitting time, the faster I work. For some workers it's the opposite. That's why Janelle is valuable. She's been here long enough to know the peak production time of every worker.

Grabbing the scissors held in place by a magnet bolted to my station, I snipped the slacks free of the machine, tossed them into the bin and readied another zipper. That's another trick I use, securing my scissors with a magnet. Some seamstresses hold theirs in the bend of their thumb, but that slows me down and I sometimes drop the scissors. If I nicked the fabric, then my work was tossed into a bin marked *SECONDS*. Cleveland Manufacturing paid less money for imperfect work.

I didn't speak, didn't waste time, and I certainly didn't pay attention to Toby, even though he lingered at my shoulder. I just focused on partnering purple cloth with a matching zipper and sewing as fast and as accurately as possible.

Chapter Six

Carole Anne

There are two kinds of students at Swain High School, those the teachers select for college, and those encouraged to find a lifelong vocation. Good jobs like working at the bank, or the county courthouse, are locked up tight. You have to wait for someone to die before those jobs come open. Even then, there's a long line of people willing to do just about anything to secure stable employment.

It's easy to figure out which category I fall under.

Behind our backs, the teachers called us rejects, students whose mom, dad—or in some cases, both—worked at Cleveland Manufacturing. Rejects were easy to spot. They wore factory seconds, remnants of clothing that couldn't be sold. Pants with pockets sewn shut and seams that snaked down the front of the leg instead of the side, shirts with crooked buttons, zippers that wouldn't stay up. Grades didn't exactly matter to rejects who were considered predestined to become second- or third-generation seamstresses and janitors. I guess that's why most rejects accepted what life offered, not daring to dream or even hope for anything other than the life they'd been born into.

At the factory, it's hard to achieve perfection while hurrying to meet production quotas. Imperfect articles of clothing get tossed into bins marked REJECTS and stored in the warehouse. Each month employees can purchase these mistakes at a discount before the Cleveland Closet's Weekend Warehouse Sale. On that weekend, the store opens to the public. A line forms before sunup made up of shoppers who had traveled from as far as two counties over, eager to grab whatever they could at a discount. Bargain hunters tugged and snatched in a frenzy, salvaging what the company couldn't sell. Women carried the defective merchandise home, repaired the imperfections, and sold clothing items at the flea market.

Nothing was wasted, not even fabric scraps. After cutting articles for sewing, workers placed the remaining tiny misshaped pieces in a bin where high school students separated them by color and bagged them. The school board called these jobs "work study classes." They were tailor-made for students who scored below average on aptitude tests, showed little interest in school, or whose parents already worked at the blue-jean plant—all of which qualified them to leave school early for work study classes. This government-funded program paid the impoverished students at Swain High minimum wage, at least until they dropped out, or graduated, whichever came first.

A familiar feeling distracted me from Mr. Potter's monotone voice. I raised my hand and asked to be excused. Mr. Potter shook his head no and then looked puzzled when I fished my jacket from inside the storage compartment of my desk, wrapped it around my waist, and whispered, "I *really* need to be excused."

When I started my period several months ago Mama explained that dogs could tell when girls have their period. She told me this to make sure I disposed of my pads properly. I suppose Mama was right about dogs. As soon as I tied my jacket around my waist Mark Foster, who'd failed science many times and wasn't nothing but a low-down dirty dog, started snickering, "She's on the rag," he said in a voice far above a whisper. Recognition flashed across Mr. Potter's face. His neck turned red. He quickly signed a hall pass, which I snatched from his hand.

"Go see Mrs. McGinnis. She's in the lounge," he commanded as I closed the door and left the giggling voices behind.

The teacher's lounge was once a place of comfort and solace where faculty escaped from worrisome students to enjoy egg salad sandwiches, smoke a cigarette, and tank up on jet-black coffee without interruption. In the morning, teachers topped off their coffee and pep-talked each other through another day of teaching the handful of students who looked forward to school. Midday, they deposited their students into the cafeteria for twenty minutes, and escaped to the comfortable teacher's lounge which, back then, boasted three couches, a refrigerator, and a bathroom. During the winter when the wind rushed through cracks in my bedroom window, I wished I could sleep in the teacher's lounge. But the teachers lock the room up tight after the last student boards the bus.

As the student population increased, there was talk of using the lounge as a classroom for those categorized as slow learners who needed extra help with reading and math. Principal Walker coordinated a planning meeting where the teachers agreed to forfeit a limited amount of square footage for storage, only if the librarian agreed to set aside space for student instruction.

The teacher's lounge now doubled as the mimeograph room and accommodates one sofa for weary teachers who do not bother to close the pop-out window perched at the tiptop of the heavy wooden door. Behind these doors, students' names travel on puffs of smoke and escape through the opening.

Standing outside the lounge with my fist knock-ready, I heard someone running a stack of dittos. The sound was undeniable. The rhythmic clack of paper jutting from the machine almost drowned out Mrs. McGinnis and Miss Love's voices. They were discussing Franklin Green who, according to Mrs. McGinnis, had "about as much promise as a flat tire." I imagine Miss Love nodding because she added, "His light bulb doesn't even screw in, much less turn on. Yes. We definitely should include him in the work study program. He could work for the maintenance department."

Mrs. McGinnis returned with, "We received more funding this year. We might want to put Carole Anne in the program too."

I froze and cocked my head toward the overhead opening.

"Are you sure? She shows promise," Miss Love said above the rapid, clack, clack, clack of the machine. "It's a shame you know. Her grades are excellent."

"Sometimes grades aren't enough," Mrs. McGinnis snapped. "You must consider the family dynamics. Statistically she doesn't have a chance. Do you really think her mama could pay for college? Do you think Carole Anne could manage one week away from home? I doubt she's ever traveled out of this county. Even if her best effort did get her into college, they couldn't afford it. They'd need loans. Do you want to saddle Carole Anne and her mother with debt? Face it. She's a reject, just like Franklin."

Mrs. McGinnis spoke like the "rejects" had a choice of where they were born, like they enjoyed going to bed with hungry bellies and wearing dirty clothes day after day. Franklin and me didn't ask to be born poor. No one does.

Anger traveled to my hand. My fist was clenched so tight the knuckles were white. Comparing me to Franklin was the worst possible insult. Franklin could barely read, but that wasn't his fault. I'm sure reading wasn't a priority in his household. He lived in the last trailer at the end of the park with mounds of trash piled high. Everyone knew they were dirt poor. His mama worked at the plant and made good money, but with eight mouths to feed the money she made just wasn't enough. She spent every dime she made as fast as it was earned. Anyone could see she struggled to survive from one day to the next. Like other women in her situation, she tried to grow food on her lot. Picking up discarded tires along the side of the road, she filled the tires with dirt then planted tomatoes and cucumbers, training the vines to run on string.

Sometimes, Franklin wore the same clothes day after day. He often smelled and was always hungry, eating anything offered to him at the lunchroom, even the peas. He'd lean over the pale blue plastic tray and shovel food in his mouth like it was the only thing he would eat that day. I guess the only reason he and his siblings didn't drop out of school was because his mama knew where her kids were each day and that their bellies were full.

"But how will any of the kids living in the trailer park have a better life if they don't pursue a higher education?" Miss Love said. Cigarette smoke leaked through the above-door window.

"Are you willing to take Carole Anne under your wing and give her the additional tutoring? She'll need to score well on the SAT. Remember now, she must travel to Asheville to take the test. If you're not willing to drive her, then Asheville might as well be the moon."

"Shouldn't we at least try to give her and the others some hope?"

"Hope?" I heard Mrs. McGinnis laugh. Another large puff of smoke escaped through the window and rolled down the hall. "Do you want me to tell you how many kids I've helped in my twenty-five years at Swain High? How many kids I've coddled and tutored and driven to Asheville. I've even driven a few to college and helped them unpack on move-in day. Want to know how many have made it? None. Zero. Want to know how many come back home with their tails tucked between their legs looking all downtrodden and depressed because they can't cut it outside of the mountains? Bryson City kids can't make it in the city. I don't know why, they just can't. Inevitably, every single one of them return back to these hills and hollers; back home to Mama."

"Like you did?" Miss Love fired back.

I wanted to kick down the door. I wanted to force them both to look at me and see me without the label they put on me. I wanted to shout, "Even rejects can control their destiny if given the chance."

"Miss Parker," Principal Walker spoke into my ear scaring me half to death. "Do you have a hall pass?"

Crap.

I unclenched my fist and presented him the crumpled slip of paper that now resembled a miniature accordion. As he examined the note, I tugged the jacket sleeves tighter around my waist and wished that *anyone* other than Principal Walker stood beside me right now.

"Womanly emergency," I muttered, unable to meet his eyes.

He glanced at my jacket, acknowledged it with a knowing nod then gave the door two solid raps and said, "Mrs. McGinnis, can you come out here for a moment?"

The door opened. Fingers of cigarette smoke carried the fragrance of purple ink and mimeograph fluid into the hallway. Mrs. McGinnis obviously expected to find only Principal Walker, as evidenced by the ear-to-ear smile she wore which quickly vanished as her gaze shifted from his golden-brown face down to my freckled one.

"Mrs. McGinnis, can you take care of Carole Anne?" Principal Walker pushed me gently toward her. His voice lowered to a whisper, "It's a womanly matter."

She scowled at the interruption, but quickly recovered and beamed at the very handsome, very single Principal Walker.

"Do come in," Mrs. McGinnis cooed, her voice filled with false concern. She placed a motherly hand on my shoulder and pulled me toward her. "Everything will be just fine."

I fought the urge to kick her. It's not like I'm new at this period stuff, but I am new to teachers acting nice just so they can impress the principal.

Inside, the room was cramped and small. She motioned to the couch and retrieved a thick Kotex from the cabinet. "Don't you keep supplies of this nature in your locker, or purse?" she asked in a biting tone while Miss Love focused on the mimeograph machine.

I nodded. "Yes, ma'am. But it's not time for me to start. This one kind of took me by surprise." I winced when a cramp seized my lower back.

A metal chair scraped across the floor as she moved it in front of me, took a seat then said, "You know, while you're here, let me give you some condoms too."

"What?" I cried. Snatching the pad from her hand, I jumped up and reached for the door. "I don't need *condoms*."

Mrs. McGinnis stood and adjusted her glasses. "Now don't be cross. I'm just trying to keep you protected. Besides, it wouldn't be the first time someone your age's gotten in trouble."

I fought back the tears that come when I'm angry. "Here's what you need to know about me. I'm not like other girls." I shoved the pad in my pocket. "I heard everything you said just now and I'm not a reject either." I slammed the door shut and rushed to the bathroom.

Chapter Seven

Barbara Parker

When the 12:15 lunch bell rang, I left my station and walked outside toward the rickety picnic tables. My eyes adjusted to the sunlight as I bent down and propped open the door with a rock. Behind me, a group of workers spilled from the building, eager to enjoy a smoke, a quick bite, and cooler air.

"Bum a cigarette?" I said to Janelle. She fished a pack of Winston's from her pocket, shook one loose, and followed with a flick of her lighter. I took a hard drag and waved off the sandwich she offered.

"Don't be stubborn," she said when I shook my head no. "You know what's mine is yours."

Janelle was always good for a cigarette and a kind word. She seemed to anticipate my finances and often packed an extra sandwich toward the end of the month. She also brought leftovers she offered while saying, "Eat this, or it'll go bad and you know it's a sin to waste food." Today, Janelle tore her sandwich in half, placed it on a paper napkin and slid it toward me. "It's my birthday and I'll do as I durned well please." She unveiled a large slice of the cake I brought that morning, forked a layer free, and pushed the top portion onto the napkin.

"Go on. Help yourself. No one else cares it's my birthday; least I can do is share." Janelle propped up her feet on the empty seat across from her. I noticed her swollen ankles. Thick socks can't hide the burden of a woman who stands all day.

Janelle chewed in silence, savoring the cinnamon and moist applesauce frosting. "Your Mama could make the best applesauce cake." Noticing my frown, Janelle tapped my leg and added, "Not that there's anything wrong with this one. It tastes so much like hers I could almost cry."

"I think her baking days are long gone." I shook my head. "Mama's baking kept a roof over my head, that's for sure. She always found a way to make an extra dollar." Stabbing a bite of cake with my fork I added, "Her coconut cakes were the best."

"Law, I know that's right. People beat a path to her door when she started adding raspberry cream filling between the layers."

"Her mixer ran nonstop after she brought a stacked apple cake to the fall festival bake sale. Remember?"

Janelle nodded while chewing. "Mmm. I remember. She could have made a fortune as a baker."

The air hung silent as I recalled the bank turning down Mama's loan. No banker in the world would float a loan to a factory worker with no collateral and a kid to raise, especially not a woman. In Mama's day, women were tethered to their husbands. Many couldn't write a check without the bank placing a call to the man of the house, just to be sure the little lady had permission to spend her husband's money. "I guess considering her mental state now, everything worked out for the best. Still, I can't help but wonder how different things might have been. It's just sad no one ever gave her a chance."

"Course you wonder Barbara. We all think like that from time to time. Around here, life ain't easy, especially not for women."

Janelle spoke from experience. She might be in a different place if her husband hadn't died in a logging accident. For her, like many of their older women workers, retirement wasn't an option.

She laughed. "Goodness, I remember right after y'all moved in with me. Pearlene bought two boxes of apples from Oliva's Orchard. She peeled and sliced so many apples the blade made marks on her thumb."

"Mama knew that dried apples made the best sauce. That was her secret. Well, that and a pinch of nutmeg." I shook my head. "Oh, I used to hate those apples. Remember how she made me put them outside on a bed sheet ... that embarrassed me to death. She'd say, 'Barbara, lay the slices flat. Don't let them touch.' And she made me spread the bedsheet on the yard. Out there in front of God and everybody."

"Well it worked," Janelle said. "People started placing their orders before the apples even dried."

Leaning close I said, "I'll let you in on a little secret. I used to sneak a slice or two. I sat in the sun and watched honeybees land on the bright white slices. After a couple hours the flesh darkened and the sugars condensed. I shooed away the bees and popped an apple slice in my mouth. They tasted better than candy."

She nodded. "I love me some apples too."

"I thought Mama wouldn't miss a couple pieces, but I'll swear she had them numbered or something. She used to wear my butt out for eating up her profit."

Janelle touched my arm. "I have a confession. You weren't the only one sneaking a slice or two. I ate my fair share." She took another bite of cake. "Yes, ma'am, I love me some apples."

"You dog," I said while swatting her hand playfully. "No wonder Mama kept blistering my hind-end."

Janelle laughed. "Remember how she used to crack open the window when she was baking?"

"Sure do. Everyone knew when Mama baked. Cooking the applesauce took forever. While the pot simmered Mama stirred the cake batter. I loved helping out. She poured in the ingredients while I held the mixer. After we spooned the batter into the pan we'd stand shoulder to shoulder, each licking a beater."

My heart sank as I remembered how quickly time passed and how short the distance is between employment and poverty.

"God, I miss those days," Janelle said while guiding another bite into her mouth.

I sighed and reached for another cigarette as Janelle focused on her sandwich. Teenage voices traveled across the parking lot. I didn't need a watch to know students were having PE classes.

Janelle turned in the direction I was looking. "It feels like only yesterday your Mama and me sat right here watching you. Do you remember when that Brown boy grabbed you on the playground?"

Her words transported me to a time I wanted to forget. I flinched when Janelle smacked the table. "I can still see her face like it was yesterday. Pearlene climbed on top of this here table. I thought your Mama was gonna jump clean over the fence and whoop some tail. Pearlene sure showed her Mama Bear side that day. Yes, she did."

Students made their way to the playground. Come football season all students spent their thirty-minute recess cramped in a tiny playground designed for elementary school children. God forbid, someone create a single divot in the football field Coach White personally manicured to perfection. Even the players couldn't use the field, except on Friday. They practiced in a dirt field behind the school while the band and cheerleaders used the gymnasium.

I watched Carole Anne walk the same path I had not so long ago. Mill workers' kids still don't socialize with trailer park kids. Oil and water, as Pearlene used to say, two things that won't ever come together. Students separated into groups: jocks and their cheerleader girlfriends on one side, Mill Town kids near the fence, outcasts in the middle, a target for both groups.

"Yeah, I remember what happened. I can still feel Connor Brown carrying me to the monkey bars while I beat my fists on his back. But mostly I remembered people laughing at me, calling me names."

Janelle reached for me, but I pulled away, distancing myself. "What you couldn't see was your Mama cheering for you. She screamed, 'Grab those bars. Wrap your hands around them. Show everyone you're just as good as they are.'"

I shook my head. "I was so dizzy. I thought I'd fall and bust my head wide open."

"Your mama threw in a few choice words I don't care to repeat," Janelle said. "She caused such a ruckus out here people thought workers were staging a strike."

"Connor did it on a dare," I said, my voice weak. "Ted dared him to pick me up and dangle me from the monkey bars. They placed bets on how long I'd hold on before falling. Connor chose me from the crowd. He could have picked anyone, but he chose me because I was the smallest and he thought I was weak."

"Guess you showed him," Janelle said as she forked another bite. "Parker women are strong. Stronger than most."

"He had to prove his loyalty and make the players on the football team think he was cool."

"Well of course he did, Barbara," Janelle said. "What choice did he have? Men are weak. They can be idjits, too, but that's a topic for another day."

I glared at her. "Don't defend him, Janelle. He embarrassed me in front of everyone."

Janelle's face fell but a brow cocked. "Honey, that was a long time ago. Those boys were high on hormones and nervous about the big game. Why are you holding on to something that don't amount to a hill of beans?"

"Connor could have dropped me. I could have been hurt," I said, even though that wasn't the real reason I was so upset.

"You weren't hurt."

"I *could* have fallen."

Janelle waved away my protest. "But you *didn't* fall. You hung on. That's what strong people do; we hang on." She patted my leg. "Now, why all this fuss? Why are you fretting about something that happened in high school? Connor was just trying to fit in, prove his worth. You're fine now."

She didn't know. No one knew what happened after Connor left me clinging to the monkey bars with sweat-slippery hands. Mama hadn't heard him whisper that I best swing or I'd fall. No one knew how hot the metal felt in the afternoon sun, or how I panicked when my hands started to slip. Pearlene didn't hear members of the football team threaten to pull down my pants and do all sorts of unmentionable things. Pearlene didn't hear the girls giggle, even the poor ones, happy they weren't the target. Their giggles were soft, relief-filled sounds that escaped their protective huddle. Mama may have been standing on the picnic table yelling encouraging words, but the jeers of my classmates drowned her out.

Lunch break was over. Splinters pierced the fabric of my pants, scratched the back of my legs as I stood and said. "Janelle, you don't know." My voice wavered. "No one knows." I ignored Janelle's puzzled expression. "Nothing was ever the same after that day." I wiped tears from my cheeks and rushed back to my station.

***

One hundred twenty-seven. That's how many pairs of zippers I had sewn by the 4:25 bell. A deafening hum vibrated through the production room as employees rushed to finish the work in front of them before calling it a day and heading to the time clock. Employees stood in line chatting about nothing important. Idle talk about the upcoming football game. I remained silent and waited my turn for the clock.

Workers piled into cars and left the parking lot in a hurry. I could catch a ride with any number of people who lived at the trailer park but would rather walk thirty minutes alone than be cooped up with someone for five. I was halfway home when Janelle's car squeaked to a stop beside me.

"Hop in. We've gotta talk," she said, her voice clipped.

I climbed inside. "What's going on?" I banged the door shut twice before it closed.

"Pull the handle toward you, then push the lock, or the door will fly open when I round the corner."

I did as instructed and then waited to see what was so important Janelle had to find me after work.

Janelle pushed the lighter until it clicked, wedged a cigarette between her lips, and tossed me the rest of the pack. "How many zippers did you sew today?" We waited as the lighter coils heated.

Her question puzzled me. Janelle wasn't the type to be in anyone's business. "One twenty-seven. Why?"

The lighter popped out, hot and ready. Janelle puffed her cigarette to life then pointed the orange coils toward me. "That's good Barbara, real good. I think you'll be safe."

"Safe? What do you mean safe?"

She signaled, turned left, and eased the car into park. "Barbara, I'm hearing talk. Something's fixing to go down at the plant." Janelle took a hard drag and held it.

"Someone's always talking. I can't get caught up in factory gossip." I wrapped my fingers around the handle. "I've gotta go."

Janelle grabbed my arm. "I'm hearing that orders are down." Her news tumbled out in a wave of smoke.

"So what? Every now and then orders slack off. It's happened before."

Moving a callused hand to my knee, Janelle said, "No, honey, I mean *way* down." Janelle's hands shook as she brought the cigarette to her lips, "I heard there'll be pink slips in tomorrow's paycheck." Janelle waited while I processed her words. "Yes. You heard me. The Eagle is cutting the work force, maybe in half. I heard him and Toby whispering when I clocked out. The looks they shot my way warned me to keep my mouth shut. I acted like I didn't hear what they were talking about, but I heard every word. Make no mistake my friend, pink slips are coming."

There was something about the way Janelle looked at me, wild-eyed and scared, that sent a shiver down my spine. I tried to remain calm. "Is that why you asked about my numbers?"

She nodded. "Nothing like this has ever happened before. I don't know how they're going to figure out who stays and who goes. I'm sure I'm out because I'm old. I don't produce anything. Heck, Toby can do my job."

My voice came out as a hiss. "Hush up now. You're the heartbeat of the place. They can't let you go."

Janelle laughed, a half-hearted gesture. We both knew layoffs spelled trouble. "Bull. Cleveland Manufacturing owns the plant. They own the building. Most days it feels like they own my soul." Janelle cracked the window and flicked ashes outside. "The way I see it Cleveland Manufacturing can do pretty much whatever they want."

"I'd like to see them try." Laying my hand on hers I said, "Don't you dare start worrying and get your blood pressure up. There'd be a backlog stacked to the ceiling if they let you go. Besides, Toby can't find his hind-end with both hands."

Janelle laughed, her eyes watery; a layoff of this nature was serious.

"Let's see what tomorrow brings. Can't do much to control the situation anyway." I spoke with fake confidence. Without our jobs Janelle and I would both be in a world of hurt, real quick. Janelle came to a stop, and I exited the car, banging the door shut. Janelle leaned over and pressed the lock down so it wouldn't fly open when she made the turn. I walked toward my tin can of a trailer with a sweet yard dog running up to greet me and prayed that tomorrow I'd still have a job, as much as I hate it. "Hey, Smokes," I said with a rub between his ears before he ambled back under the trailer.

Hinges announced my arrival with a metal-against-metal screech. Pearlene and Carole Anne sat in the kitchen sorting slips of paper. "What are you doing home so early?' Pearlene asked while cramming the pieces into a box like a kid who'd been caught doing something she shouldn't.

Forcing cheerfulness into my voice, I said, "Janelle gave me a ride. What are y'all up to?"

Pearlene and Carole Anne looked at each other. "Nothing. Just clipping some coupons," Carole Anne said innocently enough for me to know they were doing something I wouldn't approve of. But right then, I was too tired to care.

Even though I wasn't hungry, I said, "Since I forgot my lunch today, let's do something quick and easy for supper. How about soup and sandwiches?"

No one protested. They didn't exactly cheer either. Most Thursday night meals are one- dish wonders. We feasted on Friday after I cashed my check. By Wednesday, we were eating Tuna Helper.

"I'll fix it, Mama," Carole Anne volunteered while opening the refrigerator and retrieving a pack of cheese.

"Thanks, baby. Give me enough time to grab a quick bath." Eager to wash worry from my body, I ignored their surprised looks. Having an aging hot water heater meant staggering bath times so everyone enjoyed hot water. Most days, I grabbed an early morning bath. Carole Anne and Pearlene took nighttime baths.

Ivory soap floated in the water and steam filled the room as I settled deep into the tub, thinking about what Janelle had said. Made sense now why Toby had hovered at my station monitoring my production.

Maybe I could start my own business, make cakes like Mama once did.

Who am I kidding? I can't make enough money baking cakes to pay the bills.

Sinking under the water, I held my breath and considered my employment options. My hair floated free, tickling my face. Around here, the list of employers was short, basically Piggly Wiggly or the gas station. I surfaced to the sound of someone knocking on the bathroom door.

C'mon, give me one moment of peace.

"Mama, Connor Brown is here to see you?"

Water splashed as I sat up. Instinctively, I covered my breasts.

"Mama? You hear me? Connor's here."

"What does he want?" I snapped. I had no business with Connor Brown today or any other day and he certainly had no business with me.

"I'll ask." Carole Anne's footsteps sounded down the hall. I listened for the screen door, waited for the slam signaling he had left. Instead, the muffled sounds of a male voice traveled down the hall. Connor Brown was in my house.

"He says he'll wait till you get out."

Water gurgled through the slow drain as I bent to wrap my hair in a towel. Cringing as my skin made contact with the sweaty shirt, I slipped back into my work clothes. As much as I despised the feel of dirty clothes against clean skin, there was no way I would let Connor see me wearing the threadbare warm-ups I slept in. My steps echoed heavy and threatening as I walked down the hall. Pearlene and Carole Anne had abandoned the kitchen and made themselves scarce while Connor had made himself comfy on our old sofa.

"I sent them to JJ's Dairy Barn to pick up supper," he offered before I could ask.

"For your information, supper was taken care of. I don't need your help feeding my family."

"You needed my help this morning, and from what I hear you might need it again soon," Connor said, his tone solid.

"What are you talking about?" I snapped. "Haven't I done everything possible to avoid you since …" my voice broke with emotion. "Since that night."

Connor looked puzzled. "I'm talking about Carole Anne. I took her to school this morning after she missed the bus."

Anger bubbled from inside. "I told her to call one of her friends. If I had known, I wouldn't let you drive my daughter to school in a million years. I'd make her walk first." My words weren't exactly true. I didn't want Carole Anne walking anywhere in this town, but I didn't want her riding with Connor either.

Confusion flashed across his face. "She said you told me to call."

"Obviously, she lied," I snapped. "And I'll deal with her once she gets back home."

The couch groaned as he shifted his weight, "Why the hostility? I'm just trying to help."

Looking at Connor made me remember things I wanted to forget. Pain. Fear. Regret. He needed to leave.

"I heard talk about layoffs at the plant," he continued. "I thought I'd come over and see if the rumors are true."

I walked around the scratched coffee table Pearlene had picked up at a garage sale. "You know what I've always hated about living here? No one has anything better to do than run their mouth and stick their nose in my business." Janelle either told someone else, or another employee overheard the same thing about the layoffs, which was why I asked, "Do you know something I don't?"

Connor shrugged. "Thought I'd reach out in case you get bad news tomorrow, that's all."

I couldn't tell if Connor was being sincere or the bully I knew from the past. Either way, it didn't matter. The fact of the matter was that if he hadn't singled me out years ago, my life would be different.

"Get out," I said while inching toward him. "I don't need your help. The way I see it, you're the reason my life's all screwed up in the first place."

Connor pointed to his chest, "Me? What did I do?"

Wet hair tumbled around my shoulders as the towel released and fell to the floor. Angry tears pricked my eyes and threatened to reveal my weakness. "You know what you did. You and your football pals. None of your buddies would have known I existed if not for you. But you …" I pointed a shaking finger. "You ruined everything."

"Barbara, I have no idea what you're talking about." His expression told me he was working for an Oscar, but I wasn't buying a second of it.

I walked to the door. "Of course you don't. You're clueless. I'm nothing to you other than a little piece of white trash."

"White trash. What makes you say that? Hell's bells, Barbara, I live in the same trailer park as you."

Shaking my head, I continued, "I bet you and Ted probably sit around sharing a laugh, probably still call me names behind my back."

"Ted? I haven't seen Ted in years," Connor defended. "It was me they called grease monkey. Me they continually heckled and goaded … not you."

"No, Connor. You're wrong."

Connor's voice grew louder. "Look, I was just trying to fit in. I wanted acceptance—what teenaged boy doesn't? And I did stupid things. We *all* did stupid things. But that was a long, long time ago."

"I bet Ted still says what a nice little piece of …" my voice broke. I would not cry while he was in the room. I would not give Connor Brown the satisfaction. The door banged against the metal siding. "Get out. And stay away from my daughter. I don't want you, or your friends, anywhere near her."

Connor stood. With a single step we were face to face. He grabbed my arms and brought his nose nearly to mine. "What do you mean? Did something happen between you and Ted?"

I had forgotten how tall he was. Or how his body filled the room. I looked into his eyes and my breath caught. A small cry escaped as I remembered being grabbed that night, remembered fingers pinching my flesh. Connor's touch unleashed strength I didn't know I had. "Don't touch me," I said. Stronger now than I was then, I clawed at Connor's skin. Yes, I was stronger now. A hard life makes a woman strong. Pushing with all my might, I shoved him out the door.

His hair fell forward, hiding his eyes. He swept it from his forehead and took a step toward me.

"Tell me." His voice was soft now, worry-filled and his brow furrowed. "Tell me what happened between you and Ted."

I held up both hands. My strength was failing. Tremors snaked through my body as my legs threatened to give way. Wet pieces of hair slapped my face as I shook my head no.

"Go," I whispered and willed my legs to hold, willed the tears to stay pooled. "Just go."

For a moment Connor didn't budge. He examined my face for any trace of what had happened years ago. Finally, he stepped away and walked down the steps. A minute later, Connor's truck roared to life and rumbled out the driveway.

Propped against the metal doorway of my rented trailer, I watched him leave then crumpled to the floor.

Chapter Eight

Carole Anne

Granny Pearlene always said the road to hell is paved with good intentions. Now I understand why. Matchmaking Mama and Connor backfired, big time. Mama yelled at me before I could give her the cheeseburger and chocolate shake I brought back from JJ's.

"If I ever catch wind of you hanging around Connor Brown, I'll beat you till you can't sit down for a month of Sundays," Mama said, her eyes wild. Mama had lost her temper with me before, but this time she was fierce.

I trembled at her words and wondered what had happened between them while we'd been gone. I looked to Granny Pearlene for help. She just shook her head, whether to tell me to be quiet or to obey Mama, I couldn't tell. One thing's for certain, she didn't sell Connor the Oldsmobile.

Granny Pearlene didn't care that Mama grounded me. Being grounded meant no TV and no telephone for the weekend. I'm pretty sure Mama wouldn't approve of our planned trip to the landfill either. Even so, I knew that when Sunday morning rolled around Granny Pearlene would wake me early and announce it was time to start digging. I was brushing my teeth when the phone rang.

Granny Pearlene must have known by the way the phone rang that Claudette wanted to back out. She must have known it with certainty because instead of her usual "hello," she snatched the phone off the cradle and said, "Claudette, what's the problem?"

For a moment I hoped I could go back to bed. Except once Granny Pearlene gets a whiff of what she calls "easy money" a herd of elephants can't force her off the scent. She listened for a moment then said, "What do you mean you told Sheldon everything and he won't let you go?" She turned as I walked out of the bathroom. Her brow had wrinkled in anger. "I don't care if Sheldon thinks we *are* both crazy. Get yourself on over here. We're ready to roll." I hid my smile around my toothbrush when Granny Pearlene sighed deeply and said, "All right, put Sheldon on the phone. I'll talk to him."

She wrapped her fingers around the coiled telephone cord and banged it against the wall. I dashed back into the bathroom, spit and rinsed, and returned in time to hear that her tone changed. "Please Sheldon," she said using a gentle voice I sure didn't recognize. "I promise no one will see us."

She listened as Sheldon made his case then said, "Now you know I would drive myself, but the Oldsmobile isn't exactly up for an adventure."

Everyone in Bryson City knew about the Oldsmobile.

Playing on his affection for his wife Granny Pearlene added, "Now Sheldon, I know you don't like the idea of Claudette getting her good clothes all dirty down at the trash dump ..." Granny Pearlene winked at me, bringing me in on her conspiracy to convince Sheldon, a place I most definitely did not wish to be. "Yes, yes, of course church is far more important than money, but has Claudette explained how much money we stand to make each week?"

She nodded while Sheldon spoke. No doubt he was explaining all the trouble he could get into for allowing her to use his key. I wanted to snatch the phone from her hand and say, "C'mon Sheldon, stand firm," but I could tell by the look on Granny Pearlene's face I'd be digging through the garbage, like it or not.

"Well. I'm not a math expert like she is, but I figure we can make an extra fifty bucks just on the rebates alone. Now Sheldon, that's good money. Think about all the good the church could do with the extra cash Claudette puts in the collection plate."

Granny Pearlene rolled her eyes while Sheldon talked. After he had finished, she said, "If you don't want her to go that's fine. I'll make you a deal. Just let Claudette drop me and Carole Anne off at the gate. She can go on to church and pick us up after the altar call." Granny Pearlene turned to me and smiled. "Tell you what, I'll make your favorite cake as payment. You know pecans are starting to trickle in from Georgia."

Everyone knew Sheldon loved German chocolate cake and everyone knew Granny Pearlene could make the best.

"Of course, I wouldn't want to risk Claudette's car picking up any nails in her tires. Yes. Yes," Granny Pearlene said while Sheldon laid down a set of rules. "Tell you what, Claudette don't even have to drop us off at the gate. She can just pull over on the side of the road and we'll hop out."

Granny Pearlene winked then hung up the phone wearing a triumphant smile. Her eyes twinkled as she said, "Girl, fetch me my purse. We're good to go."

***

Claudette obeyed her husband's rules and let us out on the way to church. That left us a little more than an hour to find the labels and UPC codes we needed. For a moment I hoped we wouldn't find anything, but then realized Granny Pearlene would stay until midnight if she didn't find an adequate number of UPC codes. So, then I hoped we found a thousand in ten minutes.

According to Sheldon, Bryson City charged neighboring counties without a landfill a dumping fee for the privilege of using the county's space. County employees manned the property during the week, but never the weekend. That's why Granny Pearlene picked Sunday. Saturday was nonstop traffic. On Saturday folk from other counties who were eager to offload their junk without paying a fee traveled from their well-to-do homes to the poor county where Bryson City was located. They exited shiny rust-free trucks and pushed out their unwanted bulky items without a second thought. Mattresses, washing machines, refrigerators, and pieces of scrap lumber slid from truck beds and landed in a pile at the entrance. County officials knew, the sheriff knew, everyone, especially poor folk, knew about the illegal dumping.

Those who looked to make a little extra spending money arrived early to snatch up anything that could be fixed and sold at the flea market. Saturday traffic was so heavy that the county widened the entrance to allow two lanes: one for dropping off unwanted items, another for retrieving. By Saturday afternoon every item left at the gate was gone and in the process of being converted into someone's slightly used treasure. But today was Sunday, and the good people of Bryson City were right where they belonged, sitting in the Lord's house.

Shame doesn't even describe how I felt as I tumbled out of Claudette's car. Anger pressed hot in my chest as she drove away. We made our way toward the landfill. I walked slow, furious that I had no choice but to babysit Granny Pearlene on her mission.

"You know, since Sheldon and Claudette have gone yellow-bellied on us, it's just me and you and the possibility of all that hidden treasure. I can't do this without some help. I'll rip the bags open with the digger rake." The rubber boots she wore slapped against her pants as she strode beside me. "You just keep an eye out for what we need. Don't fret. The sooner we get what we need the sooner we'll be out of here. I promise." Granny Pearlene passed me a pair of rubber gloves.

"Stop being so pooch-mouthed," she said when I didn't respond. "This is a two-woman job. Trust me, I'd go at this alone if I could. Besides, think about all the money you're gonna make."

Right then, I didn't care. If someone saw me all the money in Fort Knox wouldn't buy back my dignity.

I kicked an RC Cola can then had a minute of panic when it landed near Granny Pearlene's feet. What if she figured out that bottles and cans are also worth money? She'd have me walking the roads collecting discarded cans just like Leroy the Town Drunk who turned them in for pennies on the pound.

Granny Pearlene was almost giddy in a way that makes me nervous. "You just keep an eye peeled for what we need."

Tucking the gloves into the waistband of my pants, I nodded and hoped she didn't have one of her episodes while we were there.

"You know, Carole Anne, they's a lot of people who talk about me in this town, look down their noses in judgment. Church folk especially, but that's history from before you were born. They wouldn't be caught dead at the landfill sifting through trash. You want to know what I think? Good, 'cause I'm gonna tell ya. What I'm doing beats being on the gov'mint dole. Beats getting food stamps and gov'mint cheese. Although I do fancy myself some of that delicious gov'mint cheese." Granny Pearlene stopped. "Let me tell you something, by the time you get to be my age you've got people figured out. Just because someone sits on the front pew of the church house doesn't mean they're going to heaven and it durned sure doesn't mean they're better than me or you. Going to church don't make you a good person neither. No ma'am, the devil himself is bold enough to walk into the church house, just like the rest of us sinners. Knowing the Lord is how you get a ticket into heaven. Some women just want folk to see their pretty polyester dress and polished shoes."

Here we go, I thought. *She's starting to slip.*

Granny Pearlene waited for me to catch up. "Come on slowpoke." She held out her gloved hands and waited as I crammed mine into the gloves she'd given me. They were too large. I could curl my fingers up inside the rubber. After grabbing my hand she pulled me close to her like I was six years old and needed help crossing Main Street. I stared at her for a long moment; she had applied too much Dippity-do to her hair. The curls were stiff; a strong wind couldn't move her hair, not even an inch.

"People like to say the Good Lord helps those who help themselves. Truth is, people are secretly thankful they have enough food in the pantry and a car that gets them to work."

Granny Pearlene squeezed my hand. I wanted to ask why she hated church so much, but I was afraid any conversations about church women might set her off. We stood in the middle of the dirt road with our rubber gloves bound tight. She started getting that faraway look in her eye. The one that makes my stomach fret. "Carole Anne, there's a lot of people who don't know what it feels like to look inside an empty refrigerator, or what it feels like to buy just enough heating oil to last till payday. I'd bet dollars to Dixie none of them front-pew church women have ever had their shoes resoled or prayed that the Lord would stretch the grocery money like He did with the loaves and fishes. So, while the church ladies are getting their weekly blessing from the Lord, me and you'll be browsing through their trash."

I framed my face with a noncommittal expression. I learned long ago when it comes to Granny Pearlene it's best to wait before speaking. Her hold tightened and her gaze intensified as she said, "I promise, before the end of the day you'll know more about the people of this town than you ever imagined." I saw the silver fillings in her mouth as she tilted her head back and cackled. "Remember, the Lord can meet you anywhere, even here at the trash dump. Yes ma'am. You're fixin' to get a life lesson for sure."

The landfill stank like a dark soul waiting to smother anyone who entered. The stench of rotting food mingled with warm plastic filled my nose with a disagreeable fragrance so strong it stopped me in my tracks. I held my breath for as long as possible, but quickly learned it was best to take small breaths.

When Granny Pearlene hatched this cockamamie plan, I imagined a huge mound of garbage piled several stories high; instead we approached a deep canyon carved out by heavy equipment. Finger-like streaks scarred the earth. The mouth of the canyon was pockmarked with dozer tracks. A narrow road led into the canyon with several pull-offs built along the way that allowed trucks to back in and dump their load. Four rusty bulldozers rested in a circle at the bottom. I assumed their job was to keep the pile compacted, but from where I stood, they looked like Matchbox toys. There wasn't a tree or a shrub nearby. Just dirt and garbage as far as I could see. I planned to rip off the bar codes we needed and run away from the landfill like my hair was on fire.

"Every now and then they flatten this and add a layer of dirt," Granny Pearlene explained while pointing below. "Sheldon said he offloads the household trash here first." Granny Pearlene motioned to an area near the dump trucks. "Hospital waste goes over there."

"Hospital waste?" I hadn't even considered hospital waste.

Granny Pearlene wrapped a rubber band around each wrist and

handed me two. "Here, snap these around your wrists. They'll keep the gloves from falling off." She grabbed the digger tool and poked the pile. "Wanna make sure I have solid ground before I jump in," she explained. Once satisfied, she stepped in among the trash, balanced herself, and tore into the first bag.

"Stand over there ... downwind." She used the tool as a pointer. "The breeze will keep the smell outta your nose." She raked away a grouping of thick plastic bags that I was certain held a wealth of UPC codes. "Commercial grade plastic," Granny Pearlene explained as if she were reading my mind. "Probably from the school."

I wanted to rummage through the school bags, figured I'd make more money selling tests to those who didn't have a snowball's chance of passing Mr. Arvey's biology tests. I reached out and was about to say, "Wait," but I was too slow. Shiny black bags tumbled down a mountain of trash.

She flicked the digger rake and brown paper bags flew behind her tumbling deep into the cavern. "People like us use paper sacks for their garbage. We know that their babies don't wear Pampers. No need to even look."

I nodded. Trailer park babies wore True Value brand; some still wore cotton diapers. That's why Mama didn't trust me to go to the laundromat. She's afraid I might wash our clothes in the same machine as someone who just cleaned a load of soiled diapers.

Granny Pearlene repositioned herself on another mound deeper in the hole. "Sheldon told me to look for white plastic bags. He said that's where I'd find the best trash."

I walked around the perimeter, spying white bags and instructing Granny Pearlene where to dig.

"Found something. Crest toothpaste. Pampers. Pepsi!" she shouted then tossed the empty boxes toward me.

We had decided to get as many name brand UPCs as possible. Most companies limit the rebates to one per household, but Granny Pearlene determined how to bend that rule. While we were still in Claudette's car she had said, "We'll fill out one form using my real address and one using your mama's name. On another form we'll use my maiden name, Pearlene P. Bird. That way the mailman will still deliver the check. He's known me all my life. Truth be told, he may still be a bit sweet on me. We'll mail those first. For you, we'll write Carole Anne Parker, Outbound Trailer Park, trailer number two. We'll have to wait a couple weeks to send yours to the rebate center. Just in case the same employee processes all the paperwork. No one will know that we all live together."

"What about Mama's check? You can't just walk into the bank and cash it."

Granny Pearlene smiled. "Girl, won't nobody at the bank even notice. I'll wait till four-thirty on Friday when the line of people snakes clean out the door. Then I'll ease your Mama's check in with mine. Ain't nobody gonna question me over a dollar."

It was during times like these when I realized that Granny Pearlene was a brilliant woman.

"Duncan Hines … is that on our list?" she yelled from the trash hole.

"No. We've only got coupons for cake mixes. No rebates."

An empty box landed at my feet. "There. Take it anyway. Each week brings a new batch of rebates. Who knows what Sheldon will have for us come Monday."

The sound of tires approaching filled me with panic. Leaning into the hole I yelled, "Someone is coming."

"The hell you say."

"Really. I hear a vehicle." Looking around, I realized the only place to hide was in the trash pile.

Granny Pearlene extended her arms like she could catch me. "C'mon down. If we get caught Barbara will kill us both."

I hesitated. The muffler was loud, rumbling like it was loose and bumping against the belly of a truck. Anyone traveling this far down the road owned a gate key.

"It's the cops," I hissed.

"Then you best jump on down here with me," Granny Pearlene

said. "All we need is to get arrested and be the laughingstock of town."

Part of me wanted to argue that we already were the laughingstock of town, but I heard another bang as the vehicle hit the red clay washboard ruts. Plastic groaned and bags rattled when I landed and struggled to stand. Huddled together, we listened as the noise grew louder. Tires traveled across compacted clay. A radio squawked.

"Told you it's the cops," I said. Something gooey had found its way inside my waistband. *Oh Lord, it's a messy diaper.* I thought. *Or worse, a dead rat.*

Granny Pearlene brought a gloved hand to her lips to shush me.

Just the thought of rats gave me a case of the heebie-jeebies. Ever since Granny Pearlene hatched this rebate scheme, I'd been worried about meeting up with rats the size of elephants. Everyone knows that garbage piles are a haven for the nasty beasts. Rats were a problem in the trailer park thanks to Trummie and Willie Rae's bird feeding; they forget to bring in the feeders at night. After the birds went to roost, rats gobbled up what remained then crawled inside our trailer walls to sleep, and of course, poop.

I shuddered. The cereal I had for breakfast traveled up my throat and threatened to escape. I started to shake, the kind of jitter that happens right before you puke.

Granny Pearlene grabbed my hand and squeezed hard enough to settle my stomach. A tailgate opened. Metal banged against metal. The sound echoed across the dirt and settled into the valley of garbage where we huddled. I looked up; overhead buzzards circled. We listened and we waited. The air grew silent as I held my breath. I needed to puke. I needed to pee. I needed to go home.

While we stood silent, Granny Pearlene maintained eye contact, commanding me to stand still and keep silent. What seemed like hours ticked by. For pity's sake, would whomever *ever* get done and leave? Finally, a door slammed shut, an engine revved, and tires traveling across compacted dirt faded.

"I think they're gone," I whispered.

Granny Pearlene gave me a boost while I used the digger rake to pull myself out. I wanted to remove the gloves and use my fingernails to claw out of the disgusting hole in the earth, but Lord only knew what kind of germs were in the dirt. Granny Pearlene held her hands on my backside as I inched toward the ledge and then fell back down.

"Hang on. Let me prop you up with some bags."

I pulled as she pushed. Eventually I reached solid ground only to come face to face with a headless deer carcass. Screaming, I crawled away from the body and rested hands-on-knees and tried not to cry.

"What's wrong? What is it?" Granny Pearlene's voice sounded scared from inside the trash hole.

"A deer. A dead deer."

If I stayed one minute longer I really would puke. Checking my jeans, I discovered a discolored banana mushed against my skin. Blood smeared my pants. My stomach emptied. I fought tears. I was ready to go home, ready to scrub my skin raw, ready to wash my hair in vinegar, ready for Calgon to take me far, far away.

"We gotta go," I said into the hole.

I wasn't surprised when Granny Pearlene said, "Just let me open one more bag."

My watch read 11:55. "We need to go, now. It's almost noon."

"Now don't go working yourself into a lather," Granny Pearlene said. "The Baptists never give an alter call until 12:15 or later."

More boxes landed at my feet. I ripped codes from the cardboard and crammed them into Granny Pearlene's purse.

A few minutes later, the digger rake jutted up from the edge and Granny Pearlene said, "Help pull me out."

Bambi blood rendered my gloves slippery. It took Granny Pearlene a couple tries, but she eventually emerged looking remarkably clean.

"Turn your gloves inside out when you take them off," she commanded while opening her purse. "I'll wash them when we get home. We can use them again next week."

We were hiding in the bushes when Claudette eased her car to the side of the road. "What in the world happened to you?" she asked with a sharp look at my soiled clothes, then quickly added, "Keep your feet on the newspapers." Claudette sighed then mumbled, "I knew y'all would be filthy as little pigs when you piled back in my car."

I wanted to tell her about hiding in the belly of the landfill and that a dead animal had scared me half to death, but Granny Pearlene opened her purse and said, "Look at our haul. I bet we made forty bucks, maybe more. Not bad for an hour of work."

Claudette cracked the window and gave me the stink eye through the rearview mirror. Her look warned I best keep my dirt to myself.

"That's not all I got," Granny Pearlene said while waving a magazine under Claudette's nose.

Claudette jerked the wheel. The right tire dropped off the side of the road. My feet left the newspaper as my body fell across the bench seat. Granny Pearlene laughed in delight. "I know. Shocking isn't it. Found me one of them dirty magazines right there in the landfill. Only this one is special." Granny Pearlene pointed to the pages. "You'll never guess who this belonged to."

"I can't believe you brought that trash in my car," Claudette said. "Throw it out the window."

Granny Pearlene shook her head and adjusted the rearview mirror away from the driver so she could get a good look at me without turning her head. "Carole Anne, I told you that today you were going to learn a thing or two about people." Granny Pearlene twisted the magazine into a roll and thumped the dashboard. "This little baby belonged to the preacher himself."

I leaned forward to grab the magazine.

"Oh no you don't," Granny Pearlene said while jerking the paper away from my grasp.

"How do you know it belongs to the preacher?" I asked. I could tell by the look on Claudette's face she wondered the same but hadn't yet asked.

"Well now, my first clue was the trash bag. This wasn't put in a paper sack like we use. No sir. The bag was tied up tight. Now you know I wasn't prowling. Heavens no. I'd never prowl through someone's personal business unless I was looking for a thrown away box of Crest toothpaste, which comes with a dollar rebate by the way."

Claudette said, "Hmmph."

Granny Pearlene turned sideways so she could look at both of us as she talked. "You know how men like to read while they're in the bathroom."

Claudette nodded. Because we've never had a man living with us, I shrugged.

"Well, this here dirty magazine was double bagged, tucked betwixt the Piggly Wiggly sales paper and the latest edition of the *Reader's Digest*. No proof that it belonged to the preacher, until you take a look at what he used for the bookmark."

As Granny Pearlene unfolded the magazine, an extra flap of paper secured with a weak staple unfurled from the middle. My eyes got wide.

Claudette slammed on the brakes. Granny Pearlene's body tilted forward even though she used her arms to brace for impact. It didn't matter that Claudette left black marks on the road, or that I flopped around in the back seat like a dying fish. It didn't even matter that the car was stopped dead-dog still in the middle of the road. Claudette said, "Gimme that trash" and snatched the magazine from Granny Pearlene's hands.

"What?" Granny Pearlene said innocently. "I was just trying to show you that the preacher used his sermon notes as a bookmark. You can't argue with the truth, Claudette." Granny Pearlene reached for the magazine but Claudette held it high out of her reach.

"Well maybe today's sermon was on the evils of dirty magazines," Claudette defended. "Although you'd never know seeing as how you haven't darkened the church house door in years."

Claudette's arm pumped as she rolled down the window and threw the magazine as far as she could. Too bad she didn't factor in the wind. I saw the flash of silver again as Granny Pearlene tilted her head back and cackled. Claudette gunned the engine and left a new set of black marks in the street. The magazine landed wide open in the middle of the yellow lines. The pages flapped, exposing naked boobies for all the world to see.

"Face it, Claudette, you've got a dirty-minded preacher behind the pulpit. Because I've also got the brown mailing wrapper. Found it tucked inside the magazine too." Granny Pearlene tapped her purse. "Yup. Got it right here for safe keeping. Preacher's address is printed clear as the nose on my face."

Claudette reached for the purse but Granny Pearlene wedged it between her and the passenger door. The car swerved. I yelled, "Look out!" as a large truck approached. Claudette jerked the wheel back into the correct lane and drove faster.

Granny Pearlene released another cackle. Her purse bulged with UPC codes. At that moment she was happy.

Crazier than a bedbug, but happy.

Chapter Nine

Barbara Parker

Carole Anne didn't understand why I had been so harsh. She didn't know why I couldn't tolerate the thought of her being near Connor. She didn't realize the history we shared, and even if she did, I could tell by the way her eyes lit up that he had charmed her.

Yep. Connor Brown was a charmer. He was athletic, which attracted women, and unlike other men in Bryson City, had a steady good-paying job. However, I knew him like none other. Connor Brown was no catch. He was a coward who revealed his true nature to me many years ago. For sixteen years I kept my distance from him and his cronies. Yesterday's missed bus changed all that. And while I felt guilty for snapping at Carole Anne, my job as a parent was to keep her safe. She had no idea how dangerous Connor Brown and his friends are.

Instead of watching television with Carole Anne and Pearlene, I worked to unclog the slow drain. A bottle of drain cleaner hadn't released what was probably a wad of hair. Hair. Three women can't share a bathroom without plumbing problems. I straightened a coat hanger and unscrewed the bathtub stopper. Worry about losing my job crept in my brain. The tiny bathroom walls seemed to shift and move closer around me.

Money.

Life always came down to money and the lack thereof. Pearlene received a small Social Security check each month. But we used most of that to buy her blood pressure medication, which left only a little bit left over for groceries and the occasional yard sale splurge. She didn't have extra cash to contribute toward monthly expenses.

Sliding the hanger down the drain, I scraped away layers of black goop. Months of accumulated sweat and skin bonded together. I gagged as I pulled out a glob of slime and dumped it in the trash. The only way to really clear the drain was unhook it from underneath and give the pipes a good scrubbing, but I planned on avoiding the spider-infested underbelly of the trailer as long as physically possible.

Wire banged against the pipe snagging a section in the subflooring I couldn't see. The more I tugged the less it yielded.

"C'mon now," I said speaking to the wire, hopeful my tone would frighten the hair enough to disintegrate the clog and release the hanger.

I wrapped a washcloth around the hanger, then pulled hard. The more I tugged the less the wire yielded. I wiggled the metal from side to side and wasn't one bit surprised when the coat hanger snapped.

"Great. Just great."

Now three inches of wire protruded from the drain. No way to hold water in the bathtub. My anger boiled as I stomped into the kitchen. "Where are the pliers?" I asked while slamming the cabinets. Of course, no one answered because no one knew. No one ever knew where things were when I needed them.

"Why do you need the pliers?" Pearlene asked.

"Bathroom," I said while looking under the sink. "Plumbing problem."

"Call Connor," Pearlene said. "I bet he has a pair you can borrow. Better yet, he could fix your problem. I hear he's handy."

I slammed the doors and then popped up from beneath the cabinet ready for a fight. Carole Anne sucked in air. She grabbed her grandmother's hand and patted it lightly, as if her touch could heal the brokenness inside my mother's mind.

Passing the couch, I said, "Well, there's a wire sticking out of the bathtub drain so we can't take a bath until I find the pliers." No one responded or offered to help look for the tool. "Fine then. I guess y'all will just stink." I entered my room and closed the door with a slam. The hollow door bounced against the frame and swung back open.

Stupid, stupid trailer. Even the doors aren't worth a plug nickel.

Ashamed, I used a book as a doorstop, easing it into the gap where light from the hallway seeped through underneath. I piled into bed and worried about tomorrow.

***

I was awake hours before the five-thirty whistle woke the town. Before railcars clacked past the trailer. Before the force of their wheels rattled and shook my bed. In this town, light sleepers didn't stack dishes on top of each other in cabinets where plates would clatter. Instead, dishes were washed, dried, and then laid out on the kitchen table where they waited silently to be used later. Trailer park folk don't even bother hanging pictures anymore; best to keep them safe inside a photo album.

I walked to work that morning, trying to ignore my past and not focus too much on my future. Except the future drew closer with every step. Cleveland Manufacturing came into view and I chuckled at the sight of the parking lot suddenly filled with early birds. Obviously, people had heard the layoff rumors. Unemployment is a great equalizer, blending Mill Town residents and trailer park trash into one gigantic melting pot of concern.

Believing that clocking in early today would save their jobs, a line of nervous employees waited outside. Toby stood beside the time clock, his face expressionless. That boy could win a fortune playing poker. He waited until each worker punched in and then said, "Staff meeting in ten minutes. Wait at your station."

His words hit me hard, leaving me feeling bruised and uneasy. As I walked to my area, I noticed Janelle's absence. At every station a sewing machine and the worker who operated it waited. There was no fabric. No buttons. No zippers. No thread. No bins piled ready for seamstresses. I found my station and stood like everyone else. The production floor was graveyard quiet with an occasional squeak from a rubber-soled shoe.

I wasn't the only one who noticed Janelle missing. Other employees looked around, secretly hoping she would bring work to their stations. We stood and nervously shifted our feet, waiting for the meeting to start.

Howard, The Eagle, emerged from his upstairs office we called "the nest." He'd earned the name "The Eagle" by standing on the small landing throughout the day and watching his employees work. I had worked for him for years but on the rare occasion when I bumped into him outside of work, he didn't remember my name. Names aren't important when there are orders to fill. Most days it annoyed me that he didn't know my name. Today I hoped my invisibility served me well. He motioned for us to gather beneath the landing. Reluctantly, we left our stations and stood silently waiting for his announcement.

"By now you've heard rumors that Cleveland Manufacturing will lay off some employees." Howard wrapped his hands around the black metal railing and looked across the room, not at our faces but at the back wall. "Unfortunately, the rumors are true. Several companies have moved operations overseas and are using their cheaper labor. This keeps costs low and profits high."

A grumble traveled through the room.

Howard cleared his throat. "Lower assembly costs have resulted in retail stores ordering from them instead of Cleveland Manufacturing."

More grumbles, this time louder.

"Determining who stays and who receives a pink slip is a difficult task that I don't take lightly, nor one I look forward to. Cleveland Manufacturing not only takes pride in the product you produce, but we value our workers."

Someone mumbled, "Bull."

If Howard heard, he didn't let on. "You're all excellent employees," he said, his voice shaky. "I believe we at Cleveland Manufacturing produce a superior product no other country can replicate. Obviously, everyone in this room needs a job or you wouldn't be here. But some need to work more than others. For many of you, this job provides the only income for your household. That's why I called this meeting. Instead of me arbitrarily selecting people to lay off, I gathered you together to ask for volunteers."

Behind me someone hissed, "Coward."

"I can't offer any incentives for those who volunteer. But I am sure your coworker will appreciate your kind gesture."

The Eagle's knuckles had turned white. As much as I wanted to dislike him, I did not envy him. He released the banister and ran a hand through his hair. "Now for the bad news."

Someone chuckled and said, "That was the good news?"

The Eagle surveyed us. "I need to lay off seventy-six workers by quitting time. These workers will be out for at least two weeks while management negotiates new orders."

Restless feet carried waves of disbelief across the concrete floor. One-third of the workers gone in a blink.

He held up his hands. "I know y'all hate me right now but I'm trying to be fair. This is the first time we've been faced with dwindling orders and right now management has no choice; either reduce staff, or completely shut down. I don't want to send everyone home today. When Toby comes around to your station let him know if you can take a voluntary layoff. However, if by the end of the day I don't have the number of volunteers needed, I must make decisions based on prior productivity and value to the company."

"No way am I volunteering," someone behind me said. "I'll make the bastard fire me first."

"You got that right. I can't go two weeks without pay."

In front of me, workers nudged each other, their faces shadowed with worry. I wanted to shush them. I didn't care about their words. I just wanted work. My fingers itched for fabric, thread, and slick round buttons.

"Starting today, we will not release paychecks during lunch. I know most of you are used to visiting the bank during your lunch break. But from now on, please pick up paychecks when you clock out on Friday." The Eagle took a few steps toward his office then turned as if he'd remembered something important. I tried not to worry when his eyes held mine too long and he said, "We are also suspending Saturday operations, and closing the Cleveland Closet effective immediately."

No one moved. Fact is, we barely breathed. Bryson City residents depended on the Cleveland Closet. In addition to selling imperfect rejects, Cleveland Manufacturing purchased bulk items from other manufacturers who no longer wanted the hassle of storing them. The companies didn't bother separating their unwanted remnants, they just piled everything into bins and delivered them to the loading dock.

A crowd always gathered on the first Saturday sale, eager to sift through the latest merchandise. Fabric scraps are especially valuable to women who know how to make do. These ladies focused their attention on the remnants. Picking through the scraps, they mentally matched colors with their stock at home. Some wore swatches pinned to their blouses. They gleaned seemingly insignificant pieces from the waist-high bin, performed a quick color match, and rifled through containers with nimble fingers touching each scrap. These tiny slips of fabric tossed aside by wealthy textile companies served a purpose in Bryson City. Stitched together, one cast-away fragment joined another, and another. Bound together with love and fret, make-do women transformed a discarded scrap into something purposeful. Piecing together pajamas for their children, potholders and aprons for gifts or quilts that kept family members warm during winters when the luxury of heating oil wasn't possible. Foraging through these bins provided the people of Bryson City with fabric and clothing they otherwise couldn't afford.

Closing the retail store hurt more than the workers. All of Bryson City would miss the Cleveland Closet.

Holding paychecks till the end of the day was also terrible news. That meant Cleveland Manufacturing either struggled to make payroll, or worried that workers would leave during lunch and never look back. I wanted to beg my co-workers to take a voluntary layoff, but in all these years Janelle was the only work-friend I had, and she needed a job more than me. Reality traveled deep into the pit of my stomach carrying with it a sick knowing that I'd be out of a job in just a few hours.

The Eagle's words snapped me back to attention. "Volunteers are also eligible for unemployment compensation." He glanced at his watch. "Janelle and Toby will finish delivering today's work to your stations. I'm opening my office to anyone who has questions. Otherwise, let's start sewing." His shoulders slumped as he walked inside his office and quietly closed the door.

I pushed through the crowd and found my station. Janelle came into view. Seeing her filled me with hope. Worry slid from my shoulders. If she survived the layoff, maybe I would too. Wheels squeaked as she parked a bin then left to retrieve another one. She did not look at me, didn't say a word.

My heart sank. I clutched the corner of my station and thought *Please God, let seventy-six people volunteer to go home.* Even while my mind begged for a miracle, I knew I wasn't that lucky. No employee would voluntarily take leave.

Workers were bent on assembling everything Janelle parked beside them. They sewed straight through their lunch break. The production floor hummed, as always, only this time the air crackled with tension. Seamstresses dropped their scissors. Fabric bunched in wads and needles broke as women pushed themselves and their machines as fast as both would go, trying to squeeze every possible dime out of Cleveland Manufacturing. I didn't look around to see if anyone volunteered to take a two-week layoff. And I could bet no one else looked around either.

All too soon the 4:25 whistle blew. Last call to submit my work. Time to see if I made the cut.

Chapter Ten

Carole Anne

Granny Pearlene had most of our rebates in the mail except the duplicates in my name. Those she kept tucked safely in her pocketbook, ready to mail the following week. She was giddy, in the best mood I'd seen in a while. She didn't mention another trip to the landfill, and I didn't suggest one. While she watched the television, I piled up on the bed and studied my maps.

My roadmap collection began last month after Mr. Dobson assigned a history project on North Carolina. He required us to write the governor's office requesting information about the state and then use the information gleaned for an oral presentation. Like the rest of the class, I thought I knew everything about North Carolina: tobacco is the main crop, the cardinal is the state bird, dogwood the state tree (and flower), but Mr. Dobson insisted his students learn everything possible. After writing the governor's office, we each received a brown envelope secured with a gold-embossed seal. Inside the envelope, a packet of information about the Tar Heel State along with a copy of the official State of North Carolina road map. Several students shared that they had learned that the official motto was not "First in Flight" as most believe (based on the slogan printed on the state license plate), but rather, *Esse Quam Videri* meaning *To Be Rather Than to Seem.* Luke Foster said that was a stupid motto.

I thought it was brilliant. Let Mrs. McGinnis think I'm a reject; before long I'll show her I am exceptional. While my classmates looked through their envelopes, I unfolded the road map and gazed upon a world of opportunities that waited outside Bryson City.

I'd show Mrs. McGinnis. I would show them all.

Shortly after I received my package from Raleigh, I realized I could request information from all fifty states. Mr. Dobson was pleased with my enthusiasm and mailed the envelopes for me, offering extra credit if I wrote a paper detailing what I learned about each state. Getting the maps was easy, all I had to do was explain that I had a school project and add a note at the bottom: *P.S. please include a state map.*

Granny Pearlene wasn't impressed with the amount of mail my requests generated. Ever since she began receiving Social Security checks, she'd claimed ownership of our mailbox and monitored it daily. "These trailer park buzzards will steal from anyone."

Social Security isn't a handout. Pearlene considers it reimbursement for the money she already paid into the government.

We've already been told she's walking toward the trailer. Waving a thick envelope, she'd ask, "Who do you know in Cal-a-forney and why are they writing you?"

"It's for a school project," I explained and walked toward the trailer.

"Hmmph. What in the world do you need to know about Cal-a-forney?" she said. "Just ask me. I'll tell you everything you need to know about the place. Ain't nothing out there but queers, hippies, earthquakes, and druggies." Granny Pearlene turned toward the trailer. "You sure don't need to learn about any of that godlessness. Hmmph. I don't know what to think about the education system these days. Learning about Cal-a-forney. Pshaw! We got a grocery store, beauty parlor, and even got us an undertaker right here. Bryson City's got everything a body needs."

Ignoring her comment, I walked toward the trailer. Earthquakes don't scare me. My bedroom flanks the train tracks. And as for those she called hippies and queers, well, I believe judging people is best left to the Good Lord.

Doretta arrived after cheerleading practice. I heard her open the screen door and ease down the hall. We liked to paint our fingernails, try new hairstyles, and dream about boys we wanted to date. Doretta usually had two or three boys dangling with promises. I didn't bother.

I knew Mama's opinion on dating.

"What are you doing with all those maps?" Doretta asked. She picked one up and began unfolding it.

"Hey!" I said while snatching the map of Indiana from her hands. "Be careful, they're in alphabetical order."

"Sor-ray," she whined. "It's not like I ripped them or anything." Doretta removed nail polish from her purse and a small bottle of remover. "Where did you get all these anyway?"

"I wrote the governor's office of each state. People sure seem eager to send information packets to Appalachian kids. Primarily because they know none of us have a snowball's chance of changing our circumstance. They know the best we can do is stare at a road map and wish for a way out of here."

I rearranged them into four neat piles so they wouldn't topple then said, "I'm going to paper my room with these and chart my life path. When I can't sleep, I'll look up and know exactly where my life is heading."

Doretta rifled through her purse. "Got any cotton balls?"

I nodded toward the bathroom. Doretta returned with a bag. She collected the remover and nail polish, picked up a stack of maps and said, "Let's take these outside. I want to hear more about this life path." She made quotation marks with her fingers. "Sounds like a bunch of bull hockey if you ask me."

We exited through a tiny door off the kitchen. I always wondered why they used a half-sized door at the back of the trailer. Every single trailer I've ever been in … There's no way in the world a new refrigerator would fit through when ours finally gives up the ghost. I followed Doretta down wobbly concrete steps and into our backyard, which wasn't really a yard, but more like a barren wasteland.

Train tracks cut a path behind our trailer. Thick piles of gravel and crushed rock ran alongside the rails, preventing us from growing anything back there, even grass. Instead, we stored the trash can, mop, and other items most people called junk, like the Oldsmobile.

Doretta walked around the corner to the front of our trailer and took a seat on a wooden spool. "Tell me more about this life path you're on."

"Well, for starters, people around here take what the world throws at them. But outside of Bryson City, some believe everyone has a purpose and a path to travel. Those people spend time searching for their personal path. You know, the place where they truly belong. Once they locate this path then all they need to do is walk it out."

Questions lined Doretta's face. "I don't understand how you find this path. Do you?"

"Not really. I just know that I don't like where I am right now. I don't want to end up like Mama. I don't want to spend the rest of my life worried about money all the time. I want to go to college, get a good job. You know, marry someone who doesn't dip Skoal."

Doretta nodded. I knew she didn't fully understand my unhappiness. She never mentioned leaving Bryson City. Most folk are too afraid to leave the misery they know for anything new, even if something new meant leaving poverty behind.

"These are nice." Doretta said while patting the wooden spool. "Where did these come from?"

"Connor picked them up after the power company left them at the dump. He unloaded them at the entrance of the trailer park and stapled a sign to the wood that said *free for the taking*. I rolled the largest spool into the yard then managed to get two more before people claimed the rest."

"Good thing your trailer is so close," Doretta said while removing chipped polish from her nails with a drenched cotton ball.

I nodded. In the summer when heat rose from metal-topped trailers in waves, most folk lived outside opting to inhale road dust and swat mosquitos rather than sweating half to death inside a tin can.

"Connor's here a lot," she said in an innocent tone that didn't fool me. Doretta was fishing. I wasn't the only one who knew Connor was sweet on Mama.

Ignoring the bait, I said, "By the time Mama got home from her shift I had all the spools set up. I even swept tiny pieces of gravel under the trailer."

Our trailer sat on a lot of rock-hard dirt instead of an expensive concrete pad, but I didn't care. Our seating area was nice. We'd get a lot of use out of the spools.

"I bet your Mama liked these."

"It's not fancy, but then again, neither are we." Still pleased with the way our yard looked, I kicked a stray piece of gravel and remembered how Mama's weary walk changed when she first saw the place. Seeing her smile made the painful splinters dotting my hand worth the effort. I had motioned for Mama to have a seat then balanced a pillow on top of a cinder block for her tired feet and slid an ashtray toward her.

Mama had said, "Maybe one of these days we can get one of those fancy umbrellas like rich folk use at pools." She had clicked her tongue, practicing the art of blowing smoke rings, which she'd yet to perfect. "Looks like an umbrella would fit the center of this spool just right," she'd said.

Doretta crossed her legs. "This is nice, Carole Anne, real nice. I kinda wish I had something like this at my house." Her words were sincere. She wasn't a Mill Town kid or trailer park trash like me. She was just another drop of water trying to mix in with the other kids in school. Her parents didn't worry about money like we did. Her dad worked for the electric company and her Mama worked at the bank and sold Avon on the side, not because she needed the extra income, but because she got a discount on the cosmetics.

I helped Doretta unfold the map so it wouldn't pucker and used an ashtray to hold down the corner so it wouldn't curl. "Mama said she's going to sew us some nice tablecloths when she gets the time. Watch out for splinters."

"Good idea. Tablecloths would really brighten up the place," Doretta said. "And you could get some of those candles that drive the bugs away."

I turned my attention to the maps, my fingers following the red highway lines, traveling from one end of the state to the other looking at places unknown, places full of hope and excitement. I inhaled a dusty breath. The possibilities were endless.

Doretta took a seat, drew her knees up to her chest, and pulled a long string of gum from between a gap in her front teeth. I knew this meant she was deep in thought.

"You plan on us visiting these states in alphabetical order or what?"

Shrugging a response to her question, I said, "I dunno. Anyway, what's this *us* business?" I reached for the maps. "I don't recall asking you to join me. You seem content here."

Doretta kicked away from the spool with enough force to land in the dirt with a puff. She was agile in a gymnastic sort of way, with a rubbery body that made her the world's best tree climber, or so I believed.

"Well you can't go off traveling the world by yourself. You know, it's not safe."

I rolled my eyes. "Who are you, my mother?"

"No. I'm your best friend, which is exactly why you can't abandon me here while you gallivant off on worldly adventures. No ma'am. You're not leaving me here by myself with all the Skoal dippers. Tell me, how exactly do you plan on getting to Alabama?"

My eyes darted to the Oldsmobile then quickly returned to Doretta's face.

"No way," Doretta popped another bubble. "Carole Anne. What are you thinking? You don't even know how to drive. And how would you pay for gas? Where would you sleep?"

I ignored her rapid-fire questions mainly because I didn't really have the answers. "Who said I'm going to Alabama? That's just the first map in the pile. Besides, Alabama doesn't border North Carolina. I can't get there without first traveling through Georgia."

There was no way in the world I was going to tell Doretta about the rebate scheme or my plan to take the Oldsmobile and leave Bryson City. As Granny Pearlene always says, "People don't need to know my business."

Suddenly, the back door banged against the siding and Granny Pearlene rushed out with her house shoes smacking against the concrete blocks. The black purse she always carried bumped against Doretta as she shouldered past then tipped a spool on its side and rolled it toward the road.

Doretta and I looked at each other. Doretta knew about Granny Pearlene's erratic mental condition. She also knew to play along when Granny Pearlene was confused. I knew we better stop her before she rolled it down Main Street.

Jumping in front of the spool I said, "Hey now, where are you going?"

Granny Pearlene struggled to pass. "I just heard that Albert Thomas and his wife are having a big ruckus in the middle of town." Granny Pearlene pushed the spool against me. "C'mon now," she grunted. "Help me get this thing rolling. I need something to sit on while they hash out their latest problem."

I locked my elbows and held my ground. Around here, the phone didn't need to ring for gossip to spread through Bryson City. All you needed to do was pick up the receiver and listen to the party line while people talked. That's how Granny Pearlene passed the time after her soap opera stories went off the air. The phone company warned people that a party line would make a loud click when someone else picked up, so you'd know someone else was listening to your telephone conversation. They warned that there were no private conversations. But people around here didn't care. Someone was always watching, waiting for a gesture, hiccup, or fart, anything that gave them an excuse to pick up the telephone and report their findings to someone who had nothing better to do than press their ear to the phone and listen.

Most days there's no shortage of unusual events. When Albert and Lucinda fought, Willa Rae Jameson dialed Trummie Woodard. Since Trummie's trailer was so close to ours we could almost reach into her window; Granny Pearlene heard Trummie's ringer just as good as Trummie. Granny Pearlene snatched up our phone and listened, white-knuckled, as Willa Rae reported the local gossip.

"Looks like Albert's really mad this time. He's raising all sorts of Cain." Granny Pearlene gave the spool another push. "C'mon now.

Help me get this thing rolling. We don't want to miss the excitement."

"Why don't we take these?" Doretta asked while holding three folding lawn chairs. "They'll be easier to carry."

Granny Pearlene smiled and let the spool settle to the ground. Placing her hand on Doretta's arm she said, "Let's hurry. I don't want to miss a thing."

The only good thing about living in the trailer park is our proximity to free entertainment. There's a rise at the entrance of the park where a dozer piled excess dirt after the contractor built the road and scraped out the trailer lots. The hill allows a view of the town's pitifully short Fourth of July fireworks display, and, the comings and goings of Albert Thomas and his wife Lucinda. On boring days such as these, we perched on the knoll and watched the comings and goings on Main Street. Albert and Lucinda were known for weekly arguments, which entertained Granny Pearlene almost as much as Johnny Carson.

Rite-Way Pawn is the closest thing this town has to a shopping mall. Albert Thomas likes to boast that his business helps the working man during his time of need. Truth is, when payday rolls around those with pawned items can seldom afford to get their items out of hock. Albert has, more than once, held Granny Pearlene's wedding ring until her Social Security check arrived. Before her mind got sick, she'd get her ring out with cash and a coconut cake which, Albert swore, was worth its weight in gold.

Doretta unfolded the chairs and motioned for us to sit. Frayed fibers groaned and threatened to rip as Granny Pearlene flopped down in a chair. "Got these at a yard sale for a dollar," she boasted even as a bolt loosened and tipped her to one side. She opened her purse and retrieved a box of Cracker Jack. Shaking out a handful, she passed the box to me. I poured the sweet treats into my palm and passed the box to Doretta, then adjusted my weight and tried not to move lest the chair binding give way.

"Lord-a-mercy, that Lucinda's a sight for sore eyes," Granny Pearlene said. "She should've checked her noggin' before heading out in public."

Wearing a housedress and her hair wrapped around pink rollers,

Lucinda paced the sidewalk and shouted, "Albert, pull over."

Albert slowed down long enough for Lucinda to grab the truck's door handle. Then he sped up again. Our heads turned in unison as we watched him head out of town.

"My tee-veee," Lucinda cried and crumpled to the street as the Magnavox disappeared from her sight. A pink roller loosened from her hair and rolled down the pavement.

"This is more exciting than deer season," Granny Pearlene said while chomping on her snack.

"Ooh, gross," Doretta said with a shiver. "I hate being in town during deer season."

I agreed. "Me too, seeing all those dead animals gives me the creeps." I didn't elaborate about my recent landfill encounter and hoped Granny Pearlene kept silent.

Leaning forward so she could see us both, Doretta said, "I don't understand why men feel they need to drive up and down Main Street with their kill strapped to the hood of their trucks. I mean really, who wants to eat venison that's been strapped to the hood of a truck all day. That's just disgusting."

Granny Pearlene held the Cracker Jack box to her mouth and tapped the bottom. She chewed, swallowed deliberately, and turned toward us real serious. "Girls, here's what you need to know about men." She stopped a moment to pick popcorn kernels from her teeth. "Men think with their tallywhackers; women think with their hearts. Other hunters see all those dead deer parading through town and think, by golly ole so-and-so is a manly man. I bet he's hung like a horse."

"Miss Pearlene, I'm shocked!" Doretta said, her lips quivering as she fought a smile.

"Aw now don't be. You know I speak the truth. Remember girls, anything with a tallywhacker is gonna give you trouble. Cut off a man's tallywhacker and he can't think worth a lick. He'll be weak as a kitten too."

Heat traveled up my neck. "Granny Pearlene!"

"Maybe you need to tell Lucinda that," Doretta suggested.

Granny Pearlene cupped her hands around her mouth like she was ready to holler at Lucinda. "Don't you dare," I warned while grabbing her elbow. "Doretta, stop encouraging her."

Doretta shrugged innocently. "What did I do? Anyway, I was about to say, before I was so rudely interrupted, I bet they would be happier if Albert took better care of himself. Stop drinking. Shave his hairy back."

I turned toward Doretta and before I could ask how she knew this information she said, "He cuts our neighbor's grass ... without a shirt." A shudder shook her body. "Looks like a grizzly bear out there pushing the mower. Poor Lucinda. I feel sorry for her."

"Well, I couldn't eat Bambi," I said hoping to refocus the subject. "That's just cruel."

From behind us we heard Albert's truck bounce across the rails. Instead of leaving town, he had crossed the tracks and made a sharp turn into the trailer park. He held the horn and yelled, "Hey, you nosey old biddies, I know y'all see me." He pointed to the trailers, the ones with pinched-back curtains where busybodies had been watching the ruckus and reporting their findings on the party line. We turned in our seats as Albert lingered at Trummie's place and shouted, "Don't act like you're not watching everything that goes on 'round here. Go ahead and talk. I don't care. You know that wife of mine sits on her lazy be-hind all day, just like you're doing right now."

Albert screams a lot. Cusses a lot, too. He blames it on the beer. Granny Pearlene says strong drink does that to people, makes them mean. He flung a can at Trummie's trailer. Foam oozed down the faded siding as the can landed in the birdbath.

"And folk around here call me crazy," Granny Pearlene muttered. "Girls, heed my words. Choose your husband well. Check for hairy backs and beer guts before saying your vows in the presence of God and a church full of witnesses."

Gravel pinged against the underbelly of his truck as Albert spun out of the trailer park and drove back through Main Street heading straight for his wife.

"How is that television still in one piece?" I asked as Albert made another lap.

"Lucinda's probably been praying a hedge of protection over it," Granny Pearlene said. "I don't rightly blame her. If I had me a color television, I'd sit in front of it day and night, too. She loves that television more than she loves the Lord God Almighty."

We watched Albert knock back the remnants of a Pabst Blue Ribbon then throw the empty can into the truck bed with a flick of his wrist. He wrapped both hands around the wheel and gunned the engine.

"Where in the world is Sheriff Tolliver when you need him?" Doretta asked.

"Child, that man ain't never around when there's trouble. There's a reason he's called the Coward of the County. You can't depend on him for protection. No way. No how." The lawn chair groaned as Granny Pearlene crossed one leg over the other. "But it does look like the sheriff needs to get his hind end over to Main Street before someone gets killed. Or even hurt. I'm sure Trummie's already called the station. You know how she gets when anyone bothers her birds."

Albert put the pedal to the metal. Smoke boiled from beneath the truck as he gunned the engine with one foot and held the brake with the other. Tires squealed and black marks lined the road. The rancid smell of burned rubber covered us, stinging our eyes. He released the brake and the truck jerked forward as the rusty tailpipe gave way and fell into the road. The television slid to the back and banged hard against the tailgate. By now cars had pulled over, afraid to travel lest they get in the middle of the fray. Lucinda rushed into the street while waving her arms. "Albert, *stop!*"

Albert gave the truck more gas and pressed down on the horn.

"Lord-a-mercy, he's gonna run her over," Granny Pearlene whispered. She pulled an RC Cola from her purse and popped the top. Then reached back into her purse and retrieved a pack of gum.

For a moment Lucinda stood her ground. Suddenly Albert threw the truck in reverse and spun the tires so fast that smoke boiled from the road. He whizzed past, tires screaming, and drove the truck up on the curb. Doretta giggled as two more rollers fell away from Lucinda's hair. Our heads turned to the right and then to the left like we were watching a tennis match.

Granny Pearlene passed the gum. "I've said it before, and it bears repeating. No one entertains people in this town quite like Albert and Lucinda Thomas. 'Cept maybe the preacher."

Doretta looked at me, her eyebrow arched in a question. I shook my head and hoped Granny Pearlene wouldn't elaborate.

We heard the tailgate clang and watched Lucinda cling to her husband like kudzu on a riverbank. Albert unlocked the doors of Rite-Way Pawn and manhandled the Magnavox down a wooden plank he'd wedged against the tailgate. By now, Lucinda was in a full-blown panic. We heard her say, "Albert, no!" as she grabbed one end of the television and tried to keep her beloved boob tube out of her husband's pawn shop.

Albert shook his head. A custody battle over ownership of the Magnavox ensued between Lucinda, who was attached at one end— legs locked, tugging as hard as possible—and Albert, who outweighed his wife by a good hundred pounds. Albert slid the console television across the threshold of the store and into the window of Rite-Way Pawn. He taped a FOR SALE sign across the front then stepped aside, arms crossed.

"That Albert shore is proud of hisself," Granny Pearlene said while returning the pack of gum to her purse.

Lucinda fell to the curb in a wailing heap. Drivers ignored her as traffic inched by, eager to move past the scene.

"Serves them right for being all uppity about that fancy television in the first place."

Granny Pearlene had a point. Lucinda wasn't the only one proud to own the first color television in Bryson City. Thanks to Albert's boasting, the whole town knew when their order arrived at Sears and Roebuck. After they brought it home, Lucinda hosted Tupperware parties in their modest home, casually displaying lettuce holders and hamburger patty presses atop her doily-covered walnut cabinet. Many were jealous, especially at night when she purposely opened her drapes so folk could see the colorful flicker from the Magnavox screen.

Granny Pearlene stood. "Well girls. Looks like the show's over." She glanced back at Rite-Way Pawn. I could almost hear her brain click into overdrive. She turned to me and smiled. Granny Pearlene had Lucinda's color television in her sights.

"Nothing more to see." She folded her chair and placed it in the crook of her arm. There was something about the way she held herself, confident and proud. At that moment, I knew she intended to spend our rebate money on Lucinda's Magnavox.

Chapter Eleven

Barbara Parker

I didn't need to open my paycheck to see the pink slip. The envelope told me all I needed to know. It was heavy. Thick. Bulging with bad news. I folded the paper in half and slipped it into my pocket. My hands shook as I fed the time clock and listened as the machine stamped the date and time. Four thirty-two.

Goodbye Cleveland Manufacturing. We had a good run.

Like other workers, I had complained about my job and griped when the paycheck didn't cover my bills. I now regretted those words, wished I could cram them back in my mouth and swallow my distasteful ignorance. There is a certain pride women feel after a day of factory work. I've often looked at my hands knowing they created something tangible and necessary, something others enjoy. Now those same hands shook with fear and uncertainty.

Curling my shoulders inward, I pushed past a group of workers assembled in a circle. Paper ripping and sighs of relief filled the air. For me, it sounded like nails on a chalkboard. I wanted to scream. I wanted to run. I wanted to crawl in a hole and die. Instead I told myself: *Do not cry. Not here. Not now. Not ever. You will make do, somehow.*

My pace quickened. I didn't have time for a pity party. Cashing my check and getting to the unemployment office before it closed became my priority.

The line at Northwestern Bank was long, five people deep at each teller. Taking a stack of deposit slips from a table at the front, I arranged the slips around the envelope. My callused finger slid under the flap and traveled from one end to the other. Bright pink paper flashed against my pale skin. I quickly covered the layoff notice with deposit slips, no need to read it. Folding the pages, I tucked everything in my coat pocket then waited my turn to cash my check.

When I reached the teller window Shirley welcomed me with a sympathetic smile. I signed the check and slid it toward her.

"I'm running low on twenties. Can I give you some tens?" she asked.

"Sure," I replied like I didn't have a care in the world. "It all spends."

"Yes, ma'am. Spends too fast."

Usually I make small talk with Shirley, but my former co-workers had arrived. I could feel their eyes boring into my back, heard my name on their lips. Their eager ears listening to learn whether I survived the layoffs. Taking my money, I held it in my hand for everyone to see. "See you next week," I said loud enough for those with big ears and loose tongues to hear.

My words weren't a lie. Cleveland Manufacturing still owed me for this week's work.

***

While folk stood in line at the bank, I dashed across town and prayed no one noticed. The heavy glass door with bold black letters marked EMPLOYMENT SECURITY COMMISSION opened without a sound. I couldn't help but chuckle. If employment was so secure in Bryson City, how come everyone in this town called this place the unemployment office?

Rebecca Waldron Camden looked at the clock and released a sigh so forceful it could have peeled wallpaper. She leveled her gaze and the look she shot my way said, *Who is the sloth that dares to darken my door this close to quitting time ... and on a Friday no less?*

Had I known that Rebecca Waldron worked here I probably wouldn't have come. For a minute I wanted to run, wanted to say to hell with applying for unemployment benefits. My heel was beginning to pivot when she spoke.

"Barbara Parker," Rebecca said in a tone that made me feel like I had just tracked cow manure across the freshly waxed floor. "What brings you here today?"

She knew exactly why I was there. I wasn't selling Avon, that's for certain.

Her face bore the smug expression of those who are paid to help the less fortunate. I interpreted her forced smile as saying, *I've been waiting for this moment since we were in high school. I was better than you then, and I'm still better than you.* I ran a hand over my hair, wishing I had at least put a brush to it before walking in.

An image of a younger Rebecca Waldron flashed in my mind. She wore a maroon-and-white cheerleading uniform, hair pulled back in a tight ponytail, eyelashes long and thick with mascara. Lips red. Teeth flawless and straight.

She was captain of the cheerleading squad, tailor-made for the football team's captain, Ted Camden. Standing in her presence, I recalled an image of Rebecca placing her hand in Ted's and batting those long lashes toward me in a gesture that I now realize signified their future happily ever after. *See. I can have him, and you can't,* they seemed to say. *See. He prefers me to you.*

Only I never wanted Ted. Even now the thought of him—the smell of his breath and the feel of his body crushing into mine—made me want to puke and run.

As they say, old cheerleaders never die. They live vicariously through their children. The Maroon Machine had a football game tonight as exhibited by Rebecca's white sweater, maroon vest, and a round button pinned to her chest announcing MY SON IS #12. When she turned, I caught a flash of a bruise on her neck, hidden—or so she thought—by the sweater's high collar and deep maroon-colored scarf. I shuddered. I knew whose fingerprints she wore. My hand went to my throat, my fingers touched the skin, still checking for swelling after all these years. She saw me. Saw my fingertips lightly tap my neck.

Adjusting the scarf, Rebecca trained her eyes on an insignificant piece of paper and refused to look at me. When she did finally glance my way, her glare was defiant. I knew what Ted Camden liked, so did his wife.

"I was just getting ready to lock up." She stood and shuffled papers, not to clean her desk, but to position a photo of her family so I could see. "Ted's on his way home from a business trip in Atlanta." She lifted her chin a notch. "I'm meeting him for dinner."

Behind me the clock ticked. There was plenty of time to begin my paperwork. She bent and retrieved a dusting cloth. Wiping the glass picture frame, she repositioned her perfect little family up front and center turning it just enough so I could get a good look. I almost laughed. The children in the photo were mirror images of their parents: a ponytailed cheerleader, and a freckle-faced boy destined to throw the football. Picture-perfect. But the Ted I knew was far from perfect. I could add the picture of Carole Anne when she was in kindergarten, but Mrs. Ted Camden wouldn't like that. No, she wouldn't like that one little bit.

"So, obviously I'm here because Cleveland Manufacturing just laid me off," I said, ignoring her need to clock out fifteen minutes early. I waited for my words to spur her into action, waited for her to grab a pen and slide a clipboard toward me.

"I'm sure several of my co-workers will be here soon." I hoped my words would nudge her into action.

But Rebecca wasn't the nudging kind. She stood unmoving, unlike sixteen years ago when she led the cheers as everyone mocked me on the playground. She hadn't changed. My fingers curled into a fist. Fishing the pink slip from my pocket, I didn't even look down when deposit slips escaped and fell to the floor. "Here's my layoff notice." I pushed the crumpled paper through the opening in the glass partition. "I'd like to beat the Monday rush if you don't mind. So, would you please tell me what else do you need to process my application?"

Her eyes traveled from the mess I'd made in the floor, to the clock and eventually back to me. She opened her desk drawer and retrieved an emery board. "I'd like to help you today. Really I would." She paused and blew dust from her nails. "But it takes about twenty minutes to complete an application for unemployment benefits." She pointed to the wall using the fingernail file. "As you can see, there isn't enough time."

"Couldn't you let me get started today? On Monday this place will be a madhouse. I could fill out as much as possible today then come back Monday and finish up."

"Now, Barbara," Rebecca said with a voice that made me feel like a kindergartener. "You can't rush the government."

"I could fill out part of the paperwork …" I stopped when I recognized the begging tone in my voice. I would not beg.

Rebecca shook her head. "Love to, but it's Friday and you know how important football games are." She picked up the phone and dialed. "I'm leaving for the day," she spoke into the phone using words meant for me. She tucked a leather purse under her arm, looked me straight in the eye and said, "Oh, and Harold, don't forget to take out the trash." She returned the phone to its cradle and retrieved a bottle of perfume from her purse. Spraying behind each ear, she turned and said, "Hate to dash, but Ted doesn't like it if I'm late."

I wanted to leap across the counter and mop the floor with her face. Instead I turned fast leaving deposit slips fluttering as I exited.

***

Like every payday, cars jammed the Piggly Wiggly parking lot. I grabbed the last buggy and headed straight for the meat department. Friday was usually pork chop day, but not this week. I tossed a pack of hot dogs into the buggy then grabbed some buns from the discounted day-old bread shelf and added three cans of pork 'n' beans to the cart. We needed more groceries, but my head throbbed with a mixture of worry and the stench of Rebecca's perfume. I steered the buggy down the medicine aisle and tossed in a little something extra for Rebecca on Monday.

My hands shook as I waited in the checkout line. I needed a smoke, hadn't had one since early this morning. Without my asking, Francine laid two packs on the conveyor belt just like every Friday when she rang up my groceries.

"Just one pack today," I said.

Francine arched a penciled eyebrow.

"Trying to cut back," I explained.

"Need some matches?" Francine asked. "We got a new shipment today from Corporate. They're free."

The company mascot was a fat-cheeked pig wearing a hat and a bow tie. Today's free matches featured the same character, only this time the pig wore angel wings and an innocent expression. The slogan, *Light Your Butts, Compliments of Piggly Wiggly* written in bright pink letters across the flap made me smile.

For a moment I imagined myself lighting the neatly stacked papers in Rebecca's fancy government office. I saw myself breaking the glass picture frames and holding a match to the corner of her precious family photos. The smell of sulfur and the spit of fire made me happy. I could do it. I could watch someone else struggle under the heat, watch photo paper bubble and curl as orange flames licked perfect faces until they melted and disintegrated into a pile of ash. People like Ted and Rebecca lived lives of ease. They were the kind of people who chose to scorch the earth of those around them, caring not one whit about the damage their actions caused. Their paychecks covered their bills with money left over for expensive perfume and cheerleading uniforms. Ted and Rebecca needed someone to show them the hardness of life.

They needed to be taught a lesson.

"Francine, can I have two packs of matches. One can never have too many."

She grabbed a stack from a box under the counter. "Here, love, take as many as you want. We've got plenty."

Pocketing the matches, my callused fingers caressed the angel-winged cardboard cover as I left the Piggly Wiggly and walked home.

After entertaining the thought of burning the unemployment office to the ground, a sense of reasoning took hold as I sat at the makeshift picnic area Carole Anne had created from discarded power company spools. I had thrown dinner together and left the kitchen while Carole Anne cleaned up the dishes. Putting one of the Piggly Wiggly matches to good use, I struck it hard against the sandpaper strip and inhaled the sulfur fragrance. The smell pricked my taste buds, made my mouth water even before the foam filter reached my lips and the tip glowed red. I knew I had to cut back. I really needed to quit smoking altogether, but a good smoke settled me down. Each drag makes me think a bit clearer.

Tapping ash from the end of the cigarette, I looked around. My car was rusting, the tires dry rotting, and I hadn't the energy to do much of anything other than worry. My bones were tired and my mood angry. As much as I'd like to take a day to feel sorry for myself, I was a Parker woman, and when times get tough, Parker women make do.

Chapter Twelve

Carole Anne

I know Mama told me not to talk to Connor, but it's impossible to bathe when there's half a coat hanger sticking up where the stopper goes. That's why I called him after Mama headed off to work.

Granny Pearlene was wide awake when Connor's truck rolled up the drive. She peeled back the curtains and asked, "Who's that?"

"That's Connor. He's come to fix the tub, remember?" Taking in Granny Pearlene's nightgown and housecoat, I said, "You might want to get dressed. And close the drapes when you change."

Lately we'd received some calls about Granny Pearlene traipsing around the trailer half dressed. It was hard to know whether she didn't realize what she was doing, or she was trying to aggravate the neighbors on purpose. Granny retorted with, "People can only see me if they're peering through my window. If I want to walk around in my birthday suit that's my business."

She had a point.

Instead of going to her bedroom, Granny Pearlene followed me down the hall. "What's wrong with the tub?"

"It's got a piece of wire stuck in the drain. Remember?"

Granny Pearlene fingered the scratch on her wrist like she was remembering how it got there. That's the other reason I called Connor. I must keep the trailer free of hazards, Granny-proof the bathroom, and keep harmful things tucked out of reach. The same goes for the kitchen where I've hidden the knives. They are stored in the freezer, behind the ice cube trays. Cleaning supplies stay under the sink so far in the back corner, I have to crawl inside the cabinet to retrieve them. It was pure luck Granny Pearlene had only scratched herself while trying to figure out why the stopper wouldn't work. She could have stepped on the wire and then there she'd be, confused and bleeding all over the place and me without a way to get to the doctor.

The door shook when Connor knocked. Granny Pearlene threw it open.

"Miss Pearlene, how are you this fine morning?" Connor waited for an invitation to come inside.

Granny Pearlene stared at Connor like he was a stranger. I nudged her out of the way. "Let me show you the bathroom," then mouthed *Go change* while pointing her toward her bedroom. "You sure you can get this out fast? I don't have much time before the bus comes. I can't be late this morning. I've got a big math test and besides, Mama's likely to kill us both if you drive me to school again." When I called Connor earlier, he had said it would only take a minute to pull the broken hanger out of the drain. He said he gets calls like this all the time and fixing the tub was no big deal. But I grew nervous as the clock ticked away the time.

Connor nodded. "Should have this done in a jiffy. Here, you can hold the light."

He climbed into the tub. "Tight fit," he said when his tool belt banged against the sides. "Now point the light straight in the hole so I can take a good look at what's going on down here."

I'd never been this close to Connor, not close enough for my skin to brush against his, not close enough to feel the spark when his arm touched mine.

He retrieved a pair of pliers from a pocket on his belt and clamped the tool to the piece of wire. Then he gave it a little tug, and another, harder this time.

"Feels like the metal is snagged on something. Did you unhook the hanger first, or just jab it into the drain still curled?"

Before I could answer, Granny Pearlene thundered down the hall. "What in the world is going on in here?" she said from behind me.

I turned and almost dropped the flashlight. She had changed as I asked. She was wearing what she calls her "funeral dress," complete with a fake pearl necklace and matching Sarah Coventry clip-on earrings. The only problem was she had forgotten to button the dress.

Connor quickly turned his head and tugged harder on the wire.

Gesturing for her to fix her buttons, I said, "Connor's fixing the tub. Remember? Mama broke it."

Her only response was a dead-eyed stare. I wedged the flashlight under my arm and hurried to button her up. The bus would arrive soon.

"This thing is stuck pretty good," Connor said. "Let me grab a can of WD40 from the truck." He stepped out of the bathtub, filling the room with his size.

I hoped Granny would leave, or at least turn sideways so Connor could squeeze through the door frame. Instead her face changed. Her eyes flashed angry.

"You're Connor Brown," she said while adjusting her glasses.

"Yes'm. You've known me all my life."

I smiled and nodded a confirmation, but Granny Pearlene's face had turned harsh and troubled.

Connor tapped his watch. "Now if you'll just let me pass, I'll get this fixed up and you ladies can use the bathtub again."

Granny Pearlene's eyes narrowed. "I know who you are. You're that Brown boy. The one who picked on my Barbara the other day at the playground." She took a step toward Connor. His face paled. Confused, he looked from Granny Pearlene to me.

"I beg your pardon, Miss Pearlene?"

"Don't act stupid with me boy. I've got half a mind to tan your hide right here and now." She took off her glasses and held them out for me. "You made my Barbara cry. She cried for weeks. What did you do to her?"

She unclipped her earrings like women in this area do before they are about to fight.

Connor held up his hands. "Miss Pearlene, I think you're confused. Barbara's grown now. High school was a long time ago. We've both grown up since then."

"Have you?" Granny Pearlene demanded. She was close enough to touch him.

"We were just teenagers. Not much older than Carole Anne." Connor directed his words toward me. "I had just made the football team. And I was under pressure to fit in."

"Go on boy," Granny Pearlene reached out and pushed me toward him. "Barbara's right here. Don't tell me you're sorry. You tell her. She wants to act like it's no big deal, but I can hear her crying at night."

Connor looked at me. I nodded and did my best to send him brain messages. The sooner we moved past this awkward moment and resolved whatever bothered her, the better. Granny Pearlene's doctors didn't have a good reason why she sometimes got mixed up and thought I was her daughter. I don't look like Mama all that much. Heck, most days I'd swear I was adopted, but the more we tried to explain things to Granny Pearlene, the madder she got. Mama and I always thought it best to play along until the moment passed, which it usually does.

Doctors told us that establishing a routine helps with Granny Pearlene's episodes. Each morning I placed a spoon, a bowl, and a box of cereal on the kitchen table then turned on the television before I left. That way when Granny Pearlene got out of bed everything was waiting. She only needed to pour milk from the fridge. One morning when I didn't have time to get things ready, she tore the kitchen apart, her brain unable to identify items she had used all her life. I came home from school and found her sitting naked on the kitchen floor with cereal strewn all over the place and broken pieces of glass littering the floor. Mama rushed home from work and together we patched up Granny Pearlene and then replaced most of the dishes with plastic ones. That's when we hid the knives and the cleaning supplies. Routines were essential. Connor's presence had upset the balance.

"We were on the playground. The team. Ted. The cheerleaders. Me. Everybody. Ted dared me to grab Barbara and kiss her. I guess he wanted me to prove my loyalty to the team. I don't know what else to say." Connor's shoulders slumped.

Granny Pearlene crossed her arms and gave an unimpressed grunt.

"Apologize. Go on now."

Outside, school bus brakes squealed to a stop.

Connor leaned down and said, "I'm sorry, Barbara. I didn't mean to hurt your feelings."

"I'm going to miss the bus," I mumbled while dangling the reading glasses in front of Granny Pearlene for her to take.

"Mama will kill me if I get a tardy." I touched Granny Pearlene's arm. Careful and moving slow, I nudged her into the hall just as the driver closed the bus door and drove away from the trailer park. Connor appeared beside me, "Don't worry. Give me another minute and I'll take you."

For a second I thought about his offer, but I was weary of them both. "Ya know what? Don't bother. I'll walk." I slammed the front door on my way out. Walking to school was the first step toward my independence. Perfect timing. Granny Pearlene wouldn't remember. Connor wouldn't tell, and Mama would never know.

I wiggled my shoulders until the book bag straps settled comfortably. I held my finger across the lid of the metal Holly Hobby lunchbox Granny Pearlene bought at the church yard sale. A bobby pin kept the clasp closed, but sometimes it slid away from the latch. When that happened, the lid opened, and everything fell out. I despised the durned lunchbox. Holly Hobby is so grade school, but it is still one step above a brown paper sack. These things matter in high school.

I crossed the train tracks then dashed across Main Street. To my left, First Baptist stood on the corner of Schoolhouse Hill and Main. You couldn't drag Granny Pearlene into First Baptist on Sunday, but when the church had their annual yard sale, mark my word, she'd be number one in line waiting for the doors to open.

Claudette attended First Baptist. Granny Pearlene belonged to the faithful following of Jimmy Swaggart, seen on Channel 8 every Sunday. When the newly appointed First Baptist preacher visited with the intention of wooing Granny Pearlene into his congregation, she listened, hands resting in her lap all ladylike. Then she replied, "Preacher, I already attend church. Yessir, I sit on the front row every

Sunday morning. Don't even have to wear shoes if I don't want."

Preacher argued that his messages were anointed by God Almighty and that television ministers were fond of strutting for personal glory. He had tried that pitch before but Granny Pearlene had said, "You just want my tithe. You got that big ole church to maintain and rumor has it that you're aiming for a bigger steeple. You know preacher, it's not the size of the steeple that makes a good church, it's the integrity of the folks inside. If Jesus lives in me and my body is the temple, I reckon I'm content to be my own church with a congregation of one."

After that his visits tapered off.

Across the street at Wiggins 66 Gas Station, Scott Wiggins peered inside the hood of a truck. A variety of tools lay on an oily cloth waiting for use while a gaggle of older men sat in a circle of fold-out metal chairs and offered unsolicited advice.

"Make sure you tighten those bolts down real good," one of the men said as I passed. "Ya don't want the motor falling out on account you got a screw loose." The old men chuckled at the lame joke. Scott's snowy hair bobbed as he nodded an acknowledgement. No man's hair was as lovely as Scott's. Men don't notice those things, not like me and Doretta. Nice hair matters to us.

Behind Wiggins 66, the Piggly Wiggly was already open for business catching early morning travelers and groups of walkers who had enough money to grab a fresh-baked blueberry muffin. Walking alone, I wondered why no other students joined me in the trek up Schoolhouse Hill. Living close by, most of the Mill Town kids walked to school. I started to jog when I remembered I was the last stop on the bus route. Behind me a horn sounded. I jumped, stumbled, and lost my footing. "Get on the right side of the road," someone yelled out an open window. How had I forgotten the first rule of walking? Never turn your back to oncoming traffic.

There wasn't time to cross. A line of buses whizzed past with engines groaning and exhaust pipes spitting smoke. Students pressed their noses against the glass and laughed as I climbed out of the ditch and waited to cross over to the correct side. Time slowed and the school at the top of the hill seemed small as buses disappeared from view. I still had a ways to go when three figures appeared: Mark, Luke Foster (known for skipping first period and any other class they deemed unworthy), followed by the oldest Foster boy Matthew. I wondered why Matthew was even out of the bed. He'd dropped out of school without his parents' permission. Pretty soon, I reckoned, Mark would follow in his brother's footsteps. Only Luke, who was my age, showed a hint of promise, but not when paired with his older siblings. Everyone knew the boys hid out in the woods smoking Lucky Strikes and doobies. Everyone also knew to give the Foster boys a wide berth.

For years, the trio had terrorized the student body. Before Matthew dropped out of school, the three brothers walked the halls, shoulder to shoulder and steamrolled people out of their way. The brothers stole anything that wasn't tied down, and they shot at defenseless animals. Rumor had it they belonged to a devil-worshiping cult, which their preacher father flatly denied. Rude, crude, and uncool defined their behavior and those who weren't in their group became intimately acquainted with the inner workings of the school's toilet. They pushed girls up against the wall, grinning while rough hands groped tender skin and their lips whispered, "Excuse me," like they couldn't control themselves.

They nudged each other as I neared. I didn't need to hear them to know one brother had dared another to do something to me. Probably push me off the hill and watch me tumble to my death. They'd do it too, just for a laugh.

"Hey," Mark said with a chin-lifted greeting. "You're going to be late for class." Mark was the middle sibling, the one most likely to take a dare.

Stopping for a minute to catch my breath, I answered, "Missed the bus," which was a stupid thing to say, but it wasn't like I could push through the three of them blocking the way.

"Heading for a smoke before first period. Interested?" Matthew asked.

My heart pounded at the chance of something dangerous, something my mother wouldn't allow. It wasn't that she thought smoking cigarettes was wrong. I mean, Mama smoked. She had every cigarette numbered from one payday to the next. But there was something in the way Matthew's lips curled, slick and dangerous. He wasn't talking about Lucky Strikes.

For a second, I thought about it. Thought about skipping school to hang out with the baddest boys in town.

"Um. Not today," I said, lacking the courage to rebel. "We've got a first period math test." I looked at Luke who copied from my paper every time Mr. Womick assessed our progress.

"So skip," Matthew challenged. "You ain't never gonna use math nohow."

"Can't. Mr. Womick's tests are hard. And besides, Mom'll kill me if I fail."

"Ya hear that brothers? Mom'll kill her if she fails." Matthew and Mark bent double laughing.

Luke gently took my book bag. "Don't listen to them, Carole Anne. They're just mean." Slinging the bag over his shoulder Luke said to his brothers, "Y'all go on now. Me and Carole Anne's got us a test to take." Turning, he leaned in close, his voice barely above a whisper. "I'll walk you the rest of the way. These books are too heavy for a pretty thing like you."

I blushed; I liked the way my name rolled off Luke's tongue. There was nothing special about me, certainly nothing that encouraged a second look. I wasn't considered attractive, not even to the Foster boys, whose greasy black hair and crooked teeth didn't exactly lure girls their way. The Foster boys couldn't compare with Scott Wiggins, not even close. But in Bryson City, a girl took what she could get and right now I had Luke Foster's attention. Something resembling hope crept into my heart.

It seemed like every girl in high school had a boyfriend but me. Flaunting class rings three sizes too big, girls Granny Pearlene called "loose ladies" wrapped pieces of crochet thread around their boyfriend's senior ring until they had added enough thickness so the ring fit snugly on their fingers. Then they melted scented candle wax and firmly bonded the thread, which also added a heady grape scent. I never understood why boys who worked all summer in Mr. Cochran's tobacco field wasted money on a class ring they'd never wear. Doretta called the rings "panty melters," explaining that high school relationships began with a letter jacket, progressed to a class ring, and typically fizzled out after the baby arrived and their marriage vows were forgotten.

Flashing dust-speck diamond rings purchased on credit from Rite-Way Pawn, couples in high school made out while others pretended not to notice. Everyone knew which couples were doing it. A blind man could tell by the way two people connected inseparably at the hip, unable to get enough of each other. How they rolled into the student parking lot smelling of cigarettes and sex, dashing down the hall right as the first bell rang while not even trying to hide fresh hickeys on their necks. The girls thought they were in control and that they had hooked their boyfriends for eternity. Young men eagerly made monthly payments on those dust-speck trinkets that magically unlocked the legs of their beloved ... at least until someone with a bigger trinket came along.

Even though the Health Department offered free condoms by the cases, most students attending high school didn't use birth control. Swain County boasted the highest teenage pregnancy rates in North Carolina. We also ranked number one in low wages and unemployment but that didn't deter couples from getting pregnant. By the end of the school year, mothers-to-be strutted their tight shirts and even tighter pants down the hall, all the while smirking at girls without a boyfriend and the poor homely virgins like me.

"Trust me," Doretta warned when I fretted about boys, "any girl can get pregnant. Boys around here are stupid. Girls, too, if you ask me. Bad girls make bad choices. Stay smart and in control."

"What about the bad boys?"

"Double standard," Doretta explained. "Bad boys get to do what they want. Always have. Always will. You can't fight the double standard. But you can choose well."

Doretta was right, but her words didn't ease my loneliness. Doretta kept a boy or two dangling with promise, while I couldn't get a second glance from anyone, except for the likes of the Foster boys and right now I had the attention of Luke.

While Luke's brothers scampered off through a well-worn trail, I fell in step with him. Walking toward school, our feet fell into a rhythm, perfectly in sync. Everyone was wrong about him, I thought while stealing a sideways glance. Luke possessed a sliver of goodness he only released when separated from his brothers. Perhaps Luke and I could be friends, maybe even go out. My courage grew and pushed aside the worry. He shifted the backpack to his other shoulder, freeing a hand that now hung close enough to touch. I could take his hand. I could be smart and in control. I could press my hand against his and curl my fingers tightly around his. My love would purge the bad from him. My love would pull him away from his brothers.

He must have read my thoughts. A smile formed, small at first. Mirroring him, my lips curled. When Luke slowed his pace, I followed. Reaching now, I extended my arm and straightened my fingers. Tingling at the thought of his touch, I imagined what was about to happen. We could be late. We could be like Principal Walker and Miss Love. We could be like the other couples running breathlessly to first period class smelling of cigarettes and sex.

"To hell with this," he growled, bending toward me.

I pulled him toward me, stood on tiptoe, and lifted my chin while closing my eyes. Tingling all over, I squeezed his hand and wet my lips with the tip of my tongue readying for my first kiss. My pounding heart almost blocked the sound of my book bag hitting tree limbs when Luke flung it as far as he could. Leaves rustled. Limbs snapped. I opened my eyes in time to see him vanishing through the woods to get stoned with his brothers.

Cursing my stupidity, I watched my bag swing from a limb. First bell sounded leaving me two choices: abandon my books until later or retrieve them and show up for class smelling of ignorance and virginity.

I had dried my eyes by the time I slumped into Mr. Womick's class carrying a tardy slip. He took one look at me and penciled the first unexcused absence of my life into his attendance book.

Mama would kill me.

Lifting a coffee mug, Mr. Womick slurped coffee and said, "Miss Parker, so happy you decided to join us. As you can tell, we didn't wait for you to grace us with your presence. Please take a seat. Here's a copy of the math test. Automatic five-point deduction for the tardy."

Sitting beside my empty seat, Luke Foster looked me straight in the eyes. He winked and flashed a crooked-toothed smile then gestured for me to take a seat so he could copy from my test paper. I didn't know how he beat me to class and I really didn't care. At that moment I hated him almost as much as I hated myself.

Chapter Thirteen

Barbara

I had pinned the wash to a sagging clothesline that ran from the trailer siding to a single pine tree at the edge of the yard. No need to feed quarters into the dryer. I never wasted money on a dryer anyway. At least that part of my routine wouldn't change. But if Cleveland Manufacturing didn't get some new orders soon, I'd be washing the clothes in the bathtub. Last night, I tried to figure out how to tell Carole Anne and Pearlene that I no longer had a job. Part of me hoped I wouldn't have to tell them the truth and that my situation was just a bad dream.

I perked a pot of coffee and pretended this morning was like any other workday. Before leaving, I removed my chocolate creation from the oven and wrapped it in tin foil.

Rebecca Waldron Camden had drawn a line in the sand, marked her territory, and established her superiority. Her office was her domain. Clearly, Rebecca was Queen Bossy Pants down at the unemployment office. She intended to watch me squirm and take her sweet time processing my unemployment application. The way I saw it, I had a couple choices. I could grovel at her feet or pull her through the tiny opening in her office window and beat the stuffin' out of her.

Instead I baked a little brownie delight.

Pearlene Parker raised me not to grovel, but I needed the money from an unemployment check. Rebecca knew that. Since Rebecca expected groveling, I would dig deep within the marrow of my bones and do my best to comply. I would also throw in a bribe for good measure.

The Parker women knew that chocolate opens doors better than a "please" or "thank you." No one can resist a pan of still-warm gooey brownies, especially not Rebecca, who I suspected hadn't fit into her cheerleading uniform since she was a senior in high school.

As expected, the lobby of the Employment Security Commission was packed with Cleveland Manufacturing employees who would rather be sitting at their sewing machines on this chilly morning than trapped here filling out paperwork. The brownie pan warmed my hands and gave me a feeling of power while I waited my turn. As the line moved forward, I heard Rebecca say, "Sign your name here and take a number. Fill out this form. Clip your layoff slip to this paperwork. Wait for me to call your name."

She must have already repeated the instructions several times. A flat tone without emotion or compassion replaced her superior attitude. I slid the disposable silver pan through the glass opening and forced a smile.

"Sorry we got off on the wrong foot the other day. I thought you could use a treat. It's going to be a long day." I pasted an innocent expression on my face and held her stare for a moment then looked away knowing it was only a matter of time before she, or someone in this room, leaked news of my employment status to Pearlene and Carole Anne. After my outburst over Connor I didn't have the heart to tell them I'd lost my job. Besides, talking about the layoff wouldn't help. Mama and Carole Anne couldn't change what happened years ago. They couldn't change my employment status either. No one could.

Rebecca pulled the container toward her and peeled foil from the corner. Bending, she pressed her nose to the pan and sniffed. Rebecca would tell. Today, after she ate the brownies, all of Bryson City would know. All of Bryson City would talk or listen to talk on the party line. What else is there to do in this town?

"They're still warm," I said not knowing how much longer my face would hold the fake smile. I didn't apologize for my behavior on Friday. I didn't plan to either.

The clipboard made a clanging sound as she laid it on the counter and passed it through the opening. "Fill this out. Attach your layoff slip to the form. Wait for me to call your name."

Rebecca opened her desk drawer, deposited the brownies, and readied another clipboard with a blank application.

Turning, I found only two vacant seats. Former co-workers balanced clipboards on their knees and chewed pencil erasers. I grabbed a spot in the corner near a room deodorizer that failed to mask the scent of fear oozing from the pores of thirty unemployed factory workers.

The Unemployment Benefits Claim Form was a three-page packet of wasted trees. I had expected to provide the usual important personal information: name, address, social security, number of years I had been employed (although I assumed that Cleveland Manufacturing would have provided that last part when they let me go). I didn't expect stupid questions like: *Are you currently working?* Duh, if I was, I wouldn't be sitting in the unemployment office. *Do you have a driver's license?* No. I walk to work. Or at least I did. *Do you have a commercial driver's license?* No. *Do you have any definite employment prospects?* Hell no.

I wasn't the only one frustrated. The unhappy grumblings and exhaled puffs of frustration beside me made focusing difficult. Then I remembered that many of my fellow plant workers could barely read at an elementary school level. Discouraged frowns lined weary faces.

Like most of the people in the lobby, Joanne Whitmore had worked at the plant since it opened. She dropped out of school after her dad died, when making the rent payment became a shared responsibility of her and her mother, who sat beside me. Joanne worked the day shift, her mama worked nights. Leaning over I asked, "Joanne, did you forget your glasses?" even though I knew Joanne hadn't worn glasses a single day in her life.

Relief flashed across her face as she nodded.

Tucking the clipboard under my arm, I repositioned myself beside her. Soon, others formed a circle. We worked as a team piecing together the necessary information to complete the application for benefits.

"I didn't think there would be so many forms," Joanne whispered. "I guess me and Mama didn't know what to expect. We kind of thought we'd just come in, sign a few papers, and pick up a check." Joanne jumped when her name was called.

Privacy is impossible in a packed room. Even though Rebecca spoke in a hushed tone, I could tell Joanne struggled to comprehend the instructions.

"What do you mean?" she asked.

Rebecca pushed more papers through the window opening and called the next number, which, of course, was Joanne's mother. Joanne held her place beside her mother as Rebecca repeated the same instructions. Both ladies stared at the papers. When Joanne turned, I noticed tears in her eyes. I patted the chair beside me.

"She says we have to fill out this form and turn it in next week … said we won't start getting a check for two more weeks." A tear slid down her face. "Two weeks! What am I going to do until then? I got bills to pay."

I wanted to tell Joanne not to worry, but truth was, everyone in the lobby carried their own worrisome burden. Reaching for the form, I asked, "Can I take a look?"

"I've got to turn in one of these each week in order to keep getting a check."

Beside her, Joanne's mama nodded.

The form had three sections, one for each business where you had applied for work. Practicing my most optimistic tone, I said, "Now, ladies, you still have one more check from the plant. All you need to do is write down three places where you've tried to get a job. Return this sheet and before you know it, your unemployment money will kick in."

Joanne wasn't convinced. "But she said I won't get as much money as I did with my job."

Tin foil rattled. Rebecca turned her back to those waiting in the lobby and spooned a bite of brownie into her mouth.

That's it … eat up.

There was little I could do to make Joanne, or anyone else in the room, feel better. Joanne released a shaky sigh. "I guess all we can do is pray."

I wanted to hug them both, but it was my turn to revisit the thick glass window that separated the working from the unemployed. When Rebecca called my name, I passed Joanne her paperwork and approached the counter. "Let me just take a quick look at your forms," Rebecca said with a flat tone absent any compassion.

Laughter threatened to escape my mouth when she brushed away a crumb from the corner of her mouth.

While she scanned the pages, I fingered the empty wrappers tucked inside my jacket. *Have another bite … go on, eat the whole thing. You know you want to.* Rebecca didn't thank me for the brownies. Just knowing she had taken a nibble was my satisfaction.

"Looks like everything is in order." Rebecca said while pushing a sheet of paper through the opening in the glass. "Take this with you as you look for a new job. Each week I need contact information from three places where you have applied for work. Checks are released after we receive the paperwork and are mailed from Raleigh to your home address by Wednesday of each week. Let the Employment Security Commission know if you move or fail to receive your check. Keep in mind that processing the forms isn't instantaneous and that the turnaround time could be a week to ten days. You are required by law to inform the Employment Security Commission should you find employment other than Cleveland Manufacturing. At that time all benefits cease." Rebecca looked up and asked, "Do you have any questions?" Her tone was clear. My answer best be a firm "No."

A wide smile formed. Genuine. Like the cat who swallowed the canary. "No, ma'am. Thank you, Rebecca. Enjoy the brownies."

I left the building stopping just long enough to remove the ex-lax wrappers from my pocket, pile them in the outside ashtray, strike a Piggly Wiggly match, and light the wrappers on fire.

Chapter Fourteen

Carole Anne

Bus number twenty-two stops at the Outbound Trailer Park entrance at exactly 2:58 each school day. Unless Doretta has cheerleading practice, she gets off at my stop and we do our homework together. I don't understand why she'd rather be cooped up inside our cramped trailer or sitting outside watching dust boil up from the road. I'd rather sit on Doretta's front porch overlooking a bed of petunias instead of babysitting Granny Pearlene and making dinner for Mama. If I lived in Doretta's house, I'd plant myself on the front porch with a glass of sweet tea in my hand. A real glass, not the plastic kind that comes in oatmeal containers. I'd rock back and forth in a painted white chair, might even wave when cars passed. I'd be so thankful for a real road, the absence of gravel and the dust it produced. Concrete smells different than dust, smells like progress with a pinch of hope.

Granny Pearlene says, "Carole Anne, the grass isn't greener on the other side of the tracks. Someone just fertilized it with a big ole load of manure." Of course, she had a point, but when I look outside my window, life looks a whole lot better on Doretta's side.

Riders tumbled from the bus and scattered to their trailers. Doretta and I passed them all, walking as fast as possible to Lot Number Three. I had to pee and change my pad. I hated using the bathroom at school. The janitor gives me the creeps. He lurks in the halls wearing a weird grin while hunched over the mop handle.

Doretta easily kept up. Her long legs always made me walk double-time fast, but when nature calls, I've really gotta move. Tilting my head toward the trailer, I listened for the TV while shifting my weight from one foot to the other. My bladder protested, but I ignored the discomfort. You would think by now my bladder knows it must wait for a commercial break. I can't just barge in, don't dare step foot inside and ignite Granny Pearlene's wrath unless a commercial is on, even if I had to pee so bad my eyes turned yellow.

I had just wrapped my hand on the handle when I heard Granny Pearlene say, "I ought to kill you."

I froze and listened carefully. "You heard me. I ought to shoot you dead. Draw a bead right betwixt your eyes and pull the trigger."

Pressing my finger to my lips, I eased Doretta behind me and motioned for her to listen.

"If it weren't for hellfire and brimstone, you'd be as dead as a hammer. Don't argue with me. I know what I said. Vicki Lord did *not* shoot Marco Dane. No sir. She's a good Christian woman, just like me, but even good Christian women know how to fire a gun."

Standing on tiptoe, I peered in the window to see if I needed to send Doretta next door to call the sheriff. I couldn't see a thing through the plastic we used to keep out the cold.

"That boy sniffing around my Barbara looks like Marco Dane, 'cept he don't wear fancy polyester pants and bright striped sweaters. I'm telling ya, that boy deserves a bullet, too."

Doretta whispered in my ear, "Who's she talking to?"

I shrugged. "Can't tell for certain. I don't know if someone's in there with her, or she's on the phone. Hard to tell, she might just be talking to herself."

Through the door, we heard Granny Pearlene say, "I'm telling ya, if you don't stay away from my Barbara I'll shoot you just like Vicki Lord shot Marco Dane. Yessir, you'll turn on the television and see me on the news. There'll be a big trial too, just like Vicki got."

Doretta pushed me out of the way and wrapped her hand around the door handle, her thumb pressed the latch.

Wedging my foot against the screen, I placed my hand on Doretta's.

Doretta lowered her shoulder and gave me a light shove knocking me off the cinderblock steps. "Carole Anne, quit being a coward. I know exactly what's going on in there. She's watching *One Life to Live.*

C'mon let's go before the show's over." Then she smiled, catlike. "Have I ever told you that I think Marco Dane is sexy?"

Inside, Doretta slid beside Granny Pearlene like a deep-fried chicken leg on a Styrofoam plate. Granny stiffened but didn't take her eyes off the television. Sometimes she can't tolerate physical contact. I slunk into the kitchen knowing she'd give us both a piece of her mind the moment a commercial came on. There was only one path to bladder relief, past the television and Granny Pearlene. I knew from experience I'd get my hind-end swatted if I got between Granny Pearlene and Vicki Lord.

Doretta and Granny Pearlene sat unblinking as the scene played out. My shoulders tensed as the music grew loud signaling an approaching commercial. Granny Pearlene turned toward me. Her lips pursed flat, her eyes narrow slits. Doretta picked up the TV guide and flipped through it. "Miss Pearlene, what do you think about Marco Dane?" She tapped a photo showing him wearing an orange-and-yellow sweater with dark-brown ribbing around the edges. Doretta motioned for me to approach.

Granny Pearlene looked at the TV guide. "Law child, any man dolled up like that ain't nothing but trouble. You know there's a boy sniffing around my Barbara who looks like Marco Dane, 'cept he don't wear fancy polyester pants and bright striped sweaters."

Doretta shot me a puzzled look.

I didn't care that Doretta now witnessed one of Granny Pearlene's spells, I needed the bathroom.

"After my stories end, I'm gonna pray hellfire and damnation on that boy just like the book of Proverbs instructs. Yessir. I'll pray me some coals of fire upon that boy's head, that boy with the shifty Marco Dane coal-black eyes. I try to be a good Christian woman, do what Vicki Lord and the Good Book says. But I just can't bring myself to follow all the scriptures, especially that part about giving an enemy bread to eat and water to drink. No sir. There'll be no water or drink for that boy who wants to tarnish my sweet Barbara."

Doretta paled a bit and gave me a sympathetic look. I just shrugged.

Doretta said, "Miss Pearlene, I don't think Marco Dane is dead, do you?"

This is one of the reasons why I love Doretta. She is unpredictable and brave, diffusing most situations with her charm. Her question probably saved my hind-end and my bladder.

Granny Pearlene's mouth opened. Fuss words died on her tongue as her gaze moved from me to Doretta who had crossed her legs and begun swinging her foot waiting for a response.

Seeing my chance, I dashed past them and into the bathroom.

"I don't think they really killed him off," Doretta said. "He's too handsome. Women all over the world get goo-goo eyed at the sight of him. It doesn't make sense to write him off the show."

I took my place in the brown living room chair and watched Doretta work her magic. Doretta switched legs and restarted her foot.

"Oh, I wish the men around here wore those kinds of clothes." She released a dramatic sigh. "I am so weary of seeing drab brown shirts and camouflage hunting jackets. And Marco's hair. Oh, his hair is divine. It's so black and shiny and there's never a strand out of place." Doretta wrapped a strand of her own blond hair around her finger, twirling it like she was deep in thought.

Granny Pearlene sat in stunned silence. Doretta's eyes lit up. She smiled and flashed me a look.

"Oh, my goodness," Doretta said with a grab of Granny Pearlene's hand. "I just thought of something. What if Marco Dane is dead, for real? I mean, what if he is bad sick, or worse, was disfigured in some horrible car accident on his way to the studio? Miss Pearlene, that's the only reason he would ever leave Llanview." Doretta placed her hand on her heart. "Oh, Miss Pearlene, we need to put Marco Dane on the church prayer list. Better yet, let's say a prayer right now."

Doretta released Granny Pearlene's hand and pressed her palms together into the praying hands position we learned in Bible school. She gave me a wink and clapped her hands again, which was my signal to follow her lead. "Carole Anne, we need to pray."

Granny Pearlene opened her mouth to speak, but Doretta began to pray, "Lord, we pray for Marco Dane …"

"Yes," Granny Pearlene added. "Help him, Lord."

As the commercial faded and the show resumed Doretta hissed, "Sssh! Miss Pearlene, it looks like we're gonna have to hold our prayers. Our stories are back on."

Chapter Fifteen

Barbara Parker

My life was unraveling. I was out of a job. Connor Brown was back in my life and somehow Carole Anne got mixed up with those no-good Foster boys. She knew that walking to school was not permitted, ever. I'd had to preach this to her until I was blue in the face. Walkers were a different class of students than bus riders. They left home early, giving themselves plenty of time to gather as a group, smoke a few cigarettes and pass around a doobie or two. Then they'd drag themselves into class late not caring about grades or their future.

I had just about finished celebrating my ex-lax brownie victory when a flash of orange caught my eye. A Holly Hobby lunchbox. I would recognize it anywhere. After climbing the hill behind the Piggly Wiggly, I hid behind the rhododendron. Part of me wanted to tear through the woods and help Carole Anne when the buses forced her into the ditch. But then she'd wonder why I wasn't at work. I wasn't ready to explain myself, not yet. Not when I still hoped orders might come this week and I could get my job back. I had figured to visit the plant, see if anything had changed since Friday.

A beam of light sparkled through the limbs as the Foster boys strutted down the hill looking for trouble. Silver chain links dangled from Matthew's belt loop. The kind that secured a wallet bulging with dope money. Everyone knew the Foster boys sold—and smoked— dope. Everyone except their preacher daddy who denied the rumors and presented his boys spotless and spit-shined every Sunday.

Everyone also remembered when the party line buzzed with talk of Matthew Foster dropping out of school despite his father's month-long sermon series titled, *Honoring Your Father*. Each message had gone long, well past noon. Preacher Foster quoted every scripture he could recall as his boys sat stone-faced beside their mother whose piously folded fingers were clenched so tight blood pooled at the tips. Preacher Foster had long since broken any free will lingering in his wife, but not a single one of his boys obeyed his commands.

Matthew conducted a different business than his brothers. Under the cover of darkness, he met with those who needed a little something to help them cope. When the timber industry died, men abandoned their chain saws and commuted to Kentucky working twelve-hour days in the belly of a coal mine. These men often returned home for weekend visits bitter, tired, and eager to fight. They deposited enough money into bank accounts to cover household bills while stashing a few dollars away for that certain something known to take the edge off. Even if it did turn a bitter man mean.

By the time the three-thirty rail sounded on Monday morning, a caravan of men had already made it midway to Kentucky. Punching timecards at six, the men next rode a train deep in the earth's belly while their women hid bruised cheeks and their kids nursed split lips. Sheriff Toliver knew who beat their wife, and who needed help easing the hopelessness that descends on a man whose only employment took him miles from home. That's why he looked the other way as Matthew's wallet grew fat enough to purchase a brand new 1976 Ford stepside truck. And I had long suspected the Foster boys would see an uptick in business with unemployment on the rise.

Matthew had spotted Carole Anne long before she took notice. Pranking gullible kids who walked to school fed the meanness inside his good-for-nothing soul. Now, I could have followed those boys and threatened them within an inch of their lives. I could have confronted them, told them to keep away from my daughter. But they would have known then that Carole Anne was my weakness. I saw how she looked at the youngest Foster boy, how she had leaned in, naïve and eager. They saw it too. Those boys can smell innocence and inexperience from a mile away. I could have marched myself straight over to Sheriff Toliver's office and told him what happened, but Sheriff Toliver believed boys will be boys and that talking to anyone with the last name Foster led to nothing but a waste of time. I knew that Sheriff Toliver wasn't worth a tinker's toenail. Sixteen years ago, he'd been no help. He'd taken one look at my swollen face, glancing at the purple bruises on my neck and figured I'd learned my lesson and would "use better judgment next time." He durned sure wouldn't help my daughter unless she was bleeding, or dead. Knowing this, I retrieved Carole Anne's things and decided to have a little talk with her once she got home, especially about the Foster boys.

After picking up the strewn books and cramming them into the bag, I hurried back to the Piggly Wiggly where Hoke Montgomery stood spraying window cleaner on the new glass door he had installed after an impatient customer shattered the old one with a shopping buggy. Hoke ran a squeegee across the glass and then wiped blue liquid on an apron he kept tied around his waist. He was a permanent fixture of the Piggly Wiggly; he'd started as a bag boy at age thirteen, then got himself promoted to stocker once he graduated high school and needed full-time employment. Today he ran the whole kit and caboodle and owned the building to boot.

"Good morning, Barbara," he said, catching another blue drop of cleaner with his apron. "Nice to see you on this fine day."

"Hoke, I need a job." The words erupted from my mouth in a tumble of worry and embarrassment.

"Well now, let's step into my office."

His office was built on a plywood platform stationed beside cash register number one so he could watch the register. The walls were waist-high and designed to keep out wayward children and unemployed factory workers begging for work.

Hoke Montgomery was Bryson City's most eligible bachelor. Many women had tried to get their hooks in him, but he'd always been married to the store. He kept the floor buffed so smooth you could see your reflection, but his office stayed a jumbled mess. Piles of colored paper littered the desk. I think there was a telephone buried somewhere beneath the paper because I could see a section of cord under the ledger book. He slipped his hand inside a partially open filing cabinet, presented me with a job application, and sat down in a dingy office chair.

"Know how to make change? Put up stock?" he asked.

I nodded. "I can do whatever you need."

"Barbara, I know you're a hard worker, but I've gotta tell you, we don't have enough openings for all the people who have applied since the plant laid off folk. Nothing personal, but I'm going to have to take this matter to prayer and seek an answer from the Lord."

After thanking him for his time, I waived to Francine on my way out while mentally marking Piggly Wiggly off my list. Hoke served as deacon at First Baptist. Since I only went on occasion, any opening would most likely go to a church member.

***

Back at Cleveland Manufacturing, I waited at the picnic area for Janelle to come outside for her lunch break. Before she had the chance to sit, I asked, "Any new orders come in this week?"

Janelle took the pack of matches I offered. She lit the cigarette and shook the life out of the match. "No." Her answer punched me hard in the gut. "You apply for unemployment yet?" Janelle chewed on her peanut butter sandwich while I relayed what happened during my visit with Rebecca, even the part about the ex-lax brownies.

"You didn't!" she said.

Beaming, I responded, "I did."

Janelle's hand squeezed my leg. "You done good. You make me proud. You should have also brought her some lemonade with that stuff what makes you throw up ... whadda they call it ... yippi cat?"

"Ipecac," I corrected. I didn't tell Janelle how badly I wanted to purchase a tiny bottle of the medicine, how the thoughts of Rebecca doubling over the sink somehow made me feel better about my current situation.

"Francine might wonder why I needed it," I explained. "No one looks twice at a box of ex-lax mixed in with the groceries, but ipecac raises questions."

Janelle nodded and flicked ash that gathered at the end of her smoke. "You're right. Have you told Pearlene yet?"

I ignored Janelle's question. "Let's see if you're still proud of me after Rebecca blocks my unemployment check."

"She can't do that."

"I bet she will. Mark my words. She'll try something. She'll find a reason to deny my application. Or, she'll say the paperwork got lost in the mail." Lighting my own cigarette, I said, "I let my temper get the best of me."

Janelle flicked the cigarette away from her. The smoldering nub landed in the gravel with the other yellow filters discarded by workers whose pride had been replaced with hopelessness. "Now you listen to me. If Rebecca tries something like that, I'll march down to the unemployment office and mop the floor with her. That'll give Bryson City something to talk about."

I laughed, a short dry chuckle filled with fear. "Shouldn't have done it, but she treated me like an ignorant hick. People have no right looking down their noses at any of us. Factory work is hard. Harder than her cushy desk job."

"I know that's right," Janelle agreed. "Preach, sister."

"One thing I will not tolerate is the mistreatment of hard-working folk." I took in a long draw of my smoke.

Janelle raised her chin, "Ain't no shame in factory work. Not a lick of shame in it. Where I work don't make me a lesser woman, and it durn sure don't make her a better one."

I dropped the cigarette and ground it under the toe of my shoe, then rubbed my shoulders to relieve the tension, kneading the muscles with my fingertips. "I kinda wish I hadn't done it. I wish I'd waited a week. You know, had at least one unemployment check waiting in the hopper before I fed her those brownies. Oh well, I'll know soon enough whether she retaliates or not."

"Listen to me. Sometimes you gotta stand your ground and let folk know they can't run over you." Janelle nodded toward Carole Anne's bag and said, "What ya got in there?"

"Carole Anne had an encounter with the Foster boys this morning. I fished this out of the tree."

"What's she doing hanging around them? Everyone knows they're trouble."

I shrugged. "I haven't got a clue, but I saw her walking to school this morning. I intend to find out this afternoon what's going on with her."

Janelle crumpled the brown paper bag that had held her sandwich, "You start looking for work yet?"

I didn't want to talk about the real reason why I was there—to see if there was any way I could beg The Eagle to hire me back. "Just came from the Piggly Wiggly."

"And?" Janelle pressed.

"Hoke said he'd pray on it. You know what that means."

"Sure do. Means someone from his church gets first dibs."

"Yup." I nodded. "You know how long it's going to take me to find three places to put on my unemployment forms? About a minute. Want to know how many places around here are hiring?"

"None," Janelle replied.

"Exactly. Zero. Goose egg. I guess I'll have to make something up on my paperwork because it's not like Bryson City has another factory where I can apply."

"I heard tell that some folk are listing Cleveland Manufacturing on their forms as a potential employer," Janelle offered.

Hope leapt in my chest. "Really?"

"Yup. Word is The Eagle has been talking to people. There's been a steady stream of folk picking up applications all morning. Won't do 'em no good though."

"Why not?"

Janelle frowned. "I heard this place is going to be boarded up tight by the end of the month. Heard that the whole company is moving to Mexico because labor there is cheap. Even The Eagle will be outta work. It's times like these when I wish I was older."

"What do you mean, older?"

"Don't do no good to wish for youth, because if I had my life to live over, I'd make the same choices. But if I were a couple years older, I could collect Social Security." Tears pooled in her eyes. She brushed a shaking hand across her cheek. "I'm stuck, Barbara. Too old to start over. Too young to draw Social Security. I don't know what I'll do. There's not much out there for a broken-down old woman like myself." She sighed. "But enough about me. What's going on with Carole Anne?"

"I just don't know, Janelle, but I aim to find out." My shoulders hunched now from the weight of all I carried. All I'd carried for too many years, in fact. "First," I said with determination I didn't quite feel, "I need to find a job."

Chapter Sixteen

Carole Anne

"I've gotta get out of this trailer," Granny Pearlene said while bolting for the door. Sometimes she was hard to keep up with. Sometimes she just took off, especially once an idea started rolling around in her mind. When that happened the only thing I could do was run along behind and hope she didn't hurt herself. Like now, when she bolted toward the hill overlooking Rite-Way Pawn.

Lucinda's television had been running nonstop since its arrival, more to punish Lucinda than display the working condition of the picture tube to potential buyers. "I've got it on good authority that Albert might *really* be serious about selling Lucinda's beloved television." Granny Pearlene opened her purse and retrieved a box of orange-flavored Tic Tacs. She shook one free, popped it in her mouth, then dropped the little container in my hand. "I hear she's toeing the line this time," Granny Pearlene added. "Making progress toward being a better wife."

Well, that explained why we were sitting on the rise overlooking Main Street. Granny Pearlene was keeping an eye on the television she planned on buying.

"From what I hear, Lucinda made country fried steak with green beans and mashed potatoes last night for dinner. She curled her hair, dusted off her best dress. She even greeted Albert with an ice-cold PBR."

But neither good old Albert nor the Magnavox had budged.

"How long do ya think Mr. Thomas will let it stay in the window this time?" I asked. "I think three days is the longest Lucinda's been without her television."

Granny Pearlene shrugged her shoulders. "Never know with those two. Guess it's up to Lucinda. You'd think she'd get one of those crotch pots. That way she could watch her stories and cook supper at the same time."

"You mean, croc*k* pot?"

"That's what I said. A crotch pot."

"I knew I'd find you here," Doretta said as she snapped a lawn chair in place. She blew a bright pink bubble, popped it with a click of her tongue, and sucked the gum back into her mouth. "What kind of price did he put on it, do you know?"

"Forty dollars," I replied.

Doretta whistled low and long. "Forty dollars. He really is serious."

Granny Pearlene smiled. "Not as bad as the two-hundred-dollar price tag he put on it the first time he did this. Still, forty dollars might as well be forty thousand."

"Miss Pearlene, how much you got?" Doretta asked followed by another gum pop. "Because I can hear your brain working all the way over here. You want that television real bad, don't you?"

Granny Pearlene shrugged her shoulders. "Not enough to buy it out of hock. With Albert the price is always negotiable. He'll come down if he's mad enough. I just need to make him an offer he can't refuse and make sure he stays mad at Lucinda."

"What do you have in mind?" Doretta asked after another bubble pop.

"Oh, I've got me a plan." Granny Pearlene fumbled in her purse until she found a tube of lipstick. She applied a liberal layer, rubbed her lips together and then snapped her purse closed. "C'mon girls, let's pay Mr. Rite-Way Pawn a visit." She looked over her shoulder. "First I need to get something out of the freezer. I always keep me a little cake set aside for emergencies. You know, if someone dies, or—in this case—needs a color television."

Granny Pearlene retrieved a cake from the freezer, confident of its ability to sway Albert. I worried about this cake. I hadn't seen her cook in ages. Lately, Mama had taken on all of the baking. I hoped this one was fit for human consumption, made by Mama and not Granny Pearlene who sometimes used chili powder instead of cinnamon and baking soda instead of sugar. After running a brush through my hair, I fell in line with Doretta and followed as Granny Pearlene led the way. "A smart woman knows it's best to bring a little extra incentive when wheeling and dealing," Granny Pearlene said, confidence filling every word. "Watch and learn, girls. Watch and learn."

A bell tied to the door chimed, announcing our arrival. Granny Pearlene held the door open as we entered, then followed behind wearing a sweet smile. Albert Thomas was what I called a piece of work. He boldly broke the law not only drinking and driving, but slinging beer cans all over the road. What I disliked the most was his making money off the less fortunate. He loaned money and then recouped what he loaned, plus an enormous amount of interest and was so greedy he kept the pawn shop open long after every other business had closed.

As we entered, he finger-combed his thinning hair over a growing bald spot, looked me up and down then asked, "Little lady, what can I help you with?" His faded T-shirt didn't even cover the bulge in his belly. Doretta and I exchanged a look. Doretta rolled her eyes and made a choking sound in her throat.

Granny Pearlene placed the container on the counter. "You looking to pawn your Tupperware?" he jeered with a nod toward the cake holder.

Pointing at the Magnavox Granny Pearlene said, "I'm here to talk about that beat-up ole TV you've got there in the window. I thought you and me might do a little trading."

Albert scratched his belly and picked his teeth with a toothpick he kept permanently wedged in the corner of his mouth. "Interested in an upgrade?" He waddled around the counter and came up beside Doretta. "Might want to wait till next week. I expect an increase in inventory what with the layoffs over at the plant."

Granny Pearlene eye-measured the television's cabinet and nodded that the piece would fit in our trailer. "Whadda ya want for it?" she asked, ignoring the bombshell Albert just dropped about job loss.

"Seventy-five."

"Wait," I said and stepped between them. "What about layoffs?"

Albert grinned and offered no further information.

Granny Pearlene nudged me out of the way. "Pay no attention to my granddaughter. She ain't schooled in the ways of haggling. The price tag says forty," Granny Pearlene said, pointing to Albert's own handwriting. "And I'm not paying a penny more."

"I know what it says. That was yesterday's sign." Snatching the sign off the console he said, "Storewide sale ended last week. Besides, me and the wife's been getting along better." He scratched his belly again. "I'm thinking about letting her have it back."

Granny Pearlene removed the Tupperware lid, pulled a knife and a twice-folded paper towel from her purse, then cut a thin slice of the still-frozen cake and carefully positioned the slice on the napkin. She forced her voice into a syrupy sweet tone. "Albert, I'm glad Lucinda's' coming around, I really am. I do hope her newfound affection is love for you and not her TV."

Albert folded his arms across his belly and grunted.

"How long's it been since that wife of yours made you a homemade cake?" Granny Pearlene approached, hand extended, luring Albert toward her. "You know you'll be eating frozen dinners the day after you bring that TV back home."

"Is that apple stack?" I could almost see drool forming.

Granny Pearlene nodded. "Yesiree Bob. Now Albert, I just took it from the freezer so it's still . . ."

He snatched the napkin from her hand, crammed the entire frozen slice in his mouth, and closed his eyes while chewing.

"Here's my offer," Granny Pearlene said while slicing another serving. "You let me have the Magnavox today for twenty-five cash. I'll leave this cake with you as a retainer. Every Monday for an entire month I'll bring you another one. Fresh, not frozen. Now Albert that's a good deal. You know I charge upwards of forty dollars for my cakes."

Albert chewed, swallowed, and held out the empty napkin. Granny Pearlene laid another piece in his hand. "Next week I'll bring a caramel cake, unless you prefer black walnut."

His eyes widened and crumbs escaped his mouth as he mumbled a response.

"Do we have a deal?"

Swallowing, Albert nodded and said, "Miss Pearlene, you've got yourself a deal."

They shook hands on it. "Oh, and Albert," Granny Pearlene added. "If you can find it in your heart to deliver the TV to my place before you go home to supper, Lucinda can have my black-and-white one. It still works just as good as it did on the day I bought it from you."

Albert beamed. "Miss Pearlene, you're a genius."

She retrieved twenty-five dollars from her purse while Albert wrote the bill of sale. "Now don't sell my Tupperware," Granny Pearlene said, tapping it with her fingertips. "I'll need it in a couple days." The bell chimed as we left. We waited until we crossed the tracks to whoop it up. Doretta showed Granny Pearlene how to give a high-five like the baseball players did it.

Granny Pearlene delighted in what she called "this hip celebration of happiness the youngsters do today."

Granny Pearlene reached for Doretta's hand and said, "Remember ... the way to a Magnavox Console Color TV is through Albert's stomach." She giggled and added, "Now I can watch *One Life to Live* the way God intended it—in color."

That night, I retreated to my bedroom while Granny Pearlene sat mesmerized in front of the Magnavox. Being inside the trailer made me feel like a trapped animal. The fake wood paneling and threadbare carpet suffocated me, especially after dark. Later on, while people in Bryson City slept, I walked the railroad tracks desperate to find the schoolbooks I'd lost earlier that day. Especially before Mama found out.

While I walked, I thought about Mama, about Granny Pearlene, about how being a *reject* would forever tie me here unless I did something to break away.

For most of Mama's life, she packed a peanut butter sandwich, slipped her callused feet into a pair of worn-out shoes and then walked to work. She wasn't the only one. At the break of dawn, a line of workers inched toward the plant. The rhythm of these punch-card workers is so precise I could almost hear their lives ticking away one second at a time; could almost see them standing single file holding a worn time card pinched between tobacco-stained fingers. Hanging on to a flimsy sheet of paper that bore a name and the hours each employee had worked. Slower employees did their best to hurry. Can't be late, or they'll dock your pay. Feed the time card into the clock's mouth. Wait for the loud click. Metal teeth piercing paper, recording the precise moment the plant owned you for another day of repetitive labor.

I had decided a long time ago that life wouldn't catch me dead in the plant. I will never work in a factory; never punch a clock like Granny Pearlene and Mama have for most of their lives. I'll eat dirt and die first.

Making my way up Schoolhouse Hill for the second time that day, I wondered why women in Bryson City didn't complain. Wondered why they accepted their destiny without pushing back. I understood that options around here were limited to factory work or a welfare check. Many who received welfare also had jobs. They just didn't earn enough money to survive, especially not in the winter when food and heating fuel prices skyrocketed. The proud tucked their chins and went to work, the defeated had little choice but to rely on government assistance. Well, the Parker women weren't defeated, at least not yet.

I wondered why people have always seemed to be content with this town. Why hadn't Mama tried to get a better job, or go to the community college the next county over in Jackson County? Why did students decide working in a factory was more important than finishing high school? Why didn't women grow weary of pressing fabric under the metal foot of a sewing machine day after day? Wasn't there something inside their souls urging them to make more money?

Then again, I thought as I trudged through the night, maybe the thought of life outside of Bryson City was so terrifying people felt safer living in structures with paper-thin walls and sagging roofs than dreaming of anything else. Or maybe something was wrong with *me?* Maybe I didn't belong in the town living with the women who raised me.

After shining the flashlight along the hillside for at least an hour, I gave up. My books were gone. I'd ask the librarian how much they cost, see if I had enough saved to replace them before Mama found out. I kicked a can. Buying those books would put a dent in my meager savings. I had hoped to leave Bryson City that upcoming summer, slip off and be long gone before they discovered me missing.

But that's okay; one day I'd be gone whether Mama liked it or not. Whether she gave permission or not. One day I'd leave and never look back. I ignored the guilt needling me. Yes, I would miss Granny Pearlene, but I hadn't asked to be her caregiver. I'd been assigned that duty by default.

The soles of my feet protested as I continued walking, leaving the town behind me. I wasn't ready to go home. A security light shone against concrete walls, illuminating the employee entrance of Cleveland Manufacturing. High windows, dingy and without curtains, lined the building. I never understood the reasoning behind installing windows near the roofline instead of ground level until Mama explained that large picture windows not only encouraged employees to look out, but also allowed the rest of the world a glimpse inside. She said this in a whispered tone that hinted of hunched-over work going on within those walls.

A slight vibration beneath my shoes warned it was almost three o'clock; time to head back to the trailer park. When Mama told me nothing good happens after midnight, she had spoken with a firm tone, like she had firsthand knowledge of bad things. Sometimes I walked the rails long past midnight, returning undetected in the early morning hours. Months ago, I mastered a silent exit and return. No one noticed me slipping back inside or heard me tiptoe down the hall. Mama was always too dog-tired to notice me gone and Granny Pearlene couldn't hear so good anymore. Come morning, Doretta floated into our homeroom class looking fresh and rested while dark shadows marked my tired face.

Back at the trailer, I slipped down the hall. After snuggling beneath the covers, I gazed at the road maps taped to the wall. I felt the train approach, a slight shimmy beneath me, like those earthquakes in California. Or so I supposed. California was on the list of places I would visit one day. Staring at the wall, I recalled the three-thirty engineer's face. He and I knew each other. Not by name of course, but in a friendly greeting. His, a gloved hand raised high as he sped past at twenty-five miles an hour. Mine, an eager hand stuck out the window. Sometimes with my thumb jutted out like a hopeful hitchhiker making her way across country.

How I longed to be like him with the chance to see the world and watch morning crest the horizon high above the rail. One man, small in comparison to the engine he manipulated. One man, with the ability to wake a town. As the bed shook, I closed my eyes and dreamt of my future, hoping for the courage to leave Bryson City while knowing in the deepest part of me that the odds were not in my favor.

Mama never said so, but I knew in my gut I had come into this world a mistake, an unplanned pregnancy. I could see it in the way she sometimes looked at me. Like I was a burden she didn't want. It doesn't take a mathematical genius to subtract my age from hers and determine she had me before she turned eighteen. Sure, getting pregnant as a teenager is a rite of passage around here. Some girls actually *wanted* to get pregnant before they could legally drive a car. For them, getting married while in high school seemed cool. Then they quickly learned that school takes a back seat when you have a hungry mouth to feed.

I don't know why Mama never married. I've never bothered to ask. But one of these days I'm going to find out the truth.

I've been wondering about my dad ever since the first day of kindergarten when I realized everyone else had two parents. Who he was ... where he was at. I used to imagine he was dead, killed in Vietnam when enemy fire brought down his plane. A war hero. Fearless. Brave. I liked to think of him that way. Because the alternative meant he couldn't handle having a kid in his life.

146

I hated my father when Mama's paycheck didn't cover our bills and we couldn't afford to run the blow-dryer or the heat because it cost too much money. I hated the sympathetic way the cashier nodded and smiled as we laid our bologna and white bread on the checkout counter. I hated that he didn't support us, that he didn't care enough about me to send a birthday card. Ever. Hated that I didn't even know what my father looked like. During the hating time, I focused my energy away from wanting frivolous things like Hershey's chocolate bars or new tennis shoes, focusing instead on channeling the emotion into planning my future. I wasn't exactly sure what I wanted to be when I grew up. I only knew there was no way I'd stay here in Bryson City and work in a factory.

Yep. Thoughts like this kept me awake. And sometimes, wondering about Mama's dreams kept me up. Surely, she had dreams before I came along and ruined everything. Well, now I had Mama's job to worry about as well. But, Doretta told me Albert was full of hot air and that I shouldn't listen to a word he says.

I like to think of myself as a mistake, because the alternative meant Mama deliberately chose to get pregnant instead of graduate high school. I reached for the flashlight I'd left on the bedside table, then pointed it at the road maps hanging on my bedroom wall. With me out of the way, Mama could pursue her dreams. Unless they'd been replaced with the cruel reality that, try as she might, she'd be stuck in this trailer park with the rest of Bryson City's rejects for the remainder of her life.

Chapter Seventeen

Barbara

"That Oldsmobile's gotta go," Pearlene said the minute I stepped in the trailer. She spoke before the door closed behind me, before the pocketbook strap slid from my shoulder, before I could recite the speech I had practiced on the way home.

"What?" Carole Anne jumped up from the couch. "Why do we need to sell the car? I thought you were saving it for me."

Pearlene turned to Carole Anne. "Because your mother lost her job. Isn't that right, Barbara?" Pearlene crossed her arms and waited for an answer. "Go on now, tell the truth."

Carole Anne's eyes got wide. Her mouth fell open. "Mama," she said slowly. "Is this true?"

This wasn't the way I wanted to tell them. It wasn't the way I planned on letting them know. I wanted to deliver the bad news with a positive twist. I wanted to reassure Carole Anne that everything would work out, even though I didn't know how. Sometimes mamas need to look at their daughters straight-faced and bend the truth. Sometimes we need to hear our own lies tumble from our own lips while praying things will work out.

Carole Anne looked from Pearlene to me and waited for an answer.

Addressing Pearlene, I said, "I don't know what you heard, and I don't care how you heard it. I'm not in the mood to talk about that car. We've got bigger things to worry about."

"The point is you didn't tell us," Pearlene snapped.

Ignoring Pearlene's comment, I turned to Carole Anne. "Let me explain. Almost half the workers of Cleveland Manufacturing got pink slips with their paychecks."

149

"Wouldn't have happened to me," Pearlene interrupted. "I would've sewed enough to keep my job." She turned toward Carole Anne, drawing her into the conversation. "I was the best worker at the plant. I woulda been safe."

"Mama, you don't know that," I snapped. "Things have changed. Good workers were let go. What's happening at the plant isn't about how fast you sew, or the quality of your work. New orders aren't coming in."

"Still ... I'da been safe."

"Joanne Whitmore and her daughter got pink slips too," I snapped. Smiling when shock registered on her face.

"The hell you say," Pearlene's voice lowered in disbelief.

"Yes, and Janelle is next. She said the entire place will be locked down soon. They're even shutting down the Cleveland Closet."

"Shutting down the Cleveland Closet!" Pearlene said. "What'll folks do for clothes?"

Ignoring how Mama was more worried about clothes than my lack of a job, I refocused on Carole Anne. "Don't worry. I filed for unemployment, and I have one more check coming. I have a few dollars put back. So, we aren't in a bind yet."

"From what I heard, Rebecca Camden's bowels aren't in a bind either," Pearlene added with a laugh. "Yeah, I heard all about the brownies."

Carole Anne turned seeking an explanation. I waved her off. "Don't pay her any attention. She doesn't know what she's talking about."

"I know we've got to sell that car," Pearlene gestured toward the door. "We're gonna need some money coming in here and the only thing we own of value is that piece of junk parked outside."

"It's not junk," Carole Anne insisted. "It just needs a little work."

I shook my head. "It's been sitting too long. At this point it'll take too much money to get it running."

"Not if you let Connor help," Carole Anne offered.

The room fell silent.

"Mama, I know you're mad at me for riding with him the other day, but he told me he wants to buy the car and if you don't want to sell he said he will help me get it on the road. You threw him out before he had the chance to make you an offer. He can fix just about anything. Maybe he can show us how to make the repairs."

"He doesn't have time to fool with us," I said.

"You don't know that," Carole Anne insisted. "You've never given him a chance."

"Earn more if we sold it ourselves," Pearlene said. "Don't matter if we sold it for parts or fix it up and get as much as we can for the hunk of junk. Whatever we do, we gotta act fast. Folks won't buy nothing but groceries and cigarettes now that the plant is closing."

Pearlene was right. Cleveland Manufacturing was the second largest employer in Bryson City, with the school system being the largest.

"Do we even know what's wrong with the car?" Carole Anne asked. "It might just need a new battery and air in the tires," she said, her tone hopeful. "Mama, when did you drive it last?"

Pearlene and I locked eyes. The question hung in the air, unanswered.

"I don't remember," I lied knowing the precise moment I drove the Oldsmobile was on the night Carole Anne was conceived. Pearlene crossed her arms and said, "Hmmph!"

"Why don't we start with a list of what you know is wrong with the car," Carole Anne said. "Then we can move forward from there."

"Ain't nothing wrong with the car," Pearlene said. "Not a dang thing."

"Then why aren't we driving it?" Carole Anne asked, her voice getting shrill.

I knew Carole Anne wanted the car for herself. I knew that like me she dreamed of something more. She wanted to ride away into wherever the sunset took her. But what Carole Anne didn't realize was the odds of leaving here were slim to none.

"Tell me more about the Closet," Pearlene said. "How are they going to get rid of the inventory? Do you think they'll open the Closet to employees? You know, let them have first dibs?"

"Mama, for once can you think about someone other than yourself?

Have you already forgotten I don't work there anymore? So what if they do open the Cleveland Closet. I wouldn't waste my money buying mismatched pieces of cloth."

Pearlene strode into the kitchen. "Barbara, you couldn't see a money-making opportunity if it slapped you in the face. Cleveland Manufacturing created the Cleveland Closet after realizing they could make money from their scraps and seconds. They would have never opened the Cleveland Closet, and paid someone to run it, if they weren't making money. But now that the jobs are moving overseas, the owners are done with North Carolina. They'll probably pull up stakes, unplug the machines, board up the building, and leave everything else where it is. They might find a sucker who'll come in and buy the building, but probably not. Heck, they might decide to lock the doors and start with all new equipment in Mexico. That's why I say we bust the doors wide open and take everything we can get our hands on."

I glanced toward Carole Anne. She shrugged, like me unable to tell if Pearlene was slipping, or serious. Something in my soul told me she was serious, and I needed to end this conversation before Mama's idea took root.

"Trust me, girls. I know what I'm talking about. They'll either walk away, or dump everything in the trash. All we need to do is pick it up, make an alteration here and there, sew a few quilts and aprons. We could have a yard sale the likes Bryson City has never seen. Or we could rent one of those booths at Leo's Flea Market and make a pile of money."

Neighboring Jackson County served as home to Leo's Flea Market. Last year, he commissioned the high school students to paint a mural advertisement on the side of the Smith's Dry Goods building. After paying the students a nominal fee, they spent an entire Saturday hanging on to ladders and pressing paint onto the bumpy brick building. When they finished, Leo's face greeted everyone leaving town. The words VISIT LEO'S FLEA MARKET: THE LARGEST FLEA MARKET IN THE STATE stood tall in bright white lettering.

Pearlene's eyes shone with excitement. She pulled out a drawer of sewing notions stowed in a kitchen cabinet then spent the next several minutes readying her sewing machine on the Formica kitchen table. I went to the back of the trailer, threw my purse on the bed, and changed into something a little more comfortable. When I got back to the kitchen, Pearlene was touching the wooden spools and taking inventory of buttons and snaps. "We will need navy-colored thread and zippers." Pearlene paused for a minute. "Ooh, and industrial snaps. We will definitely need those in case they throw away jeans. Jeans fetch a higher price." Pearlene grabbed her purse. "I say we head on over now and take what we can get."

Carole Anne had made her way to the door and blocked the exit with her hands raised. "Granny Pearlene, we're talking about the Oldsmobile."

I stood, mouth agape, not believing that Carole Anne for one second entertained Pearlene's idea. Carole Anne turned, just enough to make eye contact. She tilted her head ever so slightly. A signal to let her handle my mother.

"Humph," Pearlene said while pushing Carole Anne out of the way. "I ain't got time for that hunk of junk. Not when there's notions and jeans for the taking. There's far more money to be had selling clothing."

Carole Anne stepped aside and let her grandmother pass. "Fine, go ahead, but have you thought about how you will transport everything back here? Are you just going to walk down Main Street with a stack of fabric and lines of thread flapping in the wind? Because I figure if the Oldsmobile is road-ready we can load the trunk *and* the back seat. We could pack it full to the ceiling if you want." Carole Anne held open the screen door. "But if you can't wait, go ahead."

She took a seat on the sofa. Well, good land of the living. Somehow while I was busy sewing clothes for others to wear, my daughter had grown up.

"Can we *please* focus on a solution to our problem?" Carole Anne continued. "Once we make a list, we will know how much money it's going to take to put the car back on the road. Mama," she said, now turning her attention fully to me. "You could look for work out of town. You could find a better job and we could keep the car."

"Now hold your horses, Missy," Pearlene interjected. "You're getting ahead of yourself. Using the car to haul my stuff is one thing, but it takes a pile of money to drive to work every day. Why do you think so many people cram themselves in vehicles like a bunch of sardines Monday through Friday and ride to work with people they don't even like? Haven't you noticed the number of men leaving out of here before daylight?"

"That's because they're heading for tunnel work up in Kentucky." Carole Anne looked at me. "If you get a job in another county you could put an ad in the newspaper, maybe drive one or two people who can't find work here. They could pitch in on gas and keep your costs low." Her eyes were hopeful. "We can't just sit here and do nothing."

Pearlene crossed her arms tight. "Still, you can't expect this car to solve all of our problems."

"But it could make our lives easier," Carole Anne insisted. "Can't anyone think about that?" Carole Anne left and returned moments later with an envelope, which she threw on the table. "Here, I'll pay for the repairs." Tears formed in her eyes. "I'll even do the mechanic work if I have to."

I snatched the envelope off the table and leafed through it. "Where did you get all this money?"

Carole Anne lifted her chin in defiance. "I worked for it, earned every dime." Her chin trembled. "All I ask is that you give me a chance to get the car running. Don't either of you understand, if we don't fix the Oldsmobile, we will never earn enough money to buy another car. We will be stuck here forever!"

"What's going on while I'm at work? Where did she get this money?"

Pearlene didn't answer. Instead she turned to Carole Anne, her face red with emotion. "Don't you go getting high-and-mighty on me, girl. Me and your Mama have done the best we could with the hand we were dealt."

Carole Anne pointed to Pearlene. Her voice shook with emotion. "Never mind where I got the money. Take it. Take it all. Right now, I'm sick of you both." She rushed down the hall and slammed her bedroom door. Music boomed from within the walls and warned that she didn't want to be disturbed.

"Leave her be," Pearlene said when I tried to follow. "You know the problem?" my mother said. "She's just like you. Stubborn as all get out."

She was right.

Chapter Eighteen

Carole Anne

With or without the Oldsmobile, I would figure a way out of Bryson City. I just needed to take a walk and clear my head. I opened the bathroom window. It was smooth and silent, unlike the front door, which emitted a painful groan when opened and sounded like a dying calf in a hailstorm.

Positioning my foot in the crook of the hedge bush, I tested the branch with my toe then, like always, carefully applied more weight until I was certain the limb would hold. My toes found the strongest section of the branches with just enough support and flexibility to hold my weight. Later, upon my return, the low branches boosted me through the window. Many times, Mama had threatened to rip out the bushes behind the house. She hated the way the leaves smelled like cat pee, or so she claimed. To me, the shrubs beneath the bathroom window smelled like freedom.

I could travel this path with my eyes closed and sometimes I did. Stepping on one cresol-saturated railroad tie after the other. Left foot. Right foot. Left. Right. A steady rhythm without the clack or noise of an engine. My life already had so much noise—school, bus rides, fights with Mama, and unanswered questions about who I was and where my life was heading, especially now. Those were my thoughts as I walked the tracks.

When I imagined a future away from Mama and Granny Pearlene I knew my ambitions and dreams meant nothing without money. That's another reason why I walked the tracks, they took me to my secret job with Hubert. Mama and Granny Pearlene don't know about Hubert's place. The Parker women did not approve of any kind of liquor and they sure wouldn't approve of me helping Hubert.

Bryson City voters continually voted against the sale of alcohol, but that never stopped the sale of alcohol to those thirsty enough to buy it. Nor had the failed referendum prevented Hubert from converting his musty basement into a profitable business where menfolk washed away a little worry before trudging home. Hubert bought—and then resold—clear brew from Columbus Ledbetter whose corn liquor poured off clean and stout. Columbus lived on the Tennessee side of the Great Smoky Mountains, far beyond the twinkling lights of Gatlinburg, back where the woods grew dark, even at midday when clouds rolled in heavy with the smell of sour mash. Secretly, I longed to accompany Hubert on his Tennessee trips, but I knew he wouldn't allow it. He trusted me to keep an eye on the place while he was away, and besides, Johnnie Walker had dibs on the passenger seat.

Hubert drove a Ford Country Esquire modified with what he called "helper springs," thick metal coils strong enough to support the added weight. He also custom fit the station wagon's back seat with a sheet of plywood and then glued empty jars of canned food to the wood. That way, if he got pulled over while in Tennessee, an officer shining a flashlight into the back of the station wagon saw rows of food slated for delivery to those less fortunate. Truth be told, beneath the decoy cans of pork 'n' beans were cases of Budweiser and Pabst Blue Ribbon neatly stacked and ready for Hubert's thirsty customers.

These trips weren't without risk. Tucked away in the dark pull-offs and picnic areas, park rangers waited for any opportunity to capture bootleggers who kept the road hot running from the State-Line Liquor Store in Tennessee to dry towns like Bryson City. That's why Hubert paid Matthew Foster to make the Tennessee beer runs, but the Foster boys couldn't be trusted, and Old Man Ledbetter didn't sell his clear brew to strangers. Since Hubert couldn't be in two places at once, and needed someone trustworthy who wouldn't rob him blind, or drink up all the profit, he offered me a job a while back, which I accepted without a second thought.

Most folk affectionately called Hubert's place "The Hangout." This basement business began with a few men huddled around an open Johnnie Walker bottle and a deck of cards, drinking and solving the world's problems while secretly hoping Lady Luck would deal an ace. Eventually, their friendly game of cards led to friendly wagers, which, when word got out that money could be had, turned into Wednesday night poker. It doesn't really matter to me what they do while they're here. As long as I get my money, I don't care what goes on in Hubert's basement.

I picked up the pace. The quicker I arrived the more money I'd make. The door closed behind me. I hadn't even removed my coat when Hubert said, "Ole Columbus might need to start selling me some of his clear brew by the gallon. 'Cept I'm not sure the Ford's setup could accommodate those jugs. I'm pretty much at capacity now." He lined up the bottles like he was calculating how much he would pour. "Nothing like layoffs to line my pockets," he added.

He was right. Men who now dreaded going home had stopped picking up six-packs after work. Instead they came inside and sat hunched over their drinks, smoking cigarettes while I ran the popcorn popper nonstop.

"Offering free popcorn was a brilliant idea," Hubert said with a friendly nudge to my shoulder as he passed to grab a couple glasses. "A thirsty customer always drinks more. Maybe I need to put a jar of pickled pigs' feet up on the bar."

"Um, I don't think so," I said with my nose upturned. "They're nasty."

A few customers grumbled about the layoffs, but Hubert kept their drinks coming while I wiped the tables and added extra seats when the basement filled.

I'd been working at Hubert's for a while now and hoarding most of the money I made. Of course, Sheriff Tolliver knew I was here. He obviously doesn't mind. I guess he figured I was safe with Hubert. There's something about living end-to-end where one trailer almost touched another that created friction even among the best neighbors. We're blessed with good neighbors on one side, but the other neighbors are what Sheriff Tolliver called his regulars. Those who got mean drunk and acted like they were part of the WWF wrestling foundation. There's even a makeshift wrestling ring up the road where men act like they're as tough as Wahoo McDaniel while others watch and place bets. It's common to see a flash of blue lights pass by our trailer heading toward the rougher section of the trailer park when fights spill out into the road.

Yep. Sheriff Eustace Toliver knew about the bar, just like he knew about other things happening after dark in this quiet little town. Instead of busting up the beer joint and the wrestling, the fine sheriff of Bryson City believed that "a man has a right to drown his worry as long as he minds his manners and acts like somebody instead of a horse's hind-end." Besides, congregating the drinkers in one place made it easier for him to keep an eye on folk.

Sheriff Tolliver also shuttled Hubert's patrons home at closing. The moment the beer mugs and glasses began singing from the train passing, Sheriff Tolliver stood and adjusted his belt. A wordless gesture even the most inebriated customers recognized as time to go. He then eased the two-way radio out of its leather holster. Speaking into the radio using a code none of Bryson City's busybodies could interpret through their home scanners, he called Deputy Owen Blackstone and waited until he heard gravel crunching outside before herding folk into the cruiser. He didn't judge, didn't condemn, and had never made a single arrest, which was one of the reasons why he ran unopposed in every general election.

Granny Pearlene didn't have much use for Sheriff Toliver. Mama either. Granny Pearlene said he was as "useless as tits on a boar hog." Mama just shook her head and declined to elaborate. I had a feeling something had happened between them ages ago. Bad blood doesn't usually occur without justification.

I placed the crumpled dollars from tonight's work in my back pocket. With the customers gone, Hubert focused on lining the bottom of jars with sliced fruit while I stirred a concoction of apple cider, brown sugar, and spices that were warming on a portable Coleman stove. Tonight,

Hubert had promised after we were done, I could have a little taste of a product he made called Bryson City Firewater. He had added fruit and spices to the Ledbetter brew: pears, apples, figs, cinnamon, and a pinch of allspice and impatiently waited for the tasting time.

While the sugar dissolved and the mixture cooled on a new batch, I held a funnel as Hubert poured liquor into the bottom half of each jar, then carefully added a quarter cup of the syrup mixture and filled the rest of the jar with clear brew. He held the bottle to the light and swirled, watching a tornado-shaped swirl of bubbles form as flavoring mixed with liquor. Tearing off a piece of masking tape, he jotted down the date, adhered it to the jar, and then penciled a notation on his recipe card. Once, I tried to guess the combination of the safe where he kept the recipes. A woman never knows when a good Firewater recipe would come in handy.

"Let's get these bottles in the back room before we have a little taste of the first batch."

I helped him carry the hooch, knowing that the work I did really helped. Hubert paid well and more than once customers had left a dollar or two at the table as a tip.

He uncorked a bottle and poured a scant amount of Bryson City Firewater into two glasses, took a swig, and held the liquid on his tongue before swallowing.

"Here ya go," he said, while pushing a shot glass toward me. "Take a little dram of this and tell me if that don't taste like your Granny's stacked apple cake, only in liquid form."

Hubert knew Pearlene would kill us both graveyard dead if she detected even the tiniest whiff of liquor on my breath, but rules didn't exactly apply here, so I tossed back the liquid like I'd seen in the movies, and gasped as it burned a path down my throat.

"Good, ain't it?" Hubert waited for my response.

I wiped my eyes and scratched out a "yes."

"Get yourself some mustard," he told me. "A little squirt of mustard on your tongue will take the liquor smell off your breath."

"I'll be okay," I protested with a cough. "Mustard kinda makes me want to puke. I'll just chew gum."

"Suit yourself," he replied. "Just don't tell Pearlene who gave you a taste."

"Mama and Granny Pearlene don't know everything I do."

He poured himself a second taste. "Don't be so sure. Parents know more than they let on. Whadda you think? Do I need to add more cinnamon to the recipe?"

I waved off the second taste. Hubert didn't need to worry about me drinking up his profits. I hadn't the stomach for it. "Don't change a thing." I lied. He needed less cinnamon, more apples. "It's perfect."

Hubert reached deep into his pocket and retrieved a roll of twenties secured with a rubber band. He peeled one off and placed it in my hand. "Pick up five pounds of brown sugar tomorrow. I'm thinking on another recipe I want to try."

We both knew Hubert sent me to fetch sugar so the gossipy grocery store ladies would keep their nose out of his business.

"Why do you go all the way to Tennessee to buy clear brew? Seems to take so much time."

"Child, these idjits around here probably trickle their spirits through a rusty radiator. No, ma'am, I trust Columbus Ledbetter and he trusts me."

Hubert capped the bottle and headed toward the back room. "Trust is important. Perhaps the most important thing in any friendship."

His words made me think about my friendship with Doretta. She'd been my best friend for as long as I could remember. I would miss her when I left.

"This here firewater's gonna be better than anyone else's because I start with the best clear brew I can find. And I've got enough gumption to flavor it up, make something different. Carole Anne, you need gumption if you're going to make it in this life. You gotta be different, set apart from everyone else. Course, knowing Columbus Ledbetter helps. We go way back. Gumption only gets a body so far. Cash, now that's what makes the world go 'round. Cash opens doors, my dear. Lots of doors."

He was right about that.

"Listen, I know money's tight at home. I can offer more hours and after graduation, you can go full time. You'll make more money here than any other place in Bryson City. I need a partner, someone who could expand what I'm doing here. Bring in some musicians. You know, give folk something to do when football season is over and snow starts falling. Besides, the real money is in selling this stuff by the drink. I don't make but a couple dollars off these cases of beer. With your help, I could set up a bon-a-fide joint."

As much as the lure of steady money excited me, I didn't want to stay and clean up spilled beer for the rest of my life. Hubert waited, hopeful. "Wow. What a great opportunity. How about we toss around a few ideas right now."

His face lit up. "Great! Let's start with the popcorn machine. When you come on full time I'd like to get a real bar. The kind with a brass footrest. Instead of you running around from table to table, folk would come to you for their orders. Do you think I should move the machine behind the bar, or beside the door where people can smell melted butter when they first walk in?"

I had to admit, the place did need a womanly touch and I was happy to help as long as he kept paying me good.

"Let me look at the place like I'm just walking in here for the first time." I walked to the door and turned.

"Going to add more card tables over there," Hubert said while hand waving.

"The smell of popcorn entices your patrons to linger and nibble. Popcorn also masks the stench of stale cigarette smoke and mildew. I guess placement depends on whether you want people to scoop their own popcorn? That's probably not a good idea, so keeping the machine near the bar might be best."

"Agreed," Hubert said. "But I don't have any floor-mounted electrical plugs. So that's why I put the machine by the door."

"You've talked about hanging a light over the bar. Just run a beam from the floor to the ceiling and drop electrical lines beside the bar."

Hubert snapped his fingers. "I knew I was forgetting something important. I need to find me one of those fancy stained-glass lights. You know the kind that's so heavy you gotta hang it with a thick chain. What would I do without you?"

"While you're shopping for a stained-glass light, keep an eye out for a freestanding cooler with a glass front. I'm pretty sure most of your customers would buy a cold six-pack for the road." I wanted to add that most of them would drink all the beer before they arrived home, but some things are better left unsaid.

"Brilliant!" Hubert nodded and made notations on a wire pad he kept tucked in his front pocket. "You be okay while I jut out for a quick run?" He really didn't need to ask, he left me alone a lot now.

"Go ahead and slice the rest of the apples then put them in this tub of sugar water so they won't turn dark. I'll do the rest when I get back. Don't forget to lock up." Hubert patted his shirt pocket. "I've got the key."

When I'm alone in the basement bar, I take a little extra care with the bottles and glasses. Lining them in perfect rows, displaying the labels pointing out and the glasses in perfect alignment. Hubert needed me, and for now, I needed him. But my life path didn't end at Hubert's, not by a long shot. While I appreciated his offer to spend the rest of my life helping him make money my plans hadn't changed. After I got my license and a vehicle there wasn't anything stopping me from leaving.

I'd get a job wherever I landed, and if that didn't pan out, I'd set up my own little sipping business serving alcohol to the depressed and hopeless.

If gumption was all I needed to succeed, well, I had plenty of that.

Chapter Nineteen

Barbara

My eyes opened when Carole Anne eased out the window. I always knew the exact moment she left the trailer. I could feel her presence slip away, lured by the promise of excitement. She wasn't fooling me.

The first time she snuck out, I rushed to the bathroom window, my heart aching while I watched her slip into the night without a backward glance. *Don't go. Stay,* I wanted to cry out. *It's not safe ...* but deep in my soul I knew I couldn't stop her, just like I knew where she was heading: the tracks.

Ever since Norfolk Southern laid the first rail, Bryson City's youth have dreamed of hopping the train and riding it until she ran out of track. Like others before her, I knew, Carole Anne promised herself she'd get out of here. Most never made good on their promise, but Carole Anne was different. She'd board the train one day, if she could. Or she'd take the Oldsmobile and be gone.

That's the real reason why I don't want to repair the car; I am afraid Carole Anne will leave. I don't have the option of leaving, not with Pearlene's unpredictable medical condition. And I can't exactly make Pearlene tag along while I find affordable housing and a new job. I can't take a job out of town. Not without someone to check on her during the day. Only the brave leave Bryson City for places unknown; the rest of us stay put and piece together a living the best way we know how.

I watched Carole Anne walk away and realized my limited options. Even though I didn't want Carole Anne to go, looking ahead I asked myself, what future did she have after high school? Shame washed over me. I'd spent so much time focused on keeping the bills paid and a roof over our heads that I didn't know the answer. Truth be told, as much as I worried about Carole Anne leaving, part of me feared her staying even more. Staying in Bryson City meant settling for less: low wages, subpar housing, and a dating pool of young men similar to the Foster boys.

I shuddered. *Baby girl. Please, don't go.*

I sat in Carole Anne's bedroom, lit a cigarette, and weighed my options. Even though I despised the thought of raiding the Cleveland Closet, Pearlene did have a good idea. We might earn enough money to get the Oldsmobile on the road, but there wouldn't be enough to cover other expenses: rent, groceries, and the light bill. We still needed more.

The time had come to visit Wanda Jean Jewell.

Wanda Jean Jewell lived in a brick rancher high on the hill just off Buckner's Branch Road. From her front porch, one could see Bryson City's social status clearly divided with the trailer park on one side of town tucked away from view and as close to the train tracks as legally allowed. Manicured Mill Town homes were on the other side, structures shaded with trees and colorful flower beds. Wanda Jean's husband conveniently worked for the Department of Transportation, which for a short time had a satellite office on Buckner's Branch. When the Transportation Department began paving the main roads, they needed a place to dump residual concrete after a day of roadwork. Mr. Jewell had the perfect location for the excess cement: his driveway. No one thought twice when trucks backed into the driveway, emptied cement, and rinsed out the tumblers. Mr. Jewell paid the workers cash money to hammer together wooden frames and smooth out the driveway. This agreement pleased everyone, especially Wanda Jean's customers whose tires churned up the hill cutting deep ruts in the gravel, filling her pristine home with dust.

Even though I kept Pearlene's hair trimmed, she and Claudette were loyal Wanda Jean customers. They arrived as a pair, with Claudette driving up the steep incline and Pearlene reminding Claudette, "for the hundredth time," to pull the car into low gear so as not to squeal tires on the concrete. Pearlene flipped through Wanda Jean's magazines and sipped coffee while Claudette's hair processed into the platinum blond she swore was natural.

Wanda Jean closed at four o'clock but made exceptions for ladies who worked in the plant because she believed hardworking factory ladies deserved a nice cut and curl. She hadn't forgotten the trials of working women, having grown up carrying water buckets to the woodstove so her own mother could soak her tired feet.

Now approaching her late sixties, Wanda Jean booked fewer appointments. And, I figured, perhaps the plant closing would open the door to a new venture with Wanda Jean. I could wash and curl her clients' hair, a task which is hard on aging joints. She could tease, style, and finish with Aqua Net hairspray. A partnership benefiting everyone.

The bathroom window made a small sliding noise. Carole Anne had returned. I felt her ease down the hall, listened as the floor made one small creak when she exited the bathroom heading toward her room where I waited, shadowed in a corner. After she settled into bed, I stepped over and clicked on the light.

"Carole Anne, it's time we have a talk."

***

My heart hurt. I wanted to cling to her, fall against my daughter and breathe in unison as we did when I carried her in my womb. I couldn't remember the last time I sat with her, held her, told her I loved her. Carole Anne expected me to yell and demand where she'd been. Instead we talked. Talked about our situation, talked about her dreams, talked about the harshness of life. I knew she wanted an answer to the unspoken questions hovering in the room. How did we get here? And more important, could we claw our way out?

I didn't have the answers, but after we hugged and I told her I loved her, a tiny glimmer of hope flashed in my baby girl's eyes.

The next morning, after Carole Anne boarded the bus, I spent a considerable amount of time applying makeup and styling my hair, then ignored Pearlene's questioning looks as I left the trailer. I set out walking toward Wanda Jean Jewell's salon, stopping only to catch my breath when I reached the bottom of her driveway. After a steep climb on shaking legs, I discovered an empty driveway. Peeking in the glass door, I watched Wanda Jean prepare for her clients, organizing magazines and testing the fullness of Aqua Net cans. Using the window to see my reflection, I checked my hair one final time then took a deep breath and opened the door.

A brass bell chimed when I stepped inside. She welcomed me with a genuine smile and glided toward me. Wanda Jean hadn't aged a single day since the first time I saw her, which had been about twenty years ago. Her hair remained the same style—dark brown, teased, sprayed, and styled to perfection.

"Barbara, how are you doing?" she said while pulling me into a light embrace. "Pearlene called a little while ago and said she thought you'd be stopping by." She offered a genuine smile, which I accepted without restraint. "What can I do for you?" she then asked, and I knew she meant it.

"Well," I started. "I wonder if you need any help? I'm good at washing and rolling hair. That'd free you up for cuts and styles. I don't know what Mama told you, but I've been cutting people's hair for a while, as the need arises."

Wanda Jean gestured to the den located adjacent to her salon. The area was immaculate, without so much as a speck of dust anywhere. My feet sank into white wool carpet as I walked to the sofa. Right then, I realized how good life can be if you have land and money.

Rich maroon-colored brick lined the wall, floor to ceiling, with a large opening for a fireplace and a smaller opening that held the wood. Stacked perfectly, each log fit atop the other with no overlap. I sat, staring at the wood, trying to determine whether it was decorative or functional. On one end of the mantel, a shiny brass frame with a photograph of Wanda Jean and her husband, Redford, and on the other end, a purple-blooming African violet.

"Don't be fooled, Barbara," Wanda Jean said, her eyes following mine around the lush room. "Without Red's job, I'd live in the trailer park right along beside you. I don't make enough money to keep up this house." Her brown eyes stared intently into mine. "Never forget, this is a man's world. If Redford had his druthers, I would have never worked a day in my life. He'd have me waiting at five o'clock holding a gin and tonic or a vodka martini." She walked to the credenza and retrieved a pack of Virginia Slims. "Yes ma'am, Red Jewell wants to keep me locked in the 1950s catering to his every need. Just like the woman in *Housekeeping Monthly*."

My face revealed puzzlement.

"My apologies," Wanda Jean said quickly. "You caught me on a bad day. I'm not someone who discusses personal matters with customers."

"Wanda Jean, I'm not a customer. You can talk freely with me. Besides, who am I going to tell? Pearlene? In case you haven't heard, she's struggling these days with memory loss."

"Wanda. Just call me Wanda. It's almost 1980. Time to drop the middle name." With graceful hands, she removed a cigarette and offered me one. Virginia Slims weren't my brand, but I'm not one to turn down a free smoke. Then, moving to the credenza, she plugged in a stainless-steel percolator so shiny I could see my reflection from across the room. We fell silent, waiting for the coffee to perk.

"Of course you know the state won't let you cut hair without a license."

Hope faded from my body. I felt myself slump. "I thought there was an apprentice clause that allowed employment if you supervised my work." My voice shook. At that moment, working at the salon seemed my only option.

"If you so much as touch my scissors, I could lose my license."

A shrill ring sounded from the wall-mounted telephone. Wanda carefully rested the cigarette in a freestanding ashtray situated between us. "Contemporary Curls," she purred into the receiver using a velvety voice barely above a whisper. "When might I have the pleasure of serving you?"

Wanda opened a drawer of the built-in cabinet, retrieved an appointment book, and plucked a pencil from her hair. "That's lovely. I look forward to seeing you at two." Wanda returned the phone to the cradle and kneaded her neck muscles as she headed back to her chair.

"Then perhaps I could clean the salon in the afternoon. Do the laundry? Sweep the floors?" When I had to blink away tears, I realized my desperation.

"Wednesdays are the hardest," Wanda said without answering my question. She crushed out her cigarette then waited as I finished mine. Then she stood, carried the ashtray into the nearby bathroom where water ran and the lid of a metal trash can opened and then closed. After she returned, she sprayed the room with deodorizer and tucked the clean ashtray in the corner beside the fireplace.

"Red wants the salon spotless. I schedule permanents on Wednesday nights when he's at the Masonic Lodge. Even then he complains about the smell." She sat across from me again and straightened her skirt. "Red would prefer that I close down. He doesn't understand how much women depend on me ... and how much I depend on them for company."

Nodding, I clasped my hands together tight when what I really wanted was another cigarette. Another cigarette would help.

"I just booked Helen for a two o'clock perm. If you can make her happy, I'll find enough work to keep you busy."

Shaky fingers wiped the tears from where they pooled just under my eyes. I wanted to hurl myself into her arms and squeeze her tight. But before I could, Wanda stood and said, "Let me show you how I expect things to operate." She gave me a look I couldn't quite read. "And, what Red requires."

Following her like a found puppy, I memorized her instructions: "Sweep the floor after every cut ... don't leave hair in a pile ... wipe baseboards after the last customer ... no clutter in the sitting area ... collect cigarette butts tossed outside and place them in the trash." She took a breath and turned to face me head-on. "And most of all, don't gossip."

I wanted to laugh at the gossip part, but I held my tongue knowing if I wasn't careful, I'd be in trouble before the workday even started.

"The first appointment is at ten. That gives me time to get Red off to work, tidy up the house, bring in the towels, and prepare for my day. Let me show you the laundry room."

My shoes squeaked as I followed Wanda down the hall. We entered a room larger than my bedroom where a side-by-side Kenmore washer and dryer waited for today's offering. "I keep the laundry soap here," Wanda said while opening the first cabinet on the left. "And the fabric softener here. Clean towels, over there."

She opened the last cabinet revealing identically folded stacks of snow-white towels. "Throw away any towel the moment it gets dingy or stained with hair dye. I cannot abide dingy towels."

Thinking about my towels—fraying and thinning in places—I hoped she'd let me take the discards once I gained her trust. Pearlene could sew them together to form larger towels or cut them into smaller washcloth-sized pieces.

"It's best to start a load of laundry after the last customer, but that would mean staying until Red returns from work." Wanda tapped her lip with a pearl-painted fingernail. "I don't know about that just yet. It might be best for me to do the laundry. You could fold towels if we have any slack time, or when we break for lunch."

Morning sped into noon. We stumbled over each other a couple times, which frustrated me as much as Wanda. At noon, she excused herself, taking the stairs to the kitchen. I dusted the den furniture, which was still spotless, while she assembled sandwiches for our lunch. I thanked her and told her that tomorrow I'd bring my own.

"Nonsense," she insisted. "Two sandwiches are as easy to make as one." Wanda Jean Jewell did not deviate from her manners, presenting our meal on a gold-plated TV tray equipped with pull-out metal legs. She opened the credenza and refilled the percolator then retrieved milk from a tiny refrigerator I hadn't previously noticed inside the cabinet. "We'll need to brew another pot before Helen arrives, and put out a few cookies. I usually brew three or four pots a day, depending on my schedule, and the client's desire. Even if no one drinks it, I need coffee ready. My customers deserve a moment of relaxation while here. And no one likes stale coffee."

We ate in silence with me trying to mimic her ladylike chews. I didn't own cloth napkins, not the custom-made monogramed variety currently draped in my lap. Instead, when Pearlene found cotton remnants on sale at the Cleveland Closet, she stitched the multicolored scraps into squares that served as napkins and washcloths. Polyester pieces became placemats and clothing.

"Please sit up straight and look people in the eye when you're talking to them."

Rolling my shoulders back, I realized my posture did need improving.

"Sorry," I said. "Too much time spent hunched over a sewing machine."

"I don't like how we keep bumping into each other every time I turn around." She folded the napkin on top of the empty plate. "Let's try to move my old styling chair from the garage. I'm not sure we can manage, but we need two chairs for this arrangement to work."

It took some doing but we managed to heave, push, pull, and eventually roll the chair through the garage and onto the tiled salon floor. Afterward, Wanda was a sweaty mess and I wasn't exactly fresh as a daisy. Wanda excused herself to "freshen up," leaving me in the powder room wiping sweat from the back of my neck with hand towels. Hearing the side door open, I glanced at my reflection and cursed myself for not packing at least a tube of lipstick in my purse.

Helen Groenwald stood inside with a black leather bag pressed tight in the crook of her arm. Wanda told me she wouldn't discuss her client's history, said she thought it better that I form my own opinions. Looking at Helen I first thought, *Lord have mercy. She's a mess.*

Her hair seemed an extension of an angry personality. Jutting out straight from the roots, it then curled furiously with no set style.

"Where is Wanda Jean?" she asked in a tone as coarse as her hair.

Footsteps thundered down the stairs. Wanda appeared in a rush of breathless disarray. She inhaled, straightened her spine, and greeted her client.

"Helen Groenwald, you remember Barbara Parker, don't you? I've hired her as my salon assistant."

Helen's scrutiny intensified. Taking in my appearance, her gaze seemed a warning to *proceed with caution* as she said, "Of course I remember Barbara Parker."

I ignored the dig. Instead, I moved to the den and asked, "Shall I bring you a cup of coffee?" Not waiting for a response, I poured a cup, and returned, offering a tray of cookies. "Would you like cream or sugar?"

"Black," she barked while taking the cup in one hand and a cookie with the other, and never releasing her purse from the crook of her arm.

Wanda gestured to the chair. "Let's get started," she purred using her whisper-soft voice.

Standing alongside, I fed rollers and end-wrap papers, keeping one hand free to hold the water bottle Wanda needed to mist Helen's hair so the end papers would grab the unruly locks. Wanda worked fast, sectioning the hair, covering it with paper and rolling the rod until it reached the scalp. While listening for the plastic rod to click closed, I readied another end wrapper and held the next available rod. With the last rod in place, Wanda nodded toward the dryer chair. I rushed over and activated the switch while she applied the perm solution.

"Do you need to visit the restroom first?" Wanda asked.

Helen disappeared into the bathroom and I released a long breath and arched my shoulders to release tension.

Wanda busied herself adjusting the controls. Placing her hand beneath the bubble hood, she fiddled with the knob. Helen emerged from the bathroom and settled into the seat.

"Tell me if this is too hot," Wanda said while lowering the dome over Helen's rolled head.

An hour later, Helen left the salon with curls so tight it looked like she'd stuck her finger in a light socket. Wanda waved at her through the glass door, waiting until Helen's green Ford Pinto crept down the drive then said, "Thank *God* you were here. That was the fastest perm I've ever given her. That woman absolutely wears me out. I've begged her for years to let me use larger rollers, but no. She insists she gets more value from tighter curls."

Wanda swung the salon door wide, filling the room with fresh air. "I need to go upstairs before the king returns to his castle. Start the laundry before you leave." She patted my shoulder with appreciation and—dare I say—affection. "I will see you tomorrow." She held up a finger, then opened the drawer containing her appointment book. "My first appointment is at ten. Shall I expect you around nine thirty?"

Standing a bit taller, I smiled and said, "Yes, ma'am. You can count on me."

Chapter Twenty

Carole Anne

Our neighbor Trummie hosted a Tupperware party every month. People arrived early to enjoy refreshments while Trummie explained a variety of containers that, of course, were available for purchase. And every month Doretta lingered at the party, providing free lipstick samples and Avon magazines while customers mingled amidst the Tupperware. During the party, me and Mama lured her customers' husbands to our section of the trailer park for a quick haircut. I fed an extension cord outside the window while Mama placed our radio on a TV tray so customers could listen to music as she gave them a trim.

At Trummie's there was always a tray of deviled eggs and a variety of Jell-O molds, some with suspended pieces of fruit cocktail. But I wasn't allowed a single bite until everyone left. Then I'd rush over to help Trummie clean, all the while nibbling on bite-sized cucumber sandwiches. Doretta's mama worked every possible angle to convince Mama and me to sell Avon, but Mama insisted Doretta coming to the trailer park during a Tupperware party was enough.

So, men dropped their wives off at Trummie's to shop and then walked over to our side, drawn to good music, a wag of the tail from Smokey, and an affordable haircut. Mama charged five dollars, which included a neck shave and free sample of Avon cologne provided by Doretta. Tipping was most appreciated.

"Barbara, you think he's one of those queers?" Jeremiah Foster asked while Mama worked around his head. Jeremiah Foster was a regular customer. Granny Pearlene swore he gossiped more than Wanda Jean's clients.

"Beg your pardon," Mama said. "I'm not sure who you are talking about."

Mama had told me she didn't really listen to customers when they gossiped. She said she kept her comments short, "so that way I don't offend people. Folk think I'm agreeing with them, but I'm really only responding without comment. People want to be heard, but they seldom care about your opinion."

Jeremiah nodded in the direction of Trummie's Tupperware party all the while sneaking a finger sandwich to Smokey, who gobbled it up like he was some hotshot down at the country club. "That principal over there. You think he's queer? Talk around school says he's queer as a football bat."

"Of course not," Mama snapped. "Don't be ridiculous." The scissors hissed as she finished then pushed his head forward. "Chin down," she commanded. Her voice had an edge of irritation. "I've got to shave your neck. Carole Anne, run get me some shave cream."

Jeremiah complied, but continued his criticism of Principal Walker. "Best not be one of those queers. I won't have no queers luring our children, won't stand for them taking over the school. No sir. We're God-lovin', God-fearing Christian people up in here."

"You forgot gun-totin'," I added while placing a can of Barbasol in Mama's waiting hand. I twisted the metal razor handle and replaced the dull blade with the good blade we kept wrapped in wax paper. The one reserved for paying customers.

Her disapproving look reminded me that we needed his five dollars and I best keep my opinions to myself.

"What makes you think he's that way?" I asked, ignoring her warning. "And even if he is, what does that matter?"

Jeremiah's chin snapped up. Mama accidentally nicked him with the razor. "Ouch! Barbara, watch what you're doing!"

Mama and Jeremiah both glared at me while I waited for a reply. "Oh, there's plenty of talk about him," Jeremiah continued. "Folk 'round here's been watching him real close after he sashayed into town wearing those girly shoes and all that sparkly jewelry. If you ask me, he's light in the loafers. Just look at him over there fondling the Tupperware.

What kind of man needs a lettuce keeper?"

"I reckon the kind who eats salads," Mama said.

Jeremiah waved Mama away as she dabbed his neck with a dingy towel. "Even a blind man can see he all but skips down the halls. And his hair. Why he's got one of those hippie styles that's long enough to braid. I'll tell you straight up, I don't trust no man with long hair. I've got my eye on him, Barbara. Yessir. Can't be too careful who you have round your kids, especially impressionable girls like your Carole Anne here."

"You know, Jeremiah," Mama said as she placed her hands on his shoulders and gently guided him back to a seating position. She bent low and cooed into his ear, "It does my heart good knowing Carole Anne is safe under your watchful eye." Her hands kneaded his neck. "Now settle back in the chair and let me finish. We can't have you going to church with your neck half shaved. That'd be a disgrace." Jeremiah allowed Mama to tilt his head down and lather his neck. I had watched her do this before. She could coax a tip from even the cheapest customer.

I folded my arms across my chest. Who was Jeremiah to judge anyone? His boys were three of the biggest hell-raisers in the county thanks, in part, to our former Principal Hargrove, who had been more focused on retirement than discipline. He had allowed the threesome to intimidate virtually everyone in school, including the teachers.

"Wearing jewelry doesn't make you gay," I stated. "And his choice of clothing is an improvement from what most men around here wear." My eyes settled on Jeremiah's faded flannel shirt. Mama drew a sharp breath and Jeremiah looked at me hard as Mama unclipped the apron covering his shirt and handed it to me, an unspoken command to make myself invisible and shake the hairs from the apron far away from them both.

"Someone needs to teach Carole Anne to respect her elders. When I was her age, I never sassed an adult. If I had someone would have washed my mouth out with soap," Jeremiah said while fishing a folded bill from his wallet. Mama flashed a fake smile and swept stray hairs from Jeremiah's shoulder.

Turning my face away from the hairs that took flight, I flicked the apron until it was clean. When I returned, Jeremiah Foster had left, and Principal Walker sat in Mama's chair. Her fingers slid through the long waves, settling on the spot behind his ear that, thanks to Doretta, I knew curled when wet. "What do you want to do about the length?" she asked, drawing him into conversation. Mama had a way of letting customers decide what they wanted.

Principal Walker's hand grazed his ear. Sunlight winked off the gold bracelet he wore. Mama reached for the plastic apron and snapped the collar in place. Her fingertips lingered against his skin.

Jealousy pounded in my chest. I wanted to be her, wanted to feel the silky strands of his hair between my fingers, wanted to be close enough to smell his cologne, feel his breath, touch the delicate skin at the nape of his neck. My skin had gone all prickly. My heart pounded in my ears. My mind lingered at the thought of touching him. I didn't listen as they talked, didn't notice Mama picking up the scissors. I missed the gesture until it was too late. She held a long section between her fingers and lopped it off in one quick movement.

"No!" The word escaped in a panic as the duck curl fell to the ground. "You can't cut your hair. I love it . . . I mean, everyone likes your hair just the way it is."

Dimples flashed when he smiled. "Carole Anne, no need to fret. It's just hair. It will grow back. Don't worry. I'm not getting a buzz cut, just a little trim."

The scissors made a slicing sound as Mama quickly gave Principal Walker a new style.

As much as I wanted to change my life, I supposed some things needed to remain the same. I needed Principal Walker to be different than other Bryson City males. I needed to see that renegade curl behind his ear. I needed to believe he was unique and unwilling to conform to the standards others set; but most of all, I needed him to show me the world I believed existed beyond the city limits. A world with free spirits and free thinkers, a world of possibility. Today he changed his hairstyle.

What would tomorrow bring? Camouflage pants and a can of chewing tobacco forming a circle in his back pocket? I couldn't watch anymore, couldn't witness Mama's fingers working their magic, transforming him into a mirror image of everyone else in town. I needed to leave. Turning my back on them both, I headed toward the tracks.

Chapter Twenty-One

Barbara

I entered the Piggly Wiggly praying I wouldn't be seen. Dirty rubber wheels shimmied and groaned as I fought the rusty buggy intent on crashing into the apple display. I'd rather have all my teeth extracted than go to the grocery store on the fifteenth of the month, but I had no choice. We were literally out of groceries, not even a piece of cheese or a single cracker in the cabinets. Social Services issues food stamps on the fifteenth, which meant the store is packed with people who'd either had someone drive them into town or they walked to redeem a monthly stipend of government assistance.

People like me.

Shame weighed heavy on my shoulders as I maneuvered to the refrigerator section, picked up a package of Valley Farms bologna, and tossed it into the buggy. Oscar Meyer isn't an option, never will be. After my layoff from Cleveland Manufacturing, Janelle suggested I apply for temporary food stamps; I argued that I'd manage. The argument lasted only a few minutes before I realized she was right.

If Mama knew I bought milk and eggs with food stamps she'd kill me for bringing shame to the family. Mama believed accepting government assistance was a mark on a woman's personal integrity, a label telling others she failed to provide for herself and her family. My case manager told me about commodity distribution and home-delivered meals for the elderly. She told me I qualified for both and that Carole Anne was eligible for the free breakfast and lunch program at school. But there was no way I'd ever embarrass my daughter like that. It didn't matter how many times the social worker promised confidentiality, any fool could tell which children paid for their meals using cash, and who walked past the cashier wearing a look of shame. And while I could really use the help that the program offered to the elderly, I imagined the first time a Meals on Wheels staff member knocked on the trailer door Pearlene Parker would cock the hammer back on the shotgun she called "Old Betsy" and fill the worker full of lead. That's why I declined the offer of additional assistance.

Pride might have also played a part.

My case manager repeatedly assured me the names of food stamp recipients were locked up tight, but this is Bryson City; secrets stay hidden for only a short amount of time. My secret lasted only for as long as no one saw me. Around here people notice everything: where you parked, or that you exited the courthouse building housing Social Services. Then there was the checkout line, a place where you let others go ahead of you and then looked over your shoulder while fishing paper food stamps from your purse. It was only a matter of time before someone told. Maybe if the salon job worked out, I wouldn't need government assistance for long.

Grocery shopping on the fifteenth isn't a social affair. Most customers pushed their buggies with heads bent, eyes diverted away from anyone who might recognize them. They wanted to get in, get out, and get home. I held my breath while passing the meat counter. The smell of mothballs and reduced meat wafted across the aisle. According to the cashier, Sondra Smithfield, one should never buy meat on the fifteenth. "The butcher mixes day-old hamburger meat with fresh-ground and rewraps it like it is fresh," she told me one afternoon when we happened to run into each other away from the store. "Then he reduces the hamburger knowing that those food stamp customers will load up on the meat." When Sondra first told me this information neither of us knew that I'd become one of those customers.

"Hoke knows all about it too," Sondra confided. "Don't think he don't know."

Today, food stamp day coincided with the arrival of Social Security checks and payday for those lucky enough to have a government job. People packed the aisles, separated according to financial ability. As long as poor folk followed the unwritten rules and kept their hands off the fresh produce displayed for cash-paying customers, then everyone got along. Food stamp folk rarely bought fresh produce; they needed to stretch the government assistance, even if apples were priced five for a dollar. Hurrying down the canned goods aisle, I grabbed the pork 'n' beans on sale three cans for seventy-nine cents. I added a can of spaghetti sauce to the buggy. As I reached for a box of noodles I heard, "Barbara, is that you?"

I closed my eyes and exhaled. Victoria Honeycutt. I'd recognize her voice anywhere. Of all the people to meet in the grocery store while shopping with food stamps. Of course, my one-time best friend would be the one. I pasted a smile on my face and turned to meet her fake greeting with one of my own. Predictably, she struck a mannequin-like pose. She stood at a safe distance, just in case poverty was contagious. Victoria always was worried about catching some mysterious illness. In elementary school boys targeted her by leaning in for a kiss, knowing the thought of catching cooties petrified her. When mono made the rounds in high school, she refused to drink from the water fountain. But by her senior year, she became obsessed with catching a boyfriend who could become her husband and ended up with a teaching assistant named Richard who was now the high school basketball coach. With her arm gracefully bent at the elbow, she raised her hand and wiggled her pinky and ring fingers as if fanning still-wet fingernail polish— her way of reminding me she was married. Like I cared. I knew her husband Richard. I remembered him clearly after the championship win. My knowledge of him would bring Victoria's chin down a notch. She looked down at me, bent her right arm, and placed it daintily on her hip then cooed, "Oh, Barbara, it's been ages. How *are* you doing?"

The fact that Victoria Honeycutt had the nerve to speak enraged me. She only spoke to remind me of my place beneath her in the social pecking order. Everyone in town knew she was a kept woman, living off her father's money. She didn't worry about rent, food, or having enough money to pay the light bill. Choosing the menu for the bridge club and garden club meetings at the country club were her biggest concerns. My hands formed fists. For a second, I wanted to pounce on her just to smell her panic. Sure, sixteen years ago, she had been my best friend until she'd left me in town on the night the Maroon Devils won the state championship because Zeke had found her and offered her a ride to Mr. Cutshaw's barn. On the night that altered my life course she was elated to finally have attention focused on her, thrilled that our friendship provided her with an excuse to get out of the house. She had been one of the few friends who stuck with me after Pearlene and I moved into the trailer park when we could no longer afford rent at the mill house. I had been so grateful I practically fell over myself. Everyone thought I was the confident one and would go far. But, secretly, I was insecure, afraid to do anything without Victoria. In high school, she begged me to style her blond tresses to perfection. In return, she encouraged me to pick out anything I wanted from her closet and let me keep what I chose without ever returning the clothing.

She peered into my buggy and quickly inventoried the contents. "Barbara, I never see you around anymore. How have you been?" Standing there in aisle number three, she wore a pressed cotton dress with matching pink fingernails and pale lipstick. Her dry hair needed a trim and a deep conditioning treatment. I secretly hoped she would ask if I still did hair because I wanted an opportunity to let her know I didn't need her money—or friendship—anymore.

Looking at her now I knew that beneath her attractive exterior beat a coal-black heart. I blamed her *and* Connor Brown for what happened years ago.

I used to wonder if she had only used me as an excuse to get out of the house that night. If she told her parents she was meeting me or if she had lied to them too. Her parents trusted me, not because I was old enough to drive, while Victoria still had another eight months before becoming eligible, but because I had shown a level of maturity beyond what most of the kids our age had come to. Before my pregnancy, I was known as a good girl who would never get into trouble. Someone who always had her nose in a book. Everyone said I'd own my own salon one day with two or three stylists subleasing space. Looking at her now,

I knew Victoria hadn't cared about our friendship; she had been invited to a party and needed a ride. If I fell through, she would get there by any means necessary, which she did.

In high school, I wore rubber bands on my wrist and carried hairpins in my pocket so I could braid hair during school recess. Back then, Rebecca Waldron was cheer captain and asked that I stay after school and do the team's hair while she worked on their makeup. She and I were friends then, before Ted grabbed me from behind. Before I missed curfew and Mama discovered the Oldsmobile empty and frantically insisted Sheriff Tolliver search. Before he'd said, "I'm sure she's probably out celebrating with her friends." Before he reluctantly formed a search party. That was before Pearlene searched all night, finally returning home scared and exhausted only to find me rinsing blood-stained clothing in the bathroom sink and watching water carry my blood down the drain.

The next day, I took the scissors to my own hair, cropping the waist-length locks so short no one would ever wrap their paws around it, never pull it out by the roots, never use my hair as a weapon against me … ever again.

Standing in Victoria's presence now, I stared directly into her eyes. Her smile faded. For the first time I took a long look at the lines on her face, lines makeup couldn't hide. While she wore more expensive clothes and socialized in a financially comfortable circle of friends, her lifestyle had come at a cost.

She was no better. She was my equal.

Standing there in aisle number three of the Piggly Wiggly things became clear. My time at Cleveland Manufacturing was over. The job had served me well. Thanks to Wanda I had a new opportunity, a chance to do something better. Something I enjoyed. Something I was good at. Something that would make my daughter proud. There in the canned vegetable aisle beside the collards and creamed corn I realized that hating Victoria was like me swallowing poison and expecting her to get sick. She had no idea what had happened to me on that night. No one was at fault, except Ted.

And Connor … who'd started the whole thing at school that day. Connor, who'd stood by and watched …

A smile began, slow and genuine. Lifting my chin to meet hers I said, "Victoria, I am doing quite well. Thank you for asking." I turned away, leaving Victoria and those awful memories of my past behind.

Finally, I believed my little family was on the right path. We would all be fine.

Chapter Twenty-Two

Carole Anne

"A sin … wasting ain't nothing but a sin," Granny Pearlene mumbled while pivoting on her heels. "I could cut up pieces of any fabric and stitch together a quilt for sale or make one of those aprons I used to sell. Don't Cleveland Manufacturing know people around here are poor as church mice?"

She hadn't stopped talking about the Cleveland Closet since hearing about the closing. "In my day the very thought of tossing clothes into the trash was wrong," she muttered. "We gotta figure a way to get everything out of the Cleveland Closet before they lock the doors," she said with another pace across the floor.

Granny Pearlene had no need of clothing. She had so many dresses packed in her closet you couldn't wedge another item inside. Of course, every article was someone else's castoff, but a treasure to her. In addition to clothing, quilt tops and other unsewn items towered in the corner of the room. Mama called it a "junk pile." Granny Pearlene said they were "projects," and one day she'd drag out the quilt frame and teach me how to quilt. Except I had no intention of threading the first needle.

"You know, we could have a yard sale. Yes, ma'am. After we get everything; we could use those wooden spools, maybe take the kitchen table outside, fold things up real nice like a regular department store."

I wanted to point out the obvious, that we'd be selling stolen goods, but I hadn't seen Granny Pearlene this excited since the rebate checks started trickling in.

Granny Pearlene opened the fridge and poured a jelly glass full of cherry Kool-Aid. "We could price everything for a dollar. You know, if we do this right, we might earn enough money to put the Oldsmobile back on the road permanently."

Careful not to interrupt, I took the glass she offered then waited while she filled another with the bright-red, sugar-filled drink.

"What do you mean *permanently*?" I asked, cautiously waiting for the answer. No one had mentioned the car since I threw my money on the table and walked out. Money I found later that night lying in an envelope on my pillow.

"Ways I see it ..." She paused to take a sip. "We've gotta get what's over there ..." Granny Pearlene pointed in the general direction of the Cleveland Closet. "... to here." She then pointed to her feet. "We can't count on Claudette for transportation. That leaves me, you, and the Oldsmobile parked out back." A light bulb suddenly went off behind her eyes. "Call Connor Brown and tell him we need help putting the car back on the road."

I reached for the phone but hesitated. "What if Mama comes home while we're working on the vehicle? She made it clear she hates his guts."

"I don't much care for Connor and I don't much care what your mama says. You call that Brown boy and tell him to get his hind-end over here and help us crank that car. Go on now. Time's a-wasting. We've got an emergency. I'm not the only one who'll be interested in cleaning out the Cleveland Closet. We need to get a move on before those Floridians living down at Leo's Flea Market snatch up ever'thing they find. I'm sick and tired of everyone else making all the money around here. The way I see it, local folk should get the chance to make a nickel, not the Floridians. They've already bought up all the ridgelines and made the realtors a fortune, all while looking down on us like we are white trash."

I didn't want to point out that we *were* white trash.

But she had a point. Those people who rented long-term booth space at Leo's Flea Market could sniff out a bargain for miles. Most didn't live in Bryson City full time. They pulled camper trailers from Florida and parked in a field behind the building. Recognizing a money- making opportunity, Leo's built bathrooms, shower stalls, and of course charged a nominal parking fee for campers. Come Friday, the temporary flea market residents displayed their wares. You could find most everything at the flea market, if you had transportation.

Part of me wanted to comply with Granny Pearlene's latest scheme, but this time there was nowhere to hide, not like the landfill. If Mama came home and discovered us tinkering on the car, she'd have a hissy fit.

"Even if we do get the car roadworthy, it's not like we can just drive up in the middle of the day and start loading the trunk. What if the plant manager decides to give everything in the Cleveland Closet away? Or they might offer a discount to the remaining employees."

Granny Pearlene shook her head. "Don't think so. Our kind of folk don't spend money that way … can't afford the risk. Some commercial vendor will roll in here with a big truck, load everything up, and haul it straight to Florida where they'll make a pile of money. Especially with winter coming and the snowbirds heading down south. Someone will be down there living high off our work. Meanwhile, we'll eat beans and taters every night and struggle to scrape together two nickels. No! I cannot abide the thought of it. I'm getting everything I can from that place, even if I have to carry it down Main Street one armload at a time."

I knew Granny Pearlene spoke the truth, that someone would strike a deal and buy the store's contents then truck it somewhere else for a tidy profit.

"I'm telling ya, we've got to strike while the iron's hot." Granny Pearlene snatched the phone receiver off the cradle and handed it to me. "Go on now, call the boy."

Connor came quick. He was smart enough to park beside the neighbor's trailer where he could ease out undetected should Mama come home and notice the vehicle.

He grabbed one end of the tarp covering the Oldsmobile. I held the other. Together, we rolled it back enough to reveal the hood and driver's side door.

"Let's stop here," Connor said. "In case your mom shows up we can flip the tarp back over and she'll never know what's going on."

Connor opened the driver's door, bent at the waist and said, "M' lady … your chariot."

I giggled. Dust motes danced inside the stale interior as I slid across the seat. The steering wheel felt slick and dangerous.

"The battery is the best place to start. I'm sure it's dead." Connor reached down and pulled a lever beside my leg. "Need to open the hood."

Hinges groaned and the hood made a loud pop as it released. Following him like a puppy, I exited the vehicle and peered under the hood. He produced a wrench from his pocket, positioned the tool around the bolt, and gave it a turn. "Lefty Lucy. Remember that, Carole Anne."

I'm sure my face bore a blank expression because Connor quickly added, "Righty tighty. Lord girl, hasn't anyone taught you the basic rules of nuts and bolts?"

I shrugged and held my teeth together good and tight. The fewer words I spoke, the smarter I felt. Connor straightened and came around beside me. Positioning me near the battery, he placed the wrench in my hand, wrapped his strong fingers around mine, and moved the tool. "Turn left to loosen, right to tighten."

My skin tingled. Connor's breath moved my hair. A shiver walked up my spine. I wanted to fall into him, let his strength carry away my worry.

Together we tugged against the bolt. "Usually I can knock a bolt loose, but this one is pretty set." He released his hand and said, "Step aside." Connor produced a hammer from the leather belt around his waist and gave the bolts a solid rap. He extended his hand, not looking, not asking, but expecting that I had already absorbed enough knowledge to anticipate the tool he needed. My right hand produced the wrench as I grabbed the hammer he no longer needed. I stood taller. Confident.

Leaning in as he turned the bolt, Connor growled, "C'mon!"

The bolt held.

Pointing with the wrench, he said, "Go to my truck and grab a can of WD-40."

I took off, my shoes kicking up tiny pieces of gravel. "And bring me that bottle of Pepsi wedged between the seats."

He took the WD-40 first. A piece of black tape secured a tiny straw gizmo to the side of the can.

"This little feller," Connor said while pointing the straw at me, "is very important. It shoots the juice wherever need be. Lose it and you can't control the lube." He sprayed the bolts and stepped aside. "Let's give the juice a few minutes to loosen things up."

He wedged the Pepsi bottle under the hood. "If the bolts won't loosen, we'll pour Pepsi on them to eat away the corrosion. Next item: tires. You know how to change a flat?"

Connor didn't wait for my answer. He flipped the tarp out of the way from the back, opened the trunk, and gave the tire iron a twirl as he approached the driver's side. "We'll cover the proper way to jack up a vehicle after we get this baby on the road. Since we're pressed for time, just watch."

With the jack in place, it seemed like the tire lifted off the ground with only a few pumps from Connor's strong arms. He wiped his dusty hands across his jeans. "Ready to learn a little trick?"

Matching the end of the tool with the lug nut, he stepped down hard. "Leg strength always beats arm strength. You can't remove lug nuts using just your arm strength. You'll wear yourself out real fast. After loosening the nut, make sure the connection is tight and give this little baby a twirl." Connor spun the tool, caught the lug nut before it fell to the ground, and placed it in his pocket. "And whatever you do, do not lose these or you'll be in a *mell of a hess*."

He stepped back and motioned with his hand. "Now your turn."

I hesitated.

"Go on now. Pretend you've just had a flat. What's the first thing you do?"

"Call you to come save me." I laughed.

Connor folded his arms across his chest. "Be serious now. Driving is not all fun and games. I'm not letting you on the road until I know you're prepared to handle an emergency."

"Drive to the nearest station?"

Connor shook his head. "Absolutely not. Never drive on a flat. Rubber protects the rims from coming in contact with the pavement. Driving on a flat can burn the rubber clean off the rims. If that happens you could warp the wheel metal. Then you've got *real* trouble."

I liked how Connor treated me as an intelligent person. I didn't know any women who knew anything about car repairs. Obviously, Granny Pearlene didn't know how to make the Oldsmobile roadworthy or she'd keep the road hot driving here and there. It took a couple tries before I fit the lug wrench to the nut. Stepping hard like he instructed, the lug nut groaned and then loosened. I twirled the bar just like Connor.

"Great job. Since we're kinda in a rush, I'll loosen the rest. You work on the battery cables."

Moments later, Connor removed the tire while I loosened the cables. He returned with two concrete blocks, laid them beside me, then retrieved two more from the back of his truck. "We need to slide these under the car, gotta have something to hold up the frame after we get the tires off," he explained as he removed the tire and lowered the jack. Moving to the back of the vehicle he said, "Let's get 'em all off. I'll take them to the shop, along with the battery, and see if we have anything to work with. If we're lucky maybe that's all we'll need to get her roadworthy, but I doubt it."

My spirits sank. "What else do you think we'll need?"

Connor squatted at the Oldsmobile and placed his hand beneath the frame. "Brakes most definitely, and rotors. We'll probably need to drain the gas line, change the oil." He stood, repositioned the tarp, and moved to the other side of the hood. "Letting a vehicle sit is the worst thing you can do. All of the fluids kind of settle in one place." He removed the dipstick, wiped oil from it with an old rag he pulled from his back pocket, then repositioned the stick. "Sometimes water gets in the gas line." He leaned over and peered deep inside the hood. I quickly stepped alongside him to see what else was wrong with the car. "Rats move in," he said while pointing. "Build nests. Chew wires." He pointed to a ball of fluff that contained wads of Smokey's fur and bits of teaberry chewing gum wrappers.

Reaching deep, he grabbed the nest and flung it aside. Hairless newborn rats tumbled from the nest. Connor stomped them beneath the heel of his boot then kicked the dead bodies away from us.

Shuddering, I started to rethink using this vehicle. I should have known if rats lived under the trailer and in the walls, they most certainly lived inside the Oldsmobile.

Connor closed the hood with a slam. "I hate rats. Eat and piss at the same time. Leaving one long rat-piss trail for their friends to follow. Once they move in, it's hard to get rid of them. I'll bring over some traps. All sorts of bad things happen to an idle vehicle. It's better to drive one until they break than let one die a slow death."

Granny Pearlene appeared with Kool-Aid and a peanut butter and jelly sandwich cut on the diagonal. "How's it coming?" she said while offering the paper plate.

Connor waved off the sandwich, revealing dirty fingers. "Got our work cut out, that's for sure. Just found a rat's nest under the hood. God only knows what we'll find inside the interior."

Color drained from Granny Pearlene's face. "Lord, I hope not."

"What?" I asked looking from her to Connor.

"There's only one way to find out." Connor flipped the tarp, exposing the passenger side door.

Following behind, I asked again, "What?"

Connor turned quick. "Snakes, Carole Anne. Snakes eat rats."

I stepped back. "How could a snake get inside the car?"

Granny Pearlene grabbed me by the arm and pulled me toward her. "Hush now. Let him do what he's gotta do."

Connor opened the door, unlatched the glove box, and peeked inside. "Carole Anne," he said in a slow, purposeful voice, "go inside and get me a pillowcase."

"Lawd a mercy," Granny Pearlene whispered while bringing a hand to her throat. "How many?"

He kept his eyes trained on the glove box. "Pearlene. Bring me a yardstick. No, wait! A coat hanger, that'd work best. And girls, hurry."

Neither one of us argued as we stumbled toward the trailer. "Shake out my pillow and bring the pillowcase from my bed," Granny Pearlene ordered. "I'll sew another one later." The clanging of coat hangers and dresses falling from the closet filled me with panic. No way could I escape with the Oldsmobile now. No way.

"Here," Granny Pearlene said while handing me three coat hangers. "Take these." She motioned with her hand. "Go on now. Take 'em." She brought the other hand to her mouth, like she was holding back a scream trapped inside. "Hurry. I can't be out there. Snakes give me the willies."

I wanted to argue that I already had the willies, but I couldn't leave Connor outside alone. He hadn't moved since we left. He stood, feet firmly planted, with his eyes trained on whatever lived inside the glove box.

"Carole Anne, I want you to straighten out the coat hanger best you can." His words were soft and low. "Then bend the hook part like a spoon. Can you do that?"

Nodding, I tucked the pillowcase in my back pocket, dropped two of the hangers to the ground, and bent the wire I still held. It shook when I passed it to Connor.

"What I need you to do is come up alongside me real slow." His voice was lower now, almost a whisper, forcing me to step toward him in order to hear. "Good. Good. Now I need you to open the pillowcase as wide as you can."

Connor didn't break eye contact with the dashboard. He bent the wire to his liking and brought it up tight against him. "You're doing fine. I need you to ease the door open and bring the pillowcase beside me. Ready?"

Everything inside me screamed no, but I did as he asked.

He kept his eyes trained forward. "Easy. Slow and easy. You'll need to come alongside and hold the pillowcase open."

Shaking, I did as he asked.

He winced when the door squeaked. "Hang on tight to the fabric."

In one quick motion, he reached the coat hanger into the car. Weak wire bent beneath the weight of the biggest snake I'd ever seen. Squeezing my eyes closed, I held the fabric open wide, felt the creature's weight fall to the bottom of the pillowcase. Connor was fast. Covering my hands with his, he forced the fabric together, closing the creature's only escape route. Then he was off with the pillowcase running fast toward his truck. I didn't want to see what happened next, didn't want to hear what happened either. Returning to the trailer I informed Granny Pearlene she could safely go outside.

"It's the rats. Rats draw in all kinds of critters." Granny Pearlene shuddered. "I hate 'em. Durn birdfeeders. Draws rats like a picnic lures ants." She stepped outside, clipped Smokey to his lead, and brought him with her for protection.

She was right. Even though we lived in a trailer and had things packed to the ceiling, we kept the inside and outside hospital-clean. When Willa Rae Jameson and Trummie Woodard start feeding the birds, vermin flock to the ground hungry to devour scattered seeds.

"Ladies, before we do anything else," Connor said as he walked back toward us, "we need to check for anything that might crawl out from the seat while you're driving."

Granny Pearlene patted Smokey and shook her head. "Can't do it. Just can't. I'll stand watch for Barbara, but I can't go near where a snake has been."

I wanted to tell her that anybody who had stood waist-deep in the county landfill should have no problem cleaning out a few nests, but I didn't have time to argue. Mama could be home at any minute.

"Tell me what to do," I said to Connor who crouched on the ground at the passenger door.

"Run get me a trash can. Looks like I've found another nest."

Connor used the hanger to pick an old nest from beneath the seat. "Don't see any more rats, but we need to get rid of these and then toss some mothballs in here." He dumped a handful of cotton fibers, dog fur, and shelled sunflowers seeds into the pail.

"Getting close to time," Granny Pearlene warned. "We've got about ten more minutes before she gets home."

"We'll get the rest of these later," Connor said. "Let's load the battery into the truck then I'll give the belts a quick look."

He proclaimed the belts looked good and told me to add four quarts of engine oil, an oil filter, and air filter to the list.

"Tomorrow I'll bring a little gas and we'll see if she'll crank."

Hopeful, I asked, "You think we can crank her tomorrow?"

Connor draped a heavy arm around my shoulder. "I'm not making any promises, but we're sure going to try."

Chapter Twenty-Three

Barbara

Morning light broke through the plastic-covered window—I had slept through the three-thirty whistle. Didn't even stir when the five-thirty rumbled through. Rested, I stretched beneath the mound of quilts and wiggled my feet to circulate blood flow. My legs ached a bit from standing at Wanda's, but the promise of stable income eased the minor discomfort. I'd never lounged in the bed before, never had extra morning time. My previous routine had resembled chaos. Bolt from the bed, dress quickly, gulp coffee, and walk to work before sunup. This new work schedule allowed time to prepare breakfast for us all. We could finally be a normal family.

I decided it best to keep my distance from Connor. Bryson City only had one mechanic worth a flip, and he was backlogged, leaving me little choice but to trust Connor, even from a distance. He'd already started tinkering on the Oldsmobile. Pearlene wasn't fooling me. Yesterday, she or Carole Anne had invited him to start work. I immediately noticed the car resting on blocks. Not much gets past a mama's watchful eye, even hidden under a silver tarp. While Connor worked on the car, I'd get my license again, and squirrel away enough money for insurance.

I put on a pot of coffee then retrieved a box of cornflakes from the pantry. I heard Pearlene running water in the bathroom. She always brushed her teeth before breakfast, then again after. Her routine once annoyed me, today it gives comfort.

Standing in the kitchen I took a hard look at our home. Faded linoleum with holes worn through and threadbare carpet. I'd fix that first. Loosen the linoleum, even if I had to scrape it away with a razorblade. I'd rip up the carpet, toss everything old out the backdoor. I'd repaint the cabinets too, after I got a couple paychecks ahead.

I poured the cereal and smiled as Pearlene pitter-pattered toward the chair. "Good morning," I said while placing a cup of coffee beside the bowl.

She grunted and slurped.

"Heading to the salon in a few minutes. Do I need to pick up anything on the way home?"

Pearlene shook her head and spooned cereal into her mouth.

Glancing toward the alarm clock I said, "Guess Carole Anne's already at school by now."

"Guess so," Pearlene responded. "You'll need to get up earlier than you did today to catch her." She took another slurp of coffee. Swallowed hard. "That one's gonna leave us soon. You know that, right?"

I ignored her strong words, even though I knew she spoke the truth. I cleared my throat, wrapped my hands around my mug, and squeezed it for courage. "Thanks, Mom, for calling Wanda Jean. I know she's only giving me a chance because of you. Things will get better, I promise."

"Play your cards right, girl, and one day you'll own that place." Pearlene spooned another bite of cereal.

I doubted her words, even though they sounded delicious.

"Connor thinks he can have the car running in a week, maybe less," Pearlene said while I cleared the table. "He called Carole Anne and gave her a list of what needs fixing."

I wanted to apologize, to say I'm sorry for the worry I'd brought in her life. But I couldn't. The scars were too deep. Reaching for her hand, I said, "Soon as Connor fixes the Oldsmobile, I'll take you to the Cleveland Closet. First chance I get, we'll load up everything we can haul. We'll clean the place out. We'll take everything, including the lightbulbs."

I left Pearlene smiling.

Chapter Twenty-Four

Carole Anne

I skipped school the next day, choosing to go to Hubert's instead. "Once I get my license," I told him as I watched him work. "I can make the Wednesday trips for you."

Hubert responded with a grunt, then walked back to the room he called the "beer closet." He was leaving for Tennessee and wanted everything ready for the Foster boys.

"No one in the world would even suspect me," I added, my tone hopeful.

Hubert just shook his head. "Smuggling is man's business. Besides, you gotta be seventeen to purchase alcohol in Tennessee."

"But ... " I began.

He shook his head. "No. You're more valuable here helping me with the firewater." Hubert stood on tiptoe and hung a brass bell on a door hook. "I got another load of jars in the back that need cleaning. If you hear the door open, come out and let people know I'll be back soon." He patted the stack of Pabst Blue Ribbon. "The Foster boys will pick this up sometime tonight and bring me the money long after you're back home." He nodded toward the door. "I've got two twelve-packs hid under the bushes and I've turned on the night light. Folk know what to do when I'm gone. If I'm not back before you leave remember to lock up."

During Hubert's last trip to Tennessee he had acquired a night deposit box from a failed bank. The words DEPOSITORY still stood in raised lettering, despite multiple layers of paint, but he didn't mind.

"I hope someone doesn't think you robbed a bank," I said.

Hubert laughed. "Naw. Customers don't care as long as they get their brew," he explained while I held the flashlight and placed concrete screws in his outstretched hand. "They want to be in and out, preferably while their car still runs out on the street. I'd install a drive-through window if I had the chance."

During the day, regular customers placed orders that Hubert happily prepared for after-hours pickup. His system was simple. Take phone orders and stash individual bottles and larger orders under the bushes beside his house. Patrons retrieved their beer and deposited money into the stainless-steel box. This system worked particularly well for those who wanted to go unnoticed or hadn't the time for a sit-down brew inside.

I busied myself during Hubert's absence, wiping down tables and chairs then cleaning the popcorn machine. Satisfied, I stepped inside the laundry room and began filling the sink with water. I squeezed dish soap into the sink then donned plastic gloves and unscrewed the lids. I placed the last of the jars into the soaking solution and removed my gloves. My pulse quickened when I heard the bell sound. Hubert has a few customers whose sideways looks made me nervous, which is why I held back, hoping whoever was inside would quickly leave.

"Looks like we've got the place to ourselves." Mark Foster's voice—a voice I easily recognized—reached me and I stole a glance at my watch with a frown. I thought Hubert had said the Foster boys weren't coming until that night.

"He's off on another run," Matthew replied. "Let's load this up so we can head on down to Georgia. We've got customers waiting and a lot of work to do."

"While we're here, might as well have a look around," Mark said. "See if Old Hubert has anything worth taking."

"Let's not," Matthew said, surprising me that he wasn't eager to rifle through the place. "Didn't you hear me? I'm on a tight schedule."

Ignoring his brother, Mark entered the room where I stood frozen in place, all hope that I wouldn't be found now diminished. He flashed me a smile. "Well lookie here. Never took you for a liquor-running gal."

"I just help keep the place clean," I said. "Besides, I was just leaving."

Mark stepped closer. "Well now ... why don't you give us a hand loading and we'll give you a ride home."

Knowing Mama would *really* kill me if I got in the vehicle with him, I tried to think of a response that didn't make me sound like an idiot.

Matthew appeared in the doorway. "Boy. I said we gotta go. Georgia is four hours of hard driving." He picked up two cases without giving me a second look and headed for the truck.

"You coming or not?" Mark said. He walked toward me, almost daring.

This was it. The Foster boys were heading to Georgia and one of them had just said he'd give me a ride. A ride home, yes, but only if I said so. This. Was. It. My chance to leave. A chance to visit another state, do something bold and dangerous. I wished I had my money with me. I only had a few dollars in my pocket, not enough to make it far.

I eyed the safe and wished that, just once, Hubert had failed to secure the door. No such luck. I lifted a case of beer. Then I reasoned that if I rode with the Fosters to Georgia, I could keep an eye peeled for places to stay and chart a route on my map when I returned to Bryson City. Then I only had to wait and save my money until the Oldsmobile was ready.

Mark took the last case of beer, closing the door behind him. Matthew had already cranked the vehicle. Mark slid his box into a dog box bolted to the inside of the truck bed then quickly relieved me of the one I held. Closing the lid, he asked again, "Want a ride?" When I hesitated, he pushed his jacket aside, revealing a pistol tucked in the waistband of his jeans. "Girl, I wasn't exactly asking." He jerked his head toward the cab. "Get in the truck."

He grabbed my arm, squeezed, and pushed me toward the middle of the bench seat, wedging me between them both. Matthew took off before the passenger door had closed.

"I'm pretty sure y'all just kidnapped me," I said while trying to make my voice sound light. "Might as well rob a bank while we're out."

"Good idea." Mark opened a beer, sucked it dry, and pressed the empty can to his forehead to crush it. Laughing, he rolled down the window and hurled the trash outside. Matthew reached under the bench seat and retrieved a can, which he opened and chugged nearly as fast as his brother. He, too, rolled down his window and tossed the can.

In a short time, Bryson City was behind us and we were on the interstate traveling well above the posted speed limit, the warm wind whipping through the open windows and sending my hair in all directions as we crossed the Georgia border.

"I thought y'all *sold* Hubert's beer," I said when Mark opened another.

They laughed like I had just told the funniest joke ever in the history of jokes.

"We sell a few cans here and there," Matthew explained. "Enough to help out Old Hubert and earn our take." Matthew took a long drink. "We just increase the price, you know, to cover our delivery expenses. That way we get to partake a little bit every now and then for free."

He bent and fished for another can beneath the seat. The truck's front tire dropped off the edge of the pavement when Matthew took his eyes off the road. Panicking, I grabbed the wheel and righted the vehicle. "What is wrong with you?" I asked, my voice loud and scared.

Patting my leg with a heavy hand, Matthew said, "Just settle down. We'll be there before you know it. Here. Open this and take a couple swigs to settle your nerves."

I opened the can but didn't partake. "Why are you taking Hubert's beer all the way to Georgia anyway?" I asked, one hand holding the beer and the other trying to keep my hair on my head. The air in the truck was now thick and bitter. Dusty. "That doesn't make much sense if you ask me. You're not going to make any money hauling this all the way down there."

Mark tossed another empty out the window. "First, we didn't ask for your opinion. Second, we're not going to Georgia just to sell beer. We're also picking up a load of sugar. There's a place you probably never heard of called Sugar Hill. Long time known for liquor running," he continued, leaving me to wonder why he was telling me all this. And me figuring that may not be a good thing. "Me and my brother reckon it's time to start making our own corn liquor. We've got us a place laid out in the mountains and a still already built. We put it deep in the woods, over on the park side so if someone finds it, it ain't us that's gonna get in trouble. We only need some corn and some sugar."

Matthew rapped on the truck's rear window. "We'll sell all the beer and stash our ingredients in the dog box back there, bring it home and start cooking the mash." His hand returned to my knee, sending danger-tingles up my spine. I tensed. Sat up straighter knowing I was trapped in the truck. I had been wrong about leaving home. About the Foster boys being a way to Georgia. No, being kidnapped didn't make me want to sing a hallelujah. Being kidnapped made me want to call Mama.

Matthew checked his watch. "Time to get a move on." The truck lurched forward as he pressed down hard on the gas. His hand moved up my leg and squeezed.

I grasped it hard with my own, turned it over, and put the can on his palm. I wanted to say, "Keep your hands to yourself," but I figured I'd best stay quiet.

My eyes shot up to the rearview mirror where blue lights reflected in them. Matthew took a long drink, passed the can to me, and said, "Hold on." The engine roared and the tires squealed when he turned the wheel sharply. Mark tumbled into me then righted himself and grabbed the dashboard for support.

"What in the Sam Hill are you doing?"

Matthew turned to his brother and hollered across the cab, "I can't exactly pull over now, can I? Not with what we've got stashed under the seat. Besides, there's a warrant out for my arrest in Georgia. If I'm caught, they'll put me *under* the jail."

At that moment I realized that the Foster brothers had more than Pabst Blue Ribbon in the truck. "Then why in the world did you bring us to Georgia?" I dared shout over the din.

Mark kicked away a cloth on the floorboard, then lifted the handle of a storage compartment built into it. "What should I do? Throw it out?"

"And lose all our money? I'd rather go to jail."

Law enforcement activated their sirens. Matthew tightened his grip on the wheel. Without anything to hold on to my body banged between Mark and Matthew as we sped down the road taking the curves so fast the tires screamed. I pulled my knees up and pressed my feet against the dash for support. Matthew shouted, "Hang on!" then slammed the brakes. The patrol car rammed the rear bumper.

Matthew checked the rearview then gunned the engine. Without taking his eyes off the road he shouted, "Do it."

Mark tossed the bag. My breath caught as he pulled the pistol from his waistband. I twisted to look out the back window as Mark, hanging partway from the open window, turned and fired, taking out the blue lights but not the siren. I shifted forward again, pulled my knees up to my chest, and tucked my face as close to my legs as humanly possible. Mark fired the remaining shots then shifted, released the empties, and plucked ammunition from a box tucked inside the glove box.

"Here," he commanded, knocking me from my stay-safe position. "Feed 'em to me so I can keep shooting."

I looked behind me again as gunsmoke filled the cabin. Between the shots fired and the siren coming from the persistent car behind us, my ears roared even as all hope diminished that the deputy behind us might become my savior from being kidnapped.

When I didn't respond, Mark dumped the bullets in my lap and reached between my legs, picking up bullets then feeding them expertly into the metal cylinder of the weapon.

Matthew saw a side road and took it quick, pushing me away when I fell into him. The dirt road was packed, rutted, and unsuitable for high-speed driving. Rolls of dust tumbled from the back tires. I looked up again to see a flash of the cruiser reflecting in the rearview. Matthew yelled, "I'm gonna slam on the brakes. See if you can take out the driver."

"If he keeps ramming us, we're go'n' crash," Mark called back.

"You're going to get us killed," I said while clawing my way across Mark and reaching for the door handle. "Let me out!" I screamed, figuring I would roll along the packed dirt and land somewhere in the ditch near the row of foliage that grew thick on the sides of the road as natural barriers for acres of farmland.

If that battered up squad car didn't run over me first.

Matthew grabbed my hair and pulled me toward him. "Do that again and I'll *throw* you out." His fingers were still tangled in my hair when he slammed the brakes again. The cruiser rammed us again. My body brushed against Mark then slammed against the dash. I felt the truck hit a deep rut. The truck toppled out of control in a fury of metal twisting and the engine groaning. I felt like a limp washcloth in the spin cycle of a washing machine. Mark's body fell out the open window, his hands grasping at air while mine bounced around inside the cabin with cans of Pabst Blue Ribbon slamming into me. Tumbling end over end, the truck finally came to rest on the roof of the cab.

Later, I remembered crawling out the broken window, remembered Matthew calling for his brother again and again. The siren piercing the late-afternoon air—draped in dust particles and dirt—from a squad car rammed into the ditch on the other side of the road. Perhaps I was already beginning to lose consciousness as I lay in the ditch listening, hoping. Regret mingled with the soured smell of beer that had settled into my clothes. Blood blurred my vision, trickling into my eyes as I crawled up the embankment toward the road, then fell backward. I wiped my brow with my shirtsleeve, ignoring the stabbing shoulder pain. I held pressure above my brow the best I could, but the blood was slippery. A roar sounded in my ears, the kind you hear just before you pass out. I saw the silvery flash of light that faded into darkness.

I told myself that I needed to find that police officer and tell him the truth. But most of all, I needed someone to take me home, because, right then, I was about as lost as I'd ever been.

Chapter Twenty-Five

Barbara

My day passed quickly. Wanda and I fell into a rhythm. I washed and towel-dried each client's hair then directed them to sit in the salon chair where Wanda cut and styled. The third client left well before noon, then we enjoyed a leisurely lunch. Wanda allowed me to run the washing machine as long as I turned off the dryer before our first afternoon appointment arrived. I kept the coffee hot, cookies available, and the floor clean enough to pass a white-glove inspection should her husband surprise us with a visit.

When the last client left at three thirty, I retrieved a mop and cleaned the floor until it sparkled and emitted a lemony-fresh scent.

"Things went well," Wanda said while standing on the white shag carpet watching me wring out the mop. "I think we could add another client in the morning and one more in the afternoon."

"Whatever you think," I responded.

She dumped a load of towels onto the sofa and folded while I worked the mop, backing my way across the linoleum toward the carpet.

"My appointment book usually fills at least a month in advance. Opening one extra slot in the morning and afternoon means more business for me, and more money for you. I'm also thinking about closing on Monday. We could operate the salon Tuesday through Saturday. Working ladies have trouble getting an appointment with me during the week. We could fill Saturdays in a snap."

"What about Mr. Jewell? What would he think about having ladies in here on his day off?"

"Let me worry about him." Wanda sat on the sofa and patted the cushion. "Come. Sit. We've been on our feet all day." She positioned an ottoman between us. "We need to talk."

My heart sank. Even though we'd had a terrific day, deep in my heart I knew it felt too good to be true. Wanda Jean Jewell didn't really need me. She's spent years cutting hair in Bryson City without help. Pearlene once told me that Wanda had traveled all the way to Raleigh for a hair show that taught her the bouffant style.

I trudged to the couch and settled into the sofa.

"Listen carefully," Wanda began. "I've been doing hair as long as you've been on this earth."

Nodding, I folded my hands together and squeezed my fingers tight.

"I know what my clientele wants, and what looks good on them, but at the end of the day, the customer gets what the customer wants."

Replaying the day in my mind, I wondered who I had offended, who had pulled Wanda aside and complained.

Wanda leafed through a stack of magazines available for the customers, found the one she wanted, and placed it in my hand. "I want you to take a look at this cut."

I held a copy of the magazine featuring skater Dorothy Hamill but failed to understand what it had to do with me.

"This little lady has a style that's about to change the way we do business. I want you to take this magazine home. Look at it, study it as best you can because *this* hairstyle is about to become all the rage. My phone is already ringing with people wanting to know if I can cut what they call 'The Dorothy.' In the next few weeks we're going to be overrun with calls. But more important, you need to start cutting hair."

"But, I don't …"

Wanda held up her hand. "I know what you're about to say. You don't have a license. I understand. I've looked into ways to remedy that problem. Southwestern Technical College's beauty school starts classes next week and you need to register."

"But …" I began again, "I don't have …"

"The money?" Wanda interrupted. "I understand not having

tuition money, but you do have the time. The technical school has those basic educational opportunity grants. Do you understand what that means? Barbara, it's free money."

"I like working with you here." I explained, my voice weak and scared. Was she sending me home so soon?

"Barbara, I realize you've spent most of your life living day-to-day. If you can, try and look beyond today, beyond next month, next year. Ask yourself, where do I want to be ten years from now? Because anything you can picture, you can achieve with hard work and dedication." She waved a hand. "I'm not firing you. I'm handing you an opportunity you should strongly consider taking."

I glanced at the glossy image of the skater, the way each layer stacked atop each other, smooth, without harsh lines. I could cut this, easily. Truth be told, I could set up my own shop, but not many folk other than trailer park residents want to sit outside for a haircut. Principal Walker was a fluke. I figured he only came because Wanda's salon was closed on Saturday. I knew eventually someone would rat me out and the Health Department would issue a citation for operating without a license.

"They offer night classes," Wanda said, pulling me back into the conversation. "I've called. With grant money paying tuition, and an established client base, there's nothing left to do but register. Barbara, that little technical school will change your life if you let it."

My hands shook as I glanced back at the photo. I had given up on school after Carole Anne was born, settling for the only job available for high school dropouts. I'd given Cleveland Manufacturing my time and felt like I had wasted my youth hunched over a sewing machine. So much time had passed. Perhaps too much time. I couldn't help but ask myself, did I have what it takes to go back to school now as an adult?

"Do you have your GED?"

I nodded, still unable to think things fully through.

Wanda noticed my frown and lightly touched my arm. "You can do it, Barbara. I know you can. Work around your schedule, study here if you'd like. Classes are Monday and Wednesday. If I close the salon on Monday and cut back on Wednesday appointments, you'll have a manageable schedule that benefits everyone. You don't have to work all day Saturday. We could just take in a couple of clients."

I knew she meant well, but Wanda didn't know my struggles. What about Pearlene? What about transportation? I'd need a car to commute, money for gas, and insurance.

"By the time I graduate, women will be tired of The Dorothy haircut," I explained.

Wanda stood and straightened her skirt. "Hon, there is always someone famous wearing a hairstyle people want to copy." She picked up the phone and dialed a number. Waiting as it rang, she said, "I think I understand what's going on here." She twirled the cord between her fingers and said, "Yes. Good afternoon, may I speak to Cathy Randall?"

She lowered her voice to the purr she used when speaking to clients. "Cathy. It's Wanda Jean from the salon."

I arched my brow, knowing that honey-laced tone meant Wanda was up to something.

"I have this phenomenal gal helping me who wants to enroll in beauty school. Trouble is, she needs transportation."

As I approached ready to protest, Wanda held up her hand to stop me, even though I hadn't agreed to anything.

"Cathy, do you have anyone from Bryson City that's coming to Southwestern Tech? Barbara needs a ride share until we get her car back on the road."

Wanda snapped her fingers and motioned for me to pass her a notepad. I complied and stood silent while she retrieved a pencil from her sprayed-stiff hair and jotted down Cathy's responses.

"Sounds great. Yes. She's going to apply for the grant, even if I have to drive her there myself." Wanda waved me away. "Yes, Cathy, I understand. We'll be right there."

Wanda hung up the phone then retrieved her purse. "Get in the car. I'm taking you to Southwestern Technical College. Cathy said there's plenty of grant money to be had, but only one slot remains for the beauty school."

While she drove, I cried. Wanda told me part of the registration process included a placement test. I hadn't taken a test in years. She chastised that I lacked confidence, saying, "Any woman who can raise a kid while working in a factory can pass a simple admissions test." She was right. I sailed through the test, completed the application and class registration. After I finished, Wanda offered to pick up celebratory cheeseburgers from Na-Bers Drive-In, but I wanted to get back home and show Carole Anne and Pearlene the registration papers I had tucked neatly in my purse.

Patting my knee, Wanda said, "What you did today is the first step in the right direction. Carole Anne needs to see you do this. She needs to know what hope looks like. Too many girls in Bryson City have no hope."

Leaning across the car, I hugged Wanda tight then quickly brushed away tears. "Thank you," I whispered, "for giving me a chance."

My footsteps were light with the promise of a brighter future. Opening my purse, I unfolded the registration papers and hurried up the rickety concrete steps eager to share my good news. The moment I stepped inside the trailer the worried faces of Pearlene and Doretta met me. But before I could ask what was going on, Doretta blurted, "Carole Anne is missing."

Chapter Twenty-Six

Carole Anne

*M*ark Foster is dead.
What?

I opened my eyes to the orb of a full moon already peeking through a semi-dark sky, spying me through skinny dried corn stalks.

The deputy is dead. Matthew Foster is on the run ... armed and considered dangerous.

I blinked. Rolled my neck to the left, then the right. I lay in a corn field. I lay in a corn field and I hurt. I lay in a corn field and I hurt and I wasn't sure how I got there except that I'd been kidnapped and part of a high-speed chase.

I rubbed the back of my neck then stretched my arms and legs checking for broken bones. My wrist throbbed and had turned purple. A sprain, I figured, and hopefully not broken. Pieces of broken glass fell from my hair. Blood had dried and collected in the scratched places on my arms. I didn't know how long I'd been out. I only knew I was alone. Completely alone.

Willing myself to move, I forced my wobbly legs to stand, tested their strength before pulling myself upright. My head pounded. I bet this is how football players felt after they get their bell rung making a tackle. But I could see the line of knobby trees and low bushes that divided the field from the road so, at least, I knew which way to go.

I don't know how much time passed while I stood at the edge of the dirt road trying to figure out whether to go left or right. Other than pieces of broken glass dotting the clay, there wasn't much proof of an accident. The truck and squad car had been hauled away. I had no idea where the deputy or the Fosters were—dead or in jail or in a hospital somewhere—but I'd surely been left behind.

Knowing I had a fifty-fifty chance of making the wrong choice, and that thus far my choices hadn't been all that smart, I waited for guidance, an omen, any sign directing me which direction might lead to a house or a store where I could call for help.

The red dirt road was pancake flat with a treeless landscape stretching as far as I could see. From an early age, mountain folk are raised to know that rivers are our lifeblood and if you ever get lost you just need to find water and follow its flow down the hill until it reaches humanity.

Except there was no river, no stream, no water of any kind. There were only open fields and barbed wire fence rows.

With the exception of a few night bugs humming, the evening air was quiet. I ran my hand over the crown of my head; fragments of broken glass fell from my hair.

In the country, night falls fast like a turned-off light switch. One minute sunshine blisters the back of your neck, and the next you're running toward the disappearing ball in the sky screaming, "Don't leave me alone in the dark."

"Which way?" I called out. If it were daytime, I could tell east and west by the sun. That much I could do. But the station of the moon was a mystery to me.

Ignoring the pain in my bruised body and hunger pressing hard against my stomach, I started walking with the site of the accident behind me. Heading where, I had no idea.

Chapter Twenty-Seven

Barbara

The admissions paperwork fluttered to the ground.

"Matthew and Mark Foster are gone too." Doretta's eyes were wide with concern. "Luke said they haven't been seen since sometime right after lunch."

"Who gives a crap about them Foster hellions," Pearlene snapped. "We need to find Carole Anne."

"She wasn't at school today," Doretta offered.

I stared at the admission papers as if they held the answers she needed, then focused my eyes on Doretta. "Tell me what you know. Everything you know."

Doretta turned to Pearlene. "Go on now. Now ain't the time for secrets."

"Luke was late for class, which is not unusual. Except this morning he noticed Carole Anne's empty chair and pulled me aside and asked if I'd seen her. At first, I thought he was joking, you know, like the Foster boys do but there was something genuine about his concern. Then he told me."

"Told you what," I snapped. This was taking too long. I had to call the sheriff, had to find a vehicle and start looking for Carole Anne.

"That his brothers were making a run for Hubert."

"Hubert?" Pearlene said. "What'n the blazes does he have to do with Carole Anne being gone?"

Doretta hesitated, then looked from me to Pearlene.

"Go on girl, spit it out." Pearlene said. "Carole Anne could be in real danger."

"Hubert sells beer in his basement. He's been so profitable he gave

Carole Anne a job. Matthew and Mark have always helped Hubert with his beer business, selling it to seniors at school and basically anyone with money in their pocket. But they've noticed how much money Hubert makes, so they decided to start their own corn liquor business."

"The hell you say," Pearlene whispered, her voice shaky.

"It's true," Doretta said, shifting a little and all the while my heart pounding. "Luke told me he helped his brothers put the still together. They hid it in the National Park because they think no one will find it there. Matthew and Mark are ready for their first run. They just need a load of sugar and corn to get things started. Since the park rangers in Tennessee have their eyes peeled for Matthew, Luke figures they headed out to Sugar Hill, Georgia, for supplies."

"Sugar Hill," Pearlene repeated as she paced to the window and peered outside. "Lawd-a-mercy. Connor best hurry on over here. I just figured she'd run off. I didn't know she'd run off to the devil's stompin' grounds."

"Mama, what are you talking about?"

Pearlene's eyes were wild. "I'm talking about Lake Lanier. Government snatched up that land by hook or crook, just like when they formed the National Park in this county. Flooded the place. Got an entire ghost town underwater near Sugar Hill. Folk can't even cross the bridge without being scared for their life. My cousin, Della Mae Parker, has been missing since 1959. Some say her ghost walks the trestle at night."

Good Lord, now wasn't the time for Mama to have an episode. Grabbing her by the arms, I stood in front of her and forced myself to be calm. "What does *any* of that have to do with Carole Anne?"

"She gone. Don't you see? Gone just like Della Mae. Vanished. You vanished today, too. You didn't come home when you were supposed to." Pearlene wiggled herself away from me, then dashed to the front door and looked out the tiny window. "We didn't know where you were. We didn't know where Carole Anne was either. We called Wanda Jean's place, but no one answered. So we called Connor, and Sheriff Tolliver too."

"I'm *here*, Mama. We'll find Carole Anne. Don't worry." I tried to quiet the panic threatening to steal my breath. I should stay with her until she settled down but needed to start searching for Carole Anne. I *had* to because … "We can't depend on Tolliver. He won't do anything. He never does anything to help."

Pearlene turned, slow and purposeful. "He will this time. Connor will see to it."

Gravel crunching silenced us. My history with Connor pushed aside, I threw open the door and rushed toward him. "What do you know?"

"Sheriff Tolliver has sent word to other sheriffs in neighboring counties and he's convened a group of volunteers down at the town square. They're going to search here. Me and you are heading to Georgia." Connor looked over my shoulder and I turned. Doretta and Pearlene stood at the opened door, eyes wide. "Doretta, come with us. I'll drop you off downtown. Pearlene, you stay here and man the phone. We need someone here in case Carole Anne shows up or if she reaches out for help. We will call you from a pay phone once we get to Georgia. You call Tolliver and relay any news we might have." Connor looked at each of us and hurriedly said, "Miss Pearlene, can you do that?"

Tears pooled in Mama's eyes. She brought a shaking hand to her mouth and nodded. "I'll have Claudette come sit with me. We need her prayers. I ain't talked to God in a long time, but he'll listen to Claudette."

Connor grabbed my hand. I didn't protest when he squeezed it. "Let's go. Remember, Pearlene," he added, looking back at her. "Keep the phone line clear. We'll keep you updated along the way."

Pearlene retrieved a bulging change purse that once belonged to her mother. "Here, take these quarters for the pay phone and bring our Carole Anne home."

I opened the door to Connor's truck, climbed inside, then slammed it shut before he had the chance to take a seat behind the wheel.

"Move over," Doretta commanded as she hopped inside, pushing me toward the middle with her hip.

We rode in silence. I ignored the heat rolling off Connor, shocking me when my leg grazed his as he took the curves at an unsafe speed. As we passed through the edge of town, I peered out Doretta's window toward town square where a few stragglers remained. "Don't worry, Miss Parker," Doretta said as Connor brought the truck to a stop. "People look after each other in Bryson City. They make casseroles for the sick. They hold car washes and turkey shoots to fund the Youth Athletic Program." She nodded once. "We'll find Carole Anne."

I grunted, unconvinced. "Bunch of busybodies, that's all. They don't care about me."

"You're wrong. You and Carole Anne never could see good in the people who live here. These people want to help." Doretta pointed toward the square. "Look, the principal's out there. Miss Love too."

She was right. "Maybe I should stay here." I looked at Connor, whose eyes stayed on the road, then to Doretta. "What if they find her *here*? What if she's hurt?"

"Don't worry," Doretta said then headed off.

"I should stay here," I said again. "Connor, I should check the tracks just in case . . ."

Connor grabbed my arm and pulled me toward him, then gunned the engine before I could bolt. I grabbed the dash for support as he drove the vehicle across the tracks.

"I had a little talk with Hubert," he said. "Sheriff Tolliver too. Best I can gather Carole Anne's been working at Hubert's almost every night earning extra money." Connor's jawbone jutted out as he ground his teeth. "Sheriff knew all about it, too."

I noticed the knuckles on his right hand were red and swollen. I didn't ask how he gathered this information. Truth be told, I hope he punched Sheriff Tolliver square in the mouth. "Just because our fine sheriff is aware of illegal activity doesn't mean he's going to lift a finger to do anything about it," I said.

Connor didn't respond. He took the exit and headed south on the road that would take us to Georgia. "Barbara, did you know she was working with Hubert?"

Turning myself fully toward him, I said, "I most certainly did not know." I knew that she left at night, yes, but I thought that—like me— she was simply wandering … planning … "Are you implying that I'm responsible for Carole Anne running away . . . that I'm a bad mother? Because if you are, you don't know anything about me or Carole Anne."

"Probably know more about her than you do," he mumbled under his breath. "Know she's determined on getting out of here."

"Of course she is. So are a lot of teenagers."

"You don't get it, Barbara. You just don't get it. Carole Anne wants more than what you can offer."

His words stung. "You think I don't know that? Why do you think I work myself so hard? You don't know anything about my life, how impossible it is to keep up with Pearlene, to pay the bills, to survive." Tears threatened and I turned from him.

Connor hit the steering wheel. "You think I don't know?"

"Don't lecture me, Connor. You're not her father." My words died in the air. Pressing my fingertips to my lips, I turned and looked out the windshield. My voice was shaking as I whispered, "I thought she was just walking the tracks like I used to do. I didn't know she was working with Hubert."

"Do you even have a clue why she was working there? Do you even care? She was saving money to fix that dang car. Fix it up so she could get away from you!"

"Go ahead," I shouted. "Pile all the blame on me. Mothers get blamed for everything. Trust me, I can carry the load. I'm used to carrying it."

Connor steered the truck off the road, bringing it to a sudden stop. He took a deep breath. "Listen, you're stuck with me for a few hours. Frankly, I'm the only thing you've got that's even close to being a friend. So you need to get over whatever problem you have with me because I'm making a three-hour trip to Georgia, trying to help."

I looked out the windshield again, brought my hand to my lips, then went to work chewing on my nails. I'd left my smokes at home and right then I'd give anything for a cigarette.

His voice turned gentle. "What happened between you and Ted?"

"Don't act like you don't know. Don't act like you weren't there. The whole football team was there that night."

"Are you talking about the party after the game? Yeah, okay, so I was at the party. But afterward … Barbara, I found you passed out on the railroad tracks. You'd be dead if I hadn't gotten to you when I did. I put you in my truck and drove you home. Don't you remember?"

"You're lying. You were there when it happened. Ted … and the others. And those Foster boys could be doing the same thing to Carole Anne right now." I wrapped my hand around the door handle. "I can't do this. I can't be in here with you."

When Connor reached for me, I lunged at him like a wild animal. "You were there! You watched Ted. You heard them." He blocked the punches as I hurled my fists at him. "You watched and you did nothing. Nothing! And now the Foster boys are out here somewhere doing God knows what to Carole Anne."

I didn't stop fighting when he pulled me toward him, when his strong arms wrapped around me, when he started whispering, "Barbara, I'm sorry. God, I swear … I didn't know. I wasn't there, I swear. I left the party on my own and decided to take a drive near the tracks. That's when I found you … and the train coming and, yes, I grabbed you off and I drove you home so you'd be safe. But I *didn't* know."

The tears came then, a floodgate of pain and fear. Releasing the tears I had held for years, I buried my face in his shoulder. He held me until my emotions settled, until embarrassment washed over me, until I straightened, wiped my eyes, and returned to the passenger side. I didn't look at him when he said, "We'll talk about Ted later. About that night." Anger rose then disappeared from his eyes. "Right now, I want you to listen to me—we'll find her, Barbara. We'll find Carole Ann." He looked over. "Now, there's a map in the glove box and I've already marked our route." His eyes found mine. "Can you help me navigate?"

I nodded, then removed the map and prayed we found Carole Anne before the Foster boys hurt my baby. If they hadn't already, especially now with the sky growing dark and the moon hanging full … just like it had done that night. Watching.

Chapter Twenty-Eight

Carole Anne

Well, one thing was for certain, my first trip out of Bryson City didn't work out as I planned. I'd spent many nights dreaming of life beyond my tiny hometown only to find myself in a place more desolate than where I started. At least Bryson City had one traffic light, and several pay phones. This place with its boarded-up shops didn't even have decent roads.

I hadn't bothered thinking too much about Matthew or Mark. I figured if they didn't care enough about me to tell law enforcement that I was out there somewhere, then I certainly wouldn't waste any energy on them. Honestly, I'd much rather be stranded alone on a desolate backroad in the middle of a no-account town in the dark than with either one of them. I knew in my heart that if Matthew hadn't wrecked, I might be dead in a ditch somewhere, discarded by Mark like one of his crushed beer cans.

My feet kicked up red dust. Every step soiled my shoes. Dust collected on my laces and in the folds of my socks. Grime pressed against my ankles, forming an itchy layer on my skin I wanted to scrape away. The moon now shone more brightly against the darkening sky.

I wanted a bath, but I needed food more than cleanliness. Hunger pressed hard in my stomach, reminding me I hadn't eaten in a while. The red clay road offered no sustenance, not even a shamrock-shaped petal of sour grass or a dandelion like the ones we picked on our way to recess.

I stood on tiptoe and looked down the road, then turned for a quick look behind. Seeing the exact same thing both ahead and behind me made me want to cry. "Just keep walking," I said. "No time to panic. Not yet. Just pretend this road is the train tracks leading you to your life path." My stomach growled a loud and angry protest. My head hurt and my tongue was thick and dry from thirst. "I've just got to walk it out."

I walked until my canvas shoes turned red and my knees shook with a combination of fear, exhaustion, and hunger. If I could find any sign of the tracks then maybe I could also find signs telling me what road I was on. If I was headed north or south, east or west. Then again, I had no idea which direction we'd headed out of earlier in the day.

But we'd been headed for Georgia, right? Right. That meant we'd been driving south.

North. I needed to go north. North to Bryson City.

North to home.

Chapter Twenty-Nine

Barbara

"It's so dark," I whispered, speaking aloud the fear that bubbled from inside. "We aren't going to find her tonight."

Connor's jaw muscles flexed. He knew I was right.

It seemed like forever since we'd refueled the truck, emptied our bladders, and called Bryson City only to learn Carole Anne hadn't been found. Matthew and Mark Foster hadn't returned either.

"We'll be in Gwinnett County in a minute," Connor said. "We need to check the jail and the hospital. Let's start at the jail. Maybe we'll get lucky."

He drove until we pulled up in front of the Gwinnett County Sheriff's Office where Connor insisted I stay in the truck. But when I said, "I don't feel comfortable sitting here alone," he looked around and agreed.

As we took the stairs into the building, I wanted to take his hand, wanted to absorb his strength. He held open the door as I entered then whispered, "Please let me do the talking."

"All right."

And when he said, "Trust me," I realized that I could trust Connor Brown. That I always could have, if I'd only known the truth.

"Hello, I'm Connor and this is my wife Barbara." He spoke to the officer on the other side of a piece of protective glass through the built-in microphone. I opened my mouth to protest, but before I could, he opened his wallet and retrieved her school photo—one I didn't know he had—and held it up. "We've just driven down from North Carolina looking for our daughter Carole Anne. Here's a recent photo."

"Our daughter" slid off his tongue like a part of Carole Anne already belonged to him. I need only to accept it. Glancing at Connor I realized he was under no obligation to help me. But, if he cared about my daughter, perhaps even a small part of him also cared about me.

"Hold on," the department officer said, then stood, walked over to the door separating the entryway from the offices, and opened the door.

The Sheriff's department employee took the photo, gave it a good look.

"We're pretty sure she was at the wrong place at the wrong time and that Matthew and Mark Foster brought her to Georgia with them."

"She's a minor," I added. "We think they brought her against her will."

Connor nodded. "She wouldn't go with them willingly."

The employee looked again at the photo and slowly shook his head. "Haven't seen her. Arrested one of the Foster boys though." He motioned for us to follow him back into the room, where he placed the photo on his desk, then returned to his rolling chair, which he maneuvered from his desk to a second one behind him. Picking up a clipboard, he flipped through several sheets of paper. "Yup. Matthew Foster. His poppa tried bonding him out a few hours ago but he's going nowhere. Not to mention we've got him over at the hospital for observation."

"And the brother?"

"We have an APB on him. Got half the squad out looking for him though. Dogs, too."

Connor picked up the photo of Carole Anne and slid it back into his wallet. "Please sir, can you tell us where they're looking. We just want to bring our Carole Anne home."

He looked back at the paperwork, "Don't say nothing in here about a girl being with them. Just Matthew and Mark Foster. Matthew was knocked out cold in the accident. Like I said, we're looking for the other one."

I grabbed Connor's arm. "What do you mean accident? What happened to my daughter? Why isn't anyone looking for her?" My questions tumbled out, rapid-fire, giving him little chance to answer.

"Ma'am, I don't want to worry you, but if your daughter is with these boys she's hooked up with a pile of trouble." His tone was dry and direct, warning I should get a hold of my emotions and let the officers do their job. "They shot up a patrol car and darn near killed one of our deputies. The truck Matthew was driving ended up in a ditch just off Sycamore Road." He looked at me directly until something softened in his face, something that told me he was a father. A father of a teenaged daughter. That he understood how it was. "You might want to check the hospital in case someone brought her in. But she wasn't with Matthew Foster. Of course all this information is confidential; you didn't get it from me. But … they're searching the woods for Mark now. She could still be with him."

"Can you get on the radio and let them know Carole Anne … that my daughter *might* be with him?" I asked.

Connor nodded. "Sir, if could you tell me where they're searching, we'd like to do our part to help." Reaching for a pen, he asked, "May I borrow this?" Connor wrote down the contact information of Sheriff Tolliver. "If you want to call the Bryson City sheriff, he can relay details about the search that's happening right now in North Carolina for our Carole Anne."

The officer took the paper. "If you ask me those boys were headed for Old Man Perkins's place out near Buford Dam. They probably took Jimmy Dodd road." He tossed the clipboard on the desk behind him. "Round here, no one asks me though."

Looking at the name stitched across the uniform, Connor extended his hand. "Officer McClure, you've been a great help. I guess we'll be going. If you can give me directions to the hospital and the Perkins place, we'll be on our way." He turned to me. "Barbara, would you get the map from the truck?"

When I returned, I found the men chatting like old friends. They spread out the map then Officer McClure penciled a path across the map, marking Old Man Perkins's place with a dark circle. "I'm telling ya, that's where they were heading." He tapped the map. "This isn't our first rodeo with Matthew Foster. Start looking there and work your way down Jimmy Dodd Road."

"What about the hospital?" I interrupted. "I think we need to check there first."

Officer McClure shook his head, "I called while you were in the truck. She's not there."

Connor thanked Officer McClure for his help. As we left the station, Connor said, "Listen Barbara, I think we've done just about all we can for tonight. We're both exhausted and we can't exactly go door-to-door this late. I left Carole Anne's photo at the Sheriff's Department and they'll expand their search now that they know she's missing. What we need to do is get a room, get some rest, and start out bright and early tomorrow morning. Officer McClure said he'd make some calls to the locals, let people know we'll be in the area tomorrow looking for Carole Anne." Connor followed me around to the passenger side, stepping in front so he could open the door. "Listen, I know you want her home right now. But we need to let them do their job."

He was right. Even though I wanted to walk the road screaming Carole Anne's name, we didn't know the area. Prowling around after dark could get us shot. Daring myself to find the courage, I raised my chin and looked at Connor. He'd aged today, lines I hadn't noticed creased his brow. He could say the same about me. Looking at him I felt my strength begin to crumble. My baby was missing.

He caught me in his arms, pulled me toward him, and for a moment my weakness felt right. I'd spent so much of my life being strong, fighting a war without anyone to even hold my hand. I'd never had permission to be weak or allow someone to hold me, if only for a moment. Clinging to Connor, my tears came again, hot and prickly, wetting my cheeks and his shirt. His chin came to rest on the top of my head. "We'll find her," he promised.

I believed him.

We were both exhausted by the time we arrived at the Hall County Motor Lodge. Connor filled up at the gas station across the street while I stepped around back and used a pay phone to call Pearlene. "No news here," she reported. I relayed our plans for tomorrow and told her I'd call the moment I knew anything. "At least you've made some progress. Claudette's spending the night," she added. "I think that's best."

I promised to have better news tomorrow.

Dinner consisted of peanut butter crackers and cigarettes. I declined the other items Connor purchased at the gas station. "Figured I'd grab some snacks we could eat on the road tomorrow," he explained, his tone dull and bone-weary. He unstrapped the foldaway bed and moved it as far away from me as he could. There wasn't much by way of bedding, two thin sheets and a terrycloth bedspread. Wasn't much privacy either. "Listen," he said to me as I stood there looking around as though I were more lost than Carole Anne. "I know this is awkward. Let's just turn off the light and try to get some sleep."

I clicked off the light and listened as the coils creaked beneath his weight. Curling on my side, I fell asleep praying for my daughter's safety while longing to feel Connor's arms hold me, and to hear him tell me everything would be fine.

Chapter Thirty

Carole Anne

I saw the outline of the barn in the full light of the moon. With nothing to guide me toward the barn, my footsteps became shuffles. Knowing I was surrounded by barbwire fencing on either side of the road, I worried about blindly walking into the wire and becoming entangled. Or stepping into a hole and breaking my ankle.

My lips were parched and my throat scratched like sandpaper. I was so thirsty I would have lapped water from a mudhole, had one been available. Cattle called each other from inside the barn. All I had to do was follow the sound.

I've never been one who enjoyed camping. A lack of toilet facilities and too many bugs have no appeal. But I was dog-tired by this point and willing to at least take my chances inside the barn with the cows. Even if it meant lying down with crawling things ... or even spiders and mice.

Following their sounds, I continued a slow shuffle and smiled when my fingers found wood. I used my fingertips to guide me, ignoring the splinters accumulating in my skin, searching for a hinge, a latch, anything granting access inside the barn. I could have cried when I found an opening in the wall.

Manure smelled fresh and strong. I knew that come morning light, I'd discover my shoes caked with both clay and manure. The soles were slick now and more than once, I'd slid and caught myself before landing in the muck. Inching along the inside wall, my nose and fingers became my eyes. Leaving the manure smell behind, I sought the freshness of hay. My fingers found a latch and it opened without difficulty.

Climbing into the prickly bed, I curled into a ball like a barn cat and fell asleep with the hope that come morning I'd be on my way home to a hot bath, and more water than my bladder would hold.

Chapter Thirty-One

Barbara

Our faces told the story. Neither had slept very well. I quickly drank coffee while Conner washed out the thermos he had retrieved from his truck.

"Carole Anne usually pours when I drive her to school." He dried the outside of the container and carried it to dresser. "She hates coffee. Wouldn't drink it on a dare." His voice cracked with emotion and his hands shook as he filled the thermos. Connor Brown cared about my Carole Anne more than her biological father ever could. Or would.

Once we got back into the truck, Connor turned off Sycamore and drove down Jimmy Dodd Road. "Officer McClure said the truck tumbled into the ditch not long after turning off the main road."

Red dust boiled up from behind and the map buckled in my hands when he hit the washboard ruts.

"Sorry," he mumbled. "Just in a hurry to find her."

I folded the map. "Looks like we won't need this anymore. Jimmy Dodd Road leads to Buford Dam. Maybe ten miles before we get back on a paved road." I looked out the window at a two-toned landscape of towering bush and dirt so bright red it hurt my eyes. Fields of drying cornstalks ran in sad rows as far as I could see.

Connor grunted a worried response.

If Carole Anne had been injured, she could be lost in these fields. My heart beat loud in my ears. "I should have brought her pillow, or a shirt. We should have brought Bob Plott with his Plott hounds. They use them all the time to find missing people. If she's in those woods ..."

Connor slowed and maneuvered around deep holes made by trucks turning into the county landfill. "Already thought of that. I called Bob before we left Bryson. He said his dogs were being used by the Forest Service right now. Some hiker got himself lost. Officer McClure said he's assembling a search party first thing this morning. They should have their own bloodhounds."

"Think we should look there first?" My hand was already wrapped around the door handle.

He shook his head. "My gut says start with Old Man Perkins. Around here, if you live on a dirt road you know exactly who belongs and who doesn't. You can see headlights coming for a mile away."

"Thank you." I looked out the window, thoughts whirling a mile a minute. "I couldn't do this without you, Connor. I know that."

His hand reached for mine. "We're bringing Carole Anne home today."

My heart accepted his words of hope, hurting now with the anticipation of finding her. Rows of corn disappeared as we traveled on. Sagging lines of barbed wire secured to weathered locust fence posts encompassed land on both sides. The fence seemed endless, stretching for miles. "This feels right. If I was dodging the law, I'd stay off the main road and take this cut-through. Wouldn't you?"

Connor nodded. "This is farm country. Lots of cattle, poultry too. When the boll weevil wiped out the cotton crop, folk started raising chickens. Lots of corn needed to sustain livestock come winter; even more required to make corn liquor. Yes, I'd take the shortcut, especially if I knew the law was looking for me."

"The Foster boys thought they were smarter than local law enforcement. Only they didn't realize this is exactly where law enforcement would hide. It's easy to hide a patrol car around here."

"There's the barn," Connor pointed, "and the house. She could have made it to either. Let's start with the barn."

Chapter Thirty-Two

Carole Anne

It felt like someone was pulling the mattress out from under me. I rolled over and awoke to the view of a long pink tongue curling hay into the mouth. A mama cow. She was inches away, close enough to brave a touch, and on any other day I would, but on this day, I was ready to go home. During the night, more broken glass had fallen from my hair and made its way down my shirt, leaving my skin scratched. My left ankle was swollen and purple, my pulse pounded hard in my foot. My head throbbed. I needed to remove my shoe and look at it, but I knew I'd never get the shoe back on. I was hungry enough to consider eating the hay under me. I was ready to be back in my own bed, lying on the creaky mattress with coils that poked my skin through the thin sheets. Once I got out of here, I would never again complain about my saggy mattress.

The mama cow didn't move when I sat up, she just looked at me and lapped another clump of hay into her mouth. A younger cow— probably belonging to the one breathing down on me—stood not a foot behind.

I don't know much about bovines. Heck, I don't know *anything* about bovines, but I do know you should never get between any mama and her baby. Trouble was, the only way out of the haystack bed was past the mama cow. The stall was long and shallow, barely deep enough for the mama cow to turn around.

Glancing overhead, I had hoped for a two-story barn like old man Fortner has. The kind where you stack hay in the second level and drop it through a hole in the floor come feeding time. There was nothing overhead, except support beams.

"Looks like me and you need to be friends," I said to the cow. "Because I really need to get out of here without you killing me."

She turned her head and looked at the stall door. For a moment I thought I heard metal clanging and a door banging open. Listening hard, I determined it was just the other cattle leaving the barn, happy to graze at first light before the sun forced them to seek shade.

Their movement must have spooked the mama cow. She abandoned the hay, carrying long pieces of dried grass in her mouth as she turned. Approaching her calf, she bent low, gave it a sniff then gently nudged it. I had more room now, more space to stretch my legs and plan my exit. Only trouble being the short distance between her and the door and a swollen ankle that slowed me down.

"Would you let me out without stomping me to bits?" I asked, looking deep into her eyes for any trace of meanness. "Would you please let me leave. I won't hurt your baby, I promise. I just want to go home."

She turned her attention back to the calf while I eased my feet onto the sawdust floor and waited. Looking at the door, then back at the cow, I figured I could make it halfway before she noticed. But I sure couldn't run, not with my swollen foot.

Suddenly her head jerked toward the door like she had read my mind. Positioning herself in front of the calf, she stood, strong and protective.

The door bolt slid open and a metal feed bucket appeared. "Good morning, my babies."

Relief washed over me. Suddenly my knees were weak as was my voice. "Um—ma'am? Can you help me?" Pressing myself against roughhewn boards for support, I sank to my backside and began to cry.

"What in the world—" The woman dropped the bucket and started toward me, shouting, "Perkins! Perkins! Come quick!"

I dropped my face into my hands, shaking like a newborn exposed to the world for the first time.

It was then I heard it—the voice of my mama. "Carole Anne? Carole Anne?"

I stood, wobbling as the woman turned toward the open barn door. "Mama?" I made my way, best I could, toward the figure coming from the field, Connor behind her. The woman who had given me life.

And the man who would take us home.

Chapter Thirty-Three

Barbara

I stroked Carole Anne's hair, just like I had when she was a baby. I wanted to know if the Foster boys had hurt her like I'd been hurt so many years ago, but I knew she'd never tell me the truth, just as I had never told Pearlene.

Connor's arm rested across her leg. Protective, yet gentle, he kept her legs still, driving slower now so as not to wake her.

He loved my baby. That much I knew.

She had a few scratches and a large knot on her forehead. A gash above her eyebrow that probably needed stitches. I gently dabbed blood from the still oozing wound.

Connor pulled into the Waffle House and rushed in to place us an order he said we'd eat on the road. "Want me to call Pearlene?" he asked through the rolled-down window while the cook made our order.

I nodded. He came around to my side and I placed several quarters in his hand, my fingertips lingering in his palm, a thank you expressed from my fingertips to his. While Connor used the pay phone, a waitress dashed across the parking lot carrying bags of food.

"This the girl I heard about on the scanner this morning?" she asked.

I nodded.

"Sure glad they found her. Folk around here know all about those Fosters. Hope they find the other one."

Connor unfolded his wallet and plucked a few dollars from inside. The waitress waved it away.

"Your money's no good here. You just git your baby home safe."

I wiped my eyes and nodded as Conner pulled out of the parking lot.

***

Mama must have called everyone in town because Bryson City was packed. Folks stood shoulder to shoulder lining both sides of the road. I nudged Carole Anne awake the moment I saw the words WELCOME HOME CAROLE ANNE! written in dark maroon colors across a white bedsheet. Small children shook hand-painted signs and cheered like my daughter had just won some state championship. The Swain County Marching Band played while Doretta and the rest of the cheerleading squad formed the letters C A using their pompoms. Teachers, students, businessmen, even that tightwad, Albert Thomas, welcomed my baby home.

Only one was missing that I could see—Ted. Most likely his wife, too. And that was fine with me. Because the Teds in my life no longer mattered. All that really mattered was right there in that truck and the one who would be waiting for us at home.

Carole Anne

1979

They found Mark Foster's body in the woods near the landfill. After being thrown from the truck, the authorities figured, he musta run back toward the main road searching in the dark for his brother. Not realizing the extent of his injuries, he bled out while slumped against the base of a Georgia pine.

Matthew Foster is serving time for a bunch of crimes, including my kidnapping. Hubert still operates his basement bar and Sheriff Tolliver still shuttles customers home at night. In Bryson City, most things never change.

After we returned from Georgia, Connor and I fixed up and cleaned out the Oldsmobile for Mama since she needed something to drive to Southwestern Tech. She ended up graduating with honors. Mama and Granny Pearlene—along with Smokey—moved in with Wanda Jean a few months ago after Mr. Jewell died of a sudden heart attack. These days, Wanda Jean doesn't do hair. Instead, she prepares finger sandwiches and coffee for clients, entertaining as they wait for Mama. Smokey never had it so good.

Wanda Jean set up a quilt frame just off the waiting area of the salon. Now Granny Pearlene spends most of her days working on her "sewing projects." The doctors think it's good for Granny Pearlene to have contact with Mama's customers. They said piecing together fabric is much like working a puzzle, keeps the brain working. Now that Granny Pearlene finally has enough room to unpack her sewing machine and the fabric remnants she procured from the Clothing Closet, she's churning out all kinds of lovely items. She's even sold a couple quilts and several aprons she makes using blue jean and cotton remnants. Won a couple of quilting contests, too.

Granny Pearlene gossips a little too, just don't tell her I said so.

I wanted to stay in a dorm at Western Carolina University, but the rooms filled up fast and Granny Pearlene wasn't exactly thrilled with the thought of me being so close to the dorms that housed boys. Mama wasn't happy either. So, Doretta and I rented a single wide trailer on the bank of the Tuckasegee River across from the train tracks. I'm not too thrilled that I've moved from one trailer into another, but Doretta loves it, says she feels freer now than she ever has. It's easy to find our trailer; it's the one near the sycamore tree with a rope hanging from the limb. I like to climb the tree and sit over the river while Doretta launches herself from the rope and lands with a splash.

Mama, Granny Pearlene, and Connor helped us get settled in, even made sure I had transportation. Today, Connor pulled a four-speed, white Chevy Chevette into the trailer park.

"Time to learn to drive a stick," Connor said, his arm draped across Mama's shoulders.

I nudged Doretta. "Told you he was sweet on her. They need to go ahead and get married."

Taking the keys he offered, I giggled as he opened the driver's side door. "M'lady, your chariot." He hurried to the passenger side after giving Mama a quick peck on the cheek, which brought a smile, then clicked the seatbelt. I like seeing Mama smile. Life is better for her now.

"Press the clutch with your left foot. Right foot on the brake," Connor instructed. "Then turn the key."

I rolled down the window and gave a thumbs up. Granny Pearlene ran to the car and leaned inside. "Now Carole Anne, your mama didn't send you up here to get one of them MRS degrees. She's sending you up here to get you an education so you can make something outta yourself. Ain't that right, Barbara?"

Mama approached Granny Pearlene and took her by the arm. "C'mon now. It's time to let Carole Anne go."

Tears pooled in Granny Pearlene's eyes. For a moment I thought she'd latch onto the door like Lucinda had when Albert took her television away. Shaking Mama off, Granny Pearlene reached in the window and gently took my arm. "Carole Anne, I need to tell you something important. I'm gonna teach you something that big fancy college won't. There's two things that always give women a world of trouble, anything with tires or a tallywhacker." She laughed until I could see the fillings in her teeth, then smacked the hood with her hand and waved me off. "Make us proud, Carole Anne," she called out. "Make us proud."

A NOTE FROM THE AUTHOR ABOUT
BRYSON CITY

Present day Bryson City, North Carolina isn't the same small town I grew up in. There are fast-food chains, tourist shops, a bookstore, and even a brewery. The trailer park that served as the inspiration for *Outbound Train* once existed alongside the tracks. In 2016, the structures were demolished. Replaced now with a brewery frequented by locals and tourists. While town leaders are happy to be rid of the "eyesore," I hope the trailer park residents found affordable housing, which is difficult these days for the working poor in rural Appalachia.

Time travels slowly in my hometown. We are twenty years behind the times, which is a good thing. A very good thing. However, we are not immune from the fast pace of city life. One must use caution to safely cross the street, particularly when the tourist train is in town. Traffic is bumper-to-bumper all day every single day. People text and walk in the middle of the main road; they don't look up or pay attention. When you visit my hometown take it slow and easy and for Pete's sake, be respectful of locals, as many of them are elderly with slower response time and failing vision.

We've seen our share of kidnapping, murders, child abuse, and meth. Too much death, too much crime, but don't think for a moment the present-day sheriff doesn't have crime under control. Heroin floods in from Atlanta and other areas. Bryson City, in all of her Norman Rockwell glory, is not immune to big-city troubles. Her residents see— and report—crime and unlike the sheriff in *Outbound Train*, the good sheriff of Swain County does his job. He does it well.

When I was much younger, Bryson City, North Carolina ranked

number one in teenage pregnancy, unemployment, and high school dropout rates. A blanket of hopelessness covered the area. This environment of oppressive poverty didn't keep our football team from raising enough money for high-quality uniforms and equipment. Nor did poverty keep our boys from beating the dickens out of those big-city teams and winning championships, again and again. The SCHS band competes—and wins—as often as our sports team. For us, the chant "Mountain Football" and "Maroon Machine" come from a pride-filled heart. Back then, most of the students had never been out of Bryson City, never spent the night away from home, never eaten a meal that wasn't prepared by a family member. To quote a former player who sits proudly in the stands at age seventy, "No one ever did give us nothing. We earned it. Everything we got, we earned through our own sweat and blood."

Many women in my family made their living hunched over machines earning a polyester payday. Their callused hands put their children through school. The young girls in my family overcame significant poverty. They donned hand-stitched cheerleading uniforms and supported the Maroon Devils football team, but not as much as they supported each other during the tough times. Today, when you visit Bryson City and enjoy a good meal, it is most likely in the restaurant owned by my cousins—whose hands once carried heavy trays of food and wiped the tables clean.

Back when I was growing up, Swain County folk "made do." Just as they do today.

BOOK CLUB QUESTIONS:

1. Carole Anne has a plan to leave Bryson City. As a child, did you ever dream of running away? As an adult, have your responsibilities been so overwhelming you wanted to run away from them?

2. Hubert's Bar sells alcohol illegally. Why do you think Sheriff Tolliver allows Hubert to operate this illegal business without recourse? Do you agree with the sheriff's position?

3. The teachers at Carole Anne's school call her and others "rejects." Why do you think some of the teachers weren't willing to invest in the impoverished students?

4. Barbara and Pearlene once enjoyed living in a mill-town community with other factory workers, but when Pearlene couldn't afford the rent she moved into a trailer beside the railroad tracks. Why does society judge people based on where they live and where they work?

5. The Parker women possess a strong sense of pride. How do you think Pearlene would have acted had she learned that Barbara received food stamps during her period of unemployment? How would Barbara have reacted had she discovered how her mother really obtained the UPC codes for her mail-in-rebate scheme?

6. Did the women in your family once make clothing for their children? Do you know someone who once worked in the textile industry or in manufacturing? Do you think the United States will ever see a re-emergence of textile and other blue-collar jobs?

7. The economy in present day Bryson City thrives on visitors. Do you think the "tourist train" contributes monetarily to the community, or do you think tourist towns exploit impoverished areas by capitalizing on inexpensive labor?